Ninety-six days into the job, I was told The Legend. It resonated.

One hundred fifty-two days in, began daydreaming about it. Incessantly.

Ten months in, began contemplating the impossible.

Three weeks ago, decided to make my move.

In ten days, I will be escorted out of Foster's office.

The
Holden Age
of
Hollywood

The Holden Age of Hollywood

A novel by

Phil Brody

MEDALLION
P R E S S
Medallion Press, Inc.

Printed in USA

Typeset in Adobe Garmond Pro
Printed in the United States of America

ISBN # 9781605424866
10 9 8 7 6 5 4 3 2 1
First Edition

to la
i hate you i love you

Contents

	bLAh	1
1	Doing Time	5
2	Foster's Office	10
3	Legend	18
4	Rising Son	23
5	WEST, 51.4 Miles East	29
6	The Greatest Trick a Writer Ever Pulled	35
7	Suspicious Minds	47
8	Extreme Ways	50
9	How to Disappear Completely	54
10	Ten-Digit Fun	60
11	Hold for Baby Jesus	63
12	Father's Office	74
13	Routine Fuckup	83
14	Maybe True Hollywood Story	89
15	Bachman Tarantino Overdrive	99
16	Share Evidence	103
17	Quantum Mañana	108
18	MTHRFCKR	114
19	Torpedo the Ship	124
20	Psycho Writer	130
21	Cut the Kids in Half	137
22	Two Ships Passing in the Fight	142

23	Channel 5uper4ero	149
24	The Good Luck Club	154
25	Second-Half Adventure	159
26	Need a Bigger Boat	168
27	Flowers in the Addict	182
28	Version2PointZero	188
29	Throw Me the Whip, Throw You the Idol	193
30	Fish Get Drowned	201
31	Fourth Season	206
32	No Contest	216
33	Wretched Hive	220
34	All's Well, Ends Welles	225
35	Time off for Good Behavior	230
36	How to Reappear Effectively	234
37	The Space Between	245
38	McCartney-Watson-Sundance	251
39	Establishing Parting Shot	258
40	Mind the Gap	264
41	What Makes Sammy Read?	272
	Acknowledgments	281
	Author's Note	282

"You're not the kind of guy who's afraid to merge in LA, are you?"

bLAh

"*If you're looking for motivation in all this, here it is. Decided to move to Los Angeles fifteen days after I buried my father, seven days after I discovered a drawer filled with his writing— six screenplays, eleven short films, one play, a few short stories, and one unfinished book abandoned after less than four chapters. He worked in advertising as a copywriter, but I never knew he wrote like that.*

"*I read his entire body of work in two days.*

"*My dad was the only family I ever really had, besides our dog Kirby. We moved to San Francisco from Minneapolis when I was seven, and he raised me on his own. Worked his ass off to provide. Makes me wonder when he ever found the time to write anything, much less a drawer full of stuff.*

"*He was a really good writer. Pretty certain no one's aware of that but me. A stack of rejection letters postmarked Hollywood, California, led me to that assumption. Highly doubt my father tossed letters of affirmation.*

"*No one paid him to write, but he did. He did it all on*

1

spec, obviously hoping someone would like what he wrote and buy it or pay him to write something else. Neither happened for my dad.

"I should have been content to read his words, which revealed a side of him I never knew. Story should have ended there. However, something in the rejection letters didn't add up. Within those letters, I discovered the lie.

"Buried at the bottom of the drawer, I read the rejection letters last, found many discrepancies within. A lot of them were vague, mere form letters. It was the others that turned my contentment vile. The ones claiming they'd read the submission, when clearly they hadn't. They called his political farce a romantic comedy and his drama a dramedy because of their deceptive titles. I saw the discrepancies, wondered if he ever noticed.

"Sitting amidst my father's words, I was confused, irritated. Gin took the edge off, mixed with fatigue, and I gave in to slumber around three a.m.

"Kirby's panicked panting woke me about an hour later.

"The day before I discovered the drawer, six days after my dad's funeral, Kirby fell sick. He stopped eating and began to wax and wane. Throughout the day, his lethargic mood far outweighed the moments he found the strength to move.

"I forced my tired bones out of bed and moved to comfort him. In the dark, I reached to pet him, missed his head, and my hand dipped into something wet. I thought he might be bleeding, but after turning on the light, I discovered Kirby, unable to rise from the bed, had defecated in it.

"I'll never forget his eyes, the shame and weariness in them. They told me what I already knew—he was dying. Nothing I could do.

"I picked him up, carried him out to the back of the house

so I could clean him off with the garden hose. As I washed his fur, he panted, licking me whenever my skin was anywhere near his snout. I dried him off, carried him back into the house, wrapped him in my father's comforter, and laid him on the couch.

"He sniffed around the bedding, searching in vain for his best friend. When he looked up at me, confused and weary, all I could do was tell him, 'I miss him too.'

"The vet arrived two hours after I telephoned. He was one who specialized in housecalls to see if your pet is merely ill or needs to be put to sleep. He examined Kirby about thirty seconds before he said, 'It's time.'

"Two shots later, Kirby was gone.

"It was too much. I lost it. Broke down. Lamented all day.

"Decided to move to Los Angeles the following morning.

"Closed up shop, pronto. Hired a Realtor, put my dad's house up for sale. Broke the lease on my apartment. Sold everything. Everything. I had nothing. What I did take fit into my Explorer.

"Started driving toward a clear destination, uncertain where I was headed . . .

"Hey, don't look at me like that. You asked."

FOSTER FILMS, LLC

SUNSET GOWER STUDIOS / 1438 N. GOWER STREET / HOLLYWOOD, CA 90028

August 19, 1992

Dear Henry Bateman,

Let me take this opportunity to thank you for sending me a copy of your romantic comedy screenplay titled *Chase the Girl*.

After careful consideration, I feel your work is not quite right for Foster Films.

Please realize the movie business is a subjective one. Foster Films wishes you the best of luck finding placement for your work. Thank you again for the opportunity to read your script.

Sincerely,

Jon Foster

Jon Foster

Doing Time

"What are you in for?"

Fourth time tonight I'm asked this question. It's the city's trendy new way of inquiring, "What do you do?"

"Actor." Fourth different answer I've given tonight.

I'm in the Hills at an industry party hosted by a guy I despise. House is way too crowded, music's way too loud. Everyone here thinks their shit not only doesn't stink but might make a good movie. Welcome to LA.

Guy I despise is Justin Lackey, an A-list prick I work with in Development. In case your only movie experience comes in between the tearing of your ten-dollar ticket and the pissing away of six-dollar Coca-Colas, development is the process of finding, acquiring, polishing, and packaging the scripts that ultimately help fill said multiplex near you.

Lackey and I work for Jon Foster, a dinosaur in Hollywood whose last real days in the sun occurred in the late seventies. His initial success made him relevant for almost thirty years, but it's painfully obvious his days as a player in the industry are numbered. So what are we doing working for the near extinct? Biding time before we make our own moves in the game of chess that is Hollywood. That's fundamentally why we hate each other. When you're swimming with the sharks, you don't make friends. You wait for the smell of blood. Then you feast.

Shark tank of a party is wearing on me. Current conversation grates. Told I'll never be a successful actor in this town because my look is way too Kinkoed. The comment shouldn't bother me, but the chick who said it irks me, so I ask, "What's that supposed to mean?"

"Your look. It's too off-the-rack."

Speak LA, as I do now after more than a year in this wretched hive, and you'd realize this means too many actors look like me. This might resonate if I wanted to be an actor. I don't. It would also mean something if I even remotely wanted to bang this girl. I don't. She looks too Starbucked for my taste—all bitter and burned out. I like them on the chaste side. Hard to find in this town, but I aspire.

I escape to the patio, perch myself at the bar, where the bartenders can't pour the Red Bull or the Kettle One fast enough. I watch them work, mesmerized by the stampede for this overhyped mixture of depressant and upper. I know no one uses terms like that anymore—*depressant, upper.* Call me old-fashioned. Actually, call me well-rounded. Helps me do my job and deal with the reason I'm doing time in this town. *Drink to that.*

"Another gin and tonic?"

I nod once to my best friend at this party, my only friend in this fucking town—the bartender. Not this bartender per se. Every bartender. They mix a cure for what ails me. Sure, it's a momentary cure, but those are some of my happiest moments. Way it is.

Too many people. Too loud. Attitudes starting to asphyxiate. I stare at the sea of lights, the view from the Hills of this coldfuckcold city that's 75 degrees every day. It's an endless four-story grid of isolated, lock-the-door-behind-you lives, where everyone is either so wrapped up in creating their own success story or so damaged from their failure that resentment for one another is all we have in common.

Lights everywhere twinkle, look so inviting, but it's a trick. I know it.

The drug I'm sipping starts to work its magic, and my thoughts are set adrift. I ponder whether the decision I've been mulling the last few weeks, the journey I believe I'm about to embark upon, is my destiny or my density. *Destiny. Density.* Amazing how those words are so close. Just a matter of how the letters fall.

Thoughts get derailed when someone enters the picture. This tall, slender, smoking hot gotta-be-an-actress with stellar gams and straight black hair that almost meets her I-swear-sometimes-God-is-an-artist perfect ass. Love her right off the bat. Trust me, you would too.

She saunters my way. Truth told, she merely enters the crime scene that's unfolding around me. She approaches the bar where my ass has been suffocating this barstool for the last hour, while leaving incriminating fingerprints on many a glass. She busts me. I introduce myself and we shake hands. Touch of her skin confirms a smoldering attraction. The smile in her chestnut eyes ignites it.

Her name is Share. Just Share. I'm not making this up. She even spells it for me. Also confirm she's indeed an actress as I help her and her friend, who's incessantly scanning the crowd, obtain drinks. Share and I cheers, dance together with words.

"You know Justin?" she inquires.

"I work with that son of a bitch. You?"

She grins. "He is a son of a bitch."

"What kind of name is Share?"

"The kind I was given."

"Come on. Unless you were born here, there's no way."

She laughs, but I can tell she's pissed.

"Where you from? What's your real name?"

"Thanks for the drink," she says as she disregards me.

"That's it? All I get?"

"Do I owe you something?"

"No, Share," I say with sarcastic emphasis on her given name, "you don't owe me anything, for the drink or the chat. Both are overpriced anyway."

"Drinks are free. No one's paying tonight."

"You can believe that, but you're wrong. Nothing's free here. Ever."

She stares at me, pontificates, "You're not the kind of guy who's afraid to merge in LA, are you?"

Makes me laugh but also have to ask, "What are you talking about?"

Should've played the game, should have said, "Do you know who I am?" I'm nobody, but no one knows that and therein lies the secret to Coldfuckcold, California.

Share turns to her chubby, UGG-wearing friend who's not listening and says, "See?"

Her tone makes me hate her. Trust me, you'd hate her too. "See what?"

8

"You'll never be on the list."

"What list?"

"Any list."

I seethe. Take a swig of Hindsight mixed with 20/20 and lean in, making sure she can hear me. "Yeah? Well, Ass Eyes, you'll be making porn inside of a year. And not that glossy Vivid Video stuff either. It's gonna be fetish flicks and bukkake videos for you until the day you die a lonesome and disease-laden death."

"Did you just call me Ass Eyes?"

"Yeah."

"What the fuck is that?"

"Let me clarify. Your eyes. They look like shitty, brown assholes. Two of 'em. That's what the fuck that is. Now you can hurry back to the parade of delusion where, like everyone else, you're obviously somebody important."

She laughs. We talk another thirty minutes. She stares at my lips the entire time, which I hope you know is a good sign.

As her UGG-wearing friend finally pulls her away in search of a better vantage point, I garner her digits. All ten.

Watching her out-of-my-league ass sway bye-bye, I can only smile.

Welcome to LA. My lot in life.

FOSTER'S OFFICE

Jon Foster is a relic. A remnant of Tinseltown in the days before you could buy yourself a star on the Walk of Fame. Between 1968 and 1979, he produced eleven films and, in turn, built himself one of the most influential celluloid résumés in this town. Five of those films are often cited when listing the top hundred movies of all time. Two are personal favorites of mine.

He looks old school. Check that, ye olde school—silver hair, three chins, and a swollen nose charred red from the decade-long party that was Hollywood in the eighties.

Yeah, Foster might be a dinosaur, but in his day he was a T. rex. Problem is he spent the next thirty years tarnishing his reputation by producing the kind of unwatchable drivel that nourishes insomniacs. He became a joke, and this town is not kind to failure. Lambasted in the trades, then completely ignored by them, Foster vowed revenge. Over a year ago he cleaned house, except for his protégé, Justin Lackey, and hired new blood, which is when I entered the fray.

Yeah, you read that right. Been at Foster's office a year-plus. Why do I stay? To learn. It's why we all put up with Foster. Even Lackey, who with that sick home in the Hills, obviously doesn't need the cash. Assume it's power he wants. So far the assumption rings true.

Contacted Foster about an opportunity with his company when I first arrived in LA, continued to call every morning precisely at nine, left a message if it went to voice mail. Thirty-six days later, he returned my call. Actually, Lackey, the newly promoted VP of Production and Development at Foster Films telephoned and set up an interview for the following morning. That was the first time I set foot in the company's modest Culver City office. Expected to see Hollywood glitz, but Foster had been forced to leave the tinsel behind a decade before. Reality was merely two rooms, one packed with five desks for Lackey and the new staff, the other for Foster to muddle in all day every day.

Lackey dresses daily for the job he wants, not the job he has. His suits boast designer tags his paychecks clearly cannot support. Shoes always shine. Cologne offends. Even his never-a-strand-out-of-place haircut pissed me off from the moment we grudgingly shook hands.

Interview went well, but to this day I don't think Lackey would have hired me if not for an offhand movie reference he made during our conversation.

Alluding to some of the less-than-impressive candidates he'd already met, he said, "They couldn't find their dick, two hands, and a map," a modified quote from *Glengarry Glen Ross*.

"*Glengarry*. Good movie," I responded.

Lackey looked up. "You got that?"

"Sure. It's a good quote. Funny. Mamet wrote it for the screenplay, though. It's not in the source material. The play," I added. "*Glengarry* was originally a play."

"I know it was play," Lackey said, gaze falling downward to the résumé in his hands. "You were in advertising, huh? No prior industry experience?"

"That's correct."

"Why movies? Why now?"

It was an astute question. Thought for a moment about my dad and the path that led me here, but then I told Lackey what I knew he wanted to hear. "Well, a long time ago in a city not so far away, George Lucas showed me anything is possible in the movies. And why now?" I paused, pondered, searched my brain for another movie quote to thrill this obvious aficionado. "I got nowhere else to go."

Interview ended shortly thereafter. He called that evening, said they were going to take a chance on me despite my age, which apparently was about five years past the due date for the position.

I accepted the backhanded compliment along with the job, became one of four assistant development executives for Jon Foster. Said good-bye to the life I knew, enlisted in the War by the Shore.

Here's the rub. To achieve in the industry, you have to spend time in the trenches, and that's what I'm doing, even if it is with a lunatic. And Foster is a lunatic. I actually applaud these efforts at reinvention, hiring fresh minds, all of whom, except for Lackey, had no prior industry experience. Foster's intention was to mold a little army to think like him.

Good luck with that.

Again, I applaud the strategy, but his execution is flawed. The defect is the fact he's still involved in day-to-day operations. He can't let go. So day after day he sabotages the efforts of his next generation staff. Since I'm part of that team, allow me to explain precisely what we do.

First off, a development company is not a movie studio, but development is one of the stages in film production.[1]

At Foster Films, we search for viable projects to be made into motion pictures. Once we find them, we take those screenplays and work with the writers to improve or fix what they've written to the point that investors, studios, and other interested parties can be solicited to submit bids to purchase the properties. Sometimes they just buy the scripts, but other times we've put together package deals by attaching stars or directors. That's where experience and contacts like Foster's come in handy—if they still return his calls, that is.

At development companies, scripts come in daily by the boatload. When they arrive, they are logged in and then distributed. At smaller offices like Foster's, it's usually the assistant development executive's job to read the scripts. However, depending on workload, a set of readers may be employed.

Readers are the worker bees of the hive. They are often the first and only people to read the works and decide whether they're worth considering.[2] After reading a script, they provide coverage, which is a summary of a script, basi-

---

1 Film production occurs in five stages: (1) Development, (2) Preproduction, (3) Production, (4) Postproduction, (5) Sales & Distribution.

2 Successful readers are usually college educated, in tune with pop culture, and possess excellent writing skills. Above all, they have a talent in knowing what screenplay concepts, stories, and characters will strike a chord with executives, talent, and audiences.

cally the CliffsNotes of the industry. The report concludes with a verdict: RECOMMEND, CONSIDER, or PASS.

If the coverage is favorable, one of the assistant executives, myself included, gives the script a read. We then discuss viable projects at a weekly staff meeting to bring Foster up to speed.

At these meetings, Foster decides if a project lives or dies. He's the judge, jury, and witness. If Foster doesn't understand a concept—and there's a lot he doesn't comprehend—he rejects it, moves on. If he takes home a script to read and for whatever reason doesn't read it, the project gets shelved. If he doesn't like a writer's pitch or the way he dresses, the material is jettisoned. Foster's a maniac investing a lot of time and effort into finding one project that'll magically give him one more day in the sun. After being left for dead by this town, he wants to be the smarmy villain who shows up again in the third act for one more bloodbath. He's an asshole, to boot. An asshole that tends to invent his own swearwords.

"Fucktwat, we're waiting for you, and that's not good."

I scurry into Foster's office, last one to arrive, a lemming. An underappreciated, unchallenged, uninspired lemming.

Foster's seated behind his massive cherry-wood desk, which I've always suspected was bought with his first fat paycheck as a gift to himself for, well, for being the great Jon Foster.

My three assistant associates peruse the notes in their laps, making eye contact with no one in the room, par for the daily course. Kevin Mills, reformed class clown, is flipping the pages of his composition book so intently you'd think he misplaced a hundred-dollar bill inside. Warren Patrick, resident pot smoker by night, is stifling yawns with closed-mouthed jaw flexing and a lot of blinking. And Brett Stussy, perpetually praying he won't be called on, chews on the corner of his lip, most likely daydreaming about the power of invisibility.

Lackey sneers as I sit down.

"This is ass-shit, us waiting for you," Foster says.

"Sorry, sir."

"Bulldick you're sorry. Bullshitting-dick. Saying sorry don't turn back the clock. Now give us the rundown on the fucking script."

"Well, the script, while entertaining, lacks main character appeal and a character arc strong enough to attract A-list talent. Act Two meanders, and Act Three needs an overhaul."

"Gee, could you be a little less specific?"

"Sir?"

"Don't walk in here and think you can give me some cumjob. I didn't get where I am today without a keen sense for bulldick."

"Not sure what you want me to tell you. Like the reader, I'm also recommending the script, but it needs fixing."

The script being discussed was recommended by an old associate of Foster's, a retired manager doing a favor for the woman he's banging on the side. Seems her son is an aspiring screenwriter, which is how *SuperVillain* wound up in my in-box yesterday with a Post-it Note that said: *Read ASAP. Meeting to discuss Thursday 10:00 a.m.*

Foster studies me for a good twenty seconds before bellowing, "Two questions. One, why is it good?"

"It has a unique conceit. And that's rare."

Foster stares, waiting for me to explain what should be obvious to anyone who's read the script.

Lackey chimes in. "And the conceit is . . . ?"

"Ah. Sorry. Basically it's what if Superman was not on our side. Most powerful superbeing is actually a villain."

Everyone in the room reflects on this.

Lackey clears his throat.

Foster rubs his palms on his desktop. "Two, how would you fix it?"

"Well, if the villain is allowed to win instead of the preposterous happy ending climax the writer went for, he would in a sense become the protector of this city. He'd be so territorial he'd fight off every other threat that came along and, in turn, be a Superman to these people."

Foster sits there mulling my words. With each passing second, it's as if he's deep-frying them in skepticism. "Anyone else read this suckfuck story?"

"I thoroughly studied the coverage," Lackey says.

Thoroughly studied the coverage? That's like saying you saw a movie after watching the trailer. *Hack.*

"And?" Foster says.

"And I think Bateman is wasting our time. Don't believe it's a script worthy of our attention."

"Well, why were you sitting there like a titrag for the last five minutes saying nothing? Flush it. Write Brenda's son a nice note telling him I enjoyed it but the project isn't Foster Films material. Let me sign it. Now let's move on."

Just like that, *SuperVillain* is wiped from the slate of potential projects considered by this office. Guess it's partly my fault, as I didn't sell it well, but the system is also to blame. We're supposed to develop projects, polish them, fix them—not dedicate a mere five minutes to something that took Brian Sweeney months to write. Project has merit, but it means nothing now. We've moved on.

I exhale and let it go. Doesn't matter. Doesn't matter. Does not matter.

Thoughts wander . . . focus on my plan. Destiny.

Ninety-six days into the job, I was told The Legend. It resonated.

One hundred fifty-two days in, began daydreaming about it. Incessantly.

Ten months in, began contemplating the impossible.

Three weeks ago, decided to make my move.

In ten days, I will be escorted out of Foster's office.

LEGEND

Ninety-six days in, I was told The Legend. Might have flown under my radar longer if it hadn't happened over drinks. Regardless, it resonated.

Kevin Mills started working with Foster at the same time as me. My opinion, he'll never make it in Hollywood. He's too woolly. He puts time in Development with us, but he's also working on a screenplay, a flawed serial killer drama that lacks conflict. He mails dozens of headshots to casting agents every week because he wants to, as he says, "take a stab at the acting thing." One weekend out of every month, he and a few buddies make some shitty short films that are incoherent, poorly lit, and audio impaired. I'm sure when he goes home, his family and friends in whatever suburbanland he's from gush with pride at all he does. Sure, he's the star of his little town, but in Hollywood he's simply unfocused and uncertain of his vocation.

My doctrine is to find one thing, one job, one craft, one goal, set it in your sights, and go. Putting too many eggs in too many baskets waters down your focus, handicaps you.

One goal. Capture it. No distractions. My mantra, to the point of arrogance.

So when I belly up to the bar at The Culver Hotel with Kevin, I'm surprised as hell *he* teaches *me* something.

Surprised as all hell.

Three drinks in, he's slurring words and I'm starting to taxi on the runway of numb.

"Fuck Foshter. Guy treats ush like shit and worksh ush like shlaves."

Nothing a fistful of ice, a generous pour of gin, and some bubbles cannot cure.

I don't care to talk at this juncture, but he keeps babbling. Cannot tell you how thankful I am for that.

"Makesh me think he'sh jusht shearchin' for Holden."

"Meyer Holden? The writer?" Cinephile that I am, Meyer's been on my radar since I was in high school. Love his films. Haven't heard his name in a long while, though. Now I know why.

"Yesh. Meyer the writer Holden."

And just like that, everything changes. Thank you, Kevin. For this.

The greatest screenwriter this generation never read disappeared one day. Disgusted with everything Hollywood, he walked away. Vamoosed. Vanished. They think it was two years later the first Holden Ticket was placed in circulation.

Again, his name is Meyer Holden. Never heard of him? Figures. Hence the phrase, *this generation never read*. Trust me, you've seen his words on the big screen. Everyone has.

Hardly anyone's read them, though. That's because writers, no matter what anyone tells you, are below the line.

Like you, I once asked, "Fuck does that mean?" Never been afraid to ask a question but will never ask the same one twice. So when I arrived in LA, yes, I had to ask, learn, develop.

Here's the 101. The initial vision for any film springs from the minds of its creative talent—the writers, directors, actors, and producers. These individuals are above the line. Everyone else who works on the film is below the line. It's the white-collar/blue-collar of the movie industry. Having said that, if you took a poll in any suburban multiplex, you'd find the average American is able to name a plethora of actors, dozens of directors, maybe even a few producers. However, that same group of moviegoers couldn't name one screenwriter. Nada. Zilch. Zero-point-zero. Way it is.

Above the line? Try buried beneath the line.

So one day Meyer Holden, this celebrated screenwriter, said, "Fuck it, fuck you, fuck off," and walked away from the town he had come to own. Six screenplays, five of them blockbusters, and thirty-one Academy Awards spawned from his words. More important to some, those words grossed nearly two billion in domestic box office revenues.

He's not a god or some kind of magician. Holden simply knows how to write and what audiences want. That's a lethal weapon in this town. Buried beneath the line or not, screenwriting can be a profitable business for the upper echelon, and within that elite group Holden is the crème de la crème.

After selling his first four screenplays, he had what's called fuck-you money. He didn't need to write. He wanted to write. He loved to write. That's why the relationship between Holden and Hollywood was destined for a less-than-happy ending. He got sick of power brokers he despised butchering the loves of his life. Got sick of stepping in shit and scraping the crap off his boots.

So he took his money and moseyed. No one stopped him. After all, in Hollywood's eyes, he was merely a writer.

Truth told, for the first three months no one knew he was AWOL. The trades didn't catch wind for almost six. Because he was notoriously hard to reach to begin with, it seems everyone assumed he was working for someone else.

His agent and manager, uncertain of his whereabouts, took to answering all inquiries with, "Meyer Holden is unavailable at this juncture."

This spawned rumors, which ran the gamut of jail, rehab, and death, and ultimately resulted in a press release from his people.

> *The rumors of Meyer Holden's demise have been greatly exaggerated. In fact, we sat down to lunch with him at Spago last week for an in-depth discussion regarding his next project. In other words, all's well.*

Fact: Meyer Holden abhors the Hollywood scene and would never set foot in Spago. The press release was the agent and manager's obvious attempt to get Holden to call them. He never did.

Then he was a no-show at every awards ceremony. After almost a year, as the gossip was fading, those that profited most from his words—the development companies, producers, and studios he had collaborated with prior to vanishing—started getting concerned. Took some time, but box office profits were affected, and that's when all of Hollywood took notice. Holden was needed, but the man was nowhere to be found. Poof! Moseyed. That was six years ago.

Three months in, I was told The Legend. Resonated.

Seems Holden still loves to write. Doesn't need to, wants to. However, these days when his scripts are finished, he tacks on a pseudonym and creatively filters them into the system.

Clandestine.

Stealthy.

Real covert operation–like.

Doesn't notify a soul. Doesn't remotely follow the same path more than once. The industry has dubbed these scripts Holden Tickets. He puts them out there for anyone to find. It's a game he plays to fuck with Hollywood. One that can win somebody a career here in Tinseltown.

I remain emotionless as I'm told The Legend. Everyone's a rounder in this town, and a poker face keeps you swimming in open waters a lot longer than those that broadcast their emotions in high-def.

Hand is dealt. I take a peek at the cards. Hide the BOOM!BOOM!BOOM! resonating in my chest. I'll get the what, where, when, and why later, but for right now the who will do.

Meyer fuckin' Holden.

I listen. Pray Kevin's too drunk to recall story time when he sobers.

I drink it all in. Fuels my ambition. I ponder The Legend for weeks. Begin to formulate a plan. I'm mindful I'm drinking the Kool-Aid. Doesn't help, though. Gets me high, like everyone else.

Happens.

RISING SON

The Rising Sons of Mourning Park by Adrian Rutherford was discovered by two different people some seventy-two hours apart. The first, a reader, came across those golden words while working for some shantytown screenplay contest. Seems Dustin Manson, a failed LA screenwriter now living in Carefree, Arizona, founded Carefree's One-Way Ticket To Hollywood Screenplay Contest. After spending a decade in Hollywood, Manson learned a few things. Unfortunately, one of them was not how to write. He did learn how to turn a profit, though.

The submission fee for Carefree's One-Way Ticket To Hollywood Screenplay Contest was $45, and the contest received 221 submissions—not that Manson ever read any of them. Instead, the fake-phony-fraud hired a reader and paid him out of the contest's profits. The winning script was awarded $2,500 and an earmarked business card for some ICM agent who no longer returned Manson's calls.

Two hundred twenty-one entries at $45 a pop. That's $9,945. Minus $2,500 for the winner and $500 for the reader. Manson walked away with $6,945, all for writing a creative ad and placing it in a few industry trades.

Not a bad day's work, and he repeated it three times a year—spring, summer, fall.

I know all this because after the script was discovered, *Fade In* magazine did an exposé on the contest and in the process blew the lid off almost fifty will-o'-the-wisp script competitions across the country preying on hopeful/desperate writers everywhere.

I care about all this because *The Rising Sons of Mourning Park* turned out to be Holden Ticket #1.

I picked up the back issue of *Fade In* on eBay using an untraceable e-mail address. That might sound paranoid, but you don't know this town like I do. Trust me, I'm not paranoid, and the story behind Holden Ticket #2 proves it.

Not finished with numero uno, though. As I said, two people discovered *Rising Sons*, the reader for the Carefree contest being the first. The second was Billy Wise, a junior exec working at a little-known start-up development company called Shot/Cut Filmations.

Today everyone knows Shot/Cut. Finding the Holden put them on the map, and they've been an independent juggernaut ever since.

So how did Billy Wise enter the picture? Well, first off, being a lazy exec, he often let script coverage services do his work for him. Second, the reader who provided coverage for the Carefree contest double-dipped. He turned over coverage of his top five selections to Dustin Manson, as he'd been paid five hundred bucks to do. However, he also submitted his reviews of all 221 entries to HollywoodCoverage.com, an online script coverage service that paid a whopping ninety-nine cents per submitted review.

Readers everywhere double-dip, and HollywoodCoverage.com was one of the most popular dipping spots on the WorldWideInterTubes. Submissions were kept anonymous, and the action could PayPal a reader an amount somewhere between enough-for-a-candy-bar to treat-myself-to-a-few-meals, depending on the workload. It paid the Carefree reader an extra $66.33 for the sixty-seven scripts not already logged into the website's system.

Sixty-six dollars and thirty-three cents.

When *Fade In* asked what he spent the profits on, the reader was quoted as saying, "F*** you and your f***ing kiss-a** rag of a f***ing magazine."

Eloquent, but personally I think he was at his best when he reviewed *The Rising Sons of Mourning Park*: "A script that grabs hold of your attention from its first heart-pounding and blood-spattered page . . . slowly drawing you in and ultimately blowing you away with a Meyer Holden–like action spree.[3]

A Meyer Holden–like action spree.

That's all Billy Wise needed. See, one afternoon Billy wisely entered *Meyer* and *Holden* into HollywoodCoverage's search engine. That's what made the site spurt out the script's title. Billy Wise was simply looking for the *next* Meyer Holden. Instead, after making one phone call, he

---

3 Interestingly, the reader's final list for the Carefree contest slotted *Rising Sons* at number three, below *Big Bad Boogeyman*, a script catering to the trendy chase-and-slash horror craze, and the contest's grand prize winner, *A Blue X-Mas*, a "*Star 80* meets *Chasing Amy* story" that apparently struck a chord with this porn enthusiast. At least that is what he inadvertently told *Entertainment Weekly* when asked why he chose *Blue X-Mas* over *Rising Sons*. Regardless, *Boogeyman* and *Blue X-Mas* never got close to being made, but *Rising Sons* netted Billy Wise one golden ticket into the biz of show.

found the first Holden Ticket, met The Man, The Myth, The Legend, and won the lottery.

When news broke, Hollywood went into a frenzy. Overnight, readers became a valued commodity and enjoyed a raise for their now invaluable efforts and, more importantly, their loyalty and discretion in searching for another Holden Ticket.

While this frenzy was short-lived, it was merited.

The Rising Sons of Mourning Park, a streetwise epic saga of modern-day mafia, was made for a mere $12 million. Directed by Gus Van Sant, the film starred a talented gang of rising stars, launched a new generation of young Hollywood, grossed more than $165 million domestic, and was nominated for seven Oscars—Best Original Screenplay, Best Picture, Best Director, and a bevy of acting nods.

Holden did it again. Hollywood foamed at the mouth. Thus, the frenzy.

However, Holden was unhappy with the way Holden Ticket #1 went down. His game was supposed to fuck with Hollywood. Instead it uncovered more fucked-up layers within—from the Carefree moneymaking scam, to the profit-driven reader, to the search engine executive.

So unbeknownst to all, he changed things up along the way. He implemented a few shrewd hurdles in his little game to ensure the industry would play by his rules next time.

The *Fade In* article ends with *Rising Sons* in production. I garnered the rest of the facts, figures, legend from *The Smoking Gun*, *Hollywood Wiretap*, newspaper articles, and message board discussions at the now defunct meyerholdenisaneffinggenius.com.

All this research is done as I contemplate my plan. Before I even consider pushing all my chips into the middle of the table, I need to weigh the facts. Destiny or density? Mind you, I surf on the down low. Call me paranoid, but I trust nary a soul in this soulless town. I'm gathering intel on The Man—an elusive cat best described as Keyser Söze meets the Wizard of Oz. You think anyone's going to help me in my endeavor? Add in my mantra—*one goal, capture, no distractions*—and we have ourselves a bona fide quest, which I'm keeping on the hush-hush.

Aim to find myself a new apartment, a new base of operations. One criterion is ample wireless signals I can hijack. Using my iPhone, I search for available Wi-Fi as I tour potential abodes. Hit the mother lode with this place off Fountain in Hollywood, a second-floor apartment behind a house on a quiet street. One bedroom with a den, all utilities included, open-ended sublet, and the best thing is rent can be paid in cash. It's situated next to a five-story apartment complex, a home to the elderly who apparently love to surf the InterTubes but don't know jack about password protection.

Move in one idle weekend in January when most of the industry is Sundancing. Do my research on an iMac I bought with a prepaid credit card but never registered. Also utilize a refurbished laptop obtained with cash via Craigslist. Hop from signal to signal, uncover as much as possible about Meyer Holden. Every piece of intel I uncover, I copy and store digitally on a private, password-protected Tumblr site. In case this secret lair of mine is ever compromised, I choose to stow all my hard work in cyberspace, where no one can hear you scheme.

I utilize several software programs to maintain proxy

anonymity and mask my IP address whenever necessary. Untraceable, I've become a ghost, almost ready to put my plan into action.

Almost.

Hit a wall in the chronology of the Meyer Holden story, at least online. Discover there's another magazine I need to obtain, an issue of *WEST*, a supplement slipped into the Sunday edition of the *Los Angeles Times* in 2006. That year, seems *WEST* defied the unwritten rule and published a comprehensive analysis of Holden and the game he plays with the industry. The article is no longer online. Issue is not being sold anywhere. Conspiracy.

All I can find is a few low-res scans of its cover, bright red with big black letters:

Meyer Holden isn't just the best writer in Hollywood. He may be the best writer of his generation. Period.

Need. That. Magazine.

WEST, 51.4 MILES EAST

From February 5, 2006, to June 17, 2007, an issue of *WEST* was inserted into every Sunday edition of the *Los Angeles Times*. That's seventy-two issues, seventy-one of which I couldn't give a flying fuck about.

The estimated readership of the *Los Angeles Times* on May 14, 2006, was 1,253,849.[4] Some 750,000 subscribers woke with a copy of the thick newspaper waiting outside the front door. Another 500,000-plus bought copies from newsstands, bookstores, countless Starbucks locations, restaurants, airports, etc.

That's 1,253,849 copies, and all these years later I need just one.

Wish I had a list of everyone who read that paper. I'd cross-reference it with a list of current LA residents and cross-reference that with a list of suspected hoarders. Would pay those individuals a little visit, ask, "Does this cloth smell like chloroform?" Then I'd ransack their place until I

4 "Circulation and Readership: Daily & Sunday Local Comparison," *2006 Los Angeles Media Kit*, the *Los Angeles Times* online.

found a copy. My copy.

Could happen. If I were privy to that info.

Instead, I opt for strategy number B. Do some research on public libraries—know it'd be a waste of time and effort to set foot in any branch within a fifty-mile radius of the Hollywood Hills. Those copies are surely long gone. If not, they're most likely being used to lure, catch, expose the likes of me.

Too smart for them, though. Research points me to the Archibald Library in Rancho Cucamonga, California, 51.4 miles east of Hollywood, near where the I-10 and I-15 meet. The 10 takes me into LA. The 15 leads to Las Vegas. Where they intersect is where I hope to win me a rare copy of *WEST*, v.05-14-06.

Depart at 8:45 on a Saturday morning. Roads are deserted, but I'm in no hurry. Library doesn't open its doors until 10:00, and I aim to arrive at 10:10. Stop at Starbucks before hitting the highway, grab myself caffeine for the ride—grande, double cup, no room. Listen to The National the entire way. Pull in to the library parking lot at 10:07. Not bad. Check my phone. All set.

I wear a Nike ball cap and oversized hooded grey sweatshirt, sling a backpack over my shoulder. Enter, scout the librarians, find the weak link.

He's overweight, spectacled, late forties, sporting a pretty bad toupee.

Hand him a list of books I need. "I'm researching for an article I want to write on California architecture."

He squints at the list. "Article? With the melting pot of architecture in this state, you might need to write a book."

I feign amusement, happy to see my little helper straining to read the list of red herring book titles. He can't see a foot in front of his fat face. Know he'd never be able to describe me for a police sketch or pick me out of a lineup if it ever came to that. Definitely chose the right bibliotheca for this attempted heist.

I peruse the books he retrieves for a good fifty-five minutes before handing him another piece of paper. "If it's possible, I require the architecture sections from these Sunday papers."

He examines the list of dates as I take off my sweatshirt. "I'll just bring you the entire editions."

Of course you will.

He returns with them in under eleven minutes. Good little helper.

Begin reading the edition on top, all the while eyeing the issue on the bottom of the pile. *Sunday, May 14, 2006.* As fate would have it, the issue of the *WEST* is peeking out from the folds. Would know the cover anywhere, pics from the Internet branded in my brain. Spy the bright red, part of the word *Period.*

BOOM!BOOM!BOOM! *Almost there. Almost there.*

Continue to read, moving to the next paper after fifteen minutes. Allow another twenty-five to pass as I take notes on a few of the articles. About to move on to the most important edition when my curator of the printed word moseys over.

"Find everything you need okay?"

"Yes. Yes, I did." I never look up.

He waddles away, disappearing into a graveyard of Dewey Decimals. Never look over to see if he might be watching, spying from the bookshelves. He might be on to me, but I keep my head down. A mere glance would confirm his suspicions. Calls would be made. People informed. Who knows how long I'd have before they'd arrive. Won't allow that to happen. Not when I'm this close.

At three minutes after noon, what I predicted would happen does happen. My spectacled friend is relieved so he can shuffle off to the nearest fast-food joint for a feed. He's replaced by his antithesis, a thin, ancient skeleton of a man. Safe to say Bones here would have a hard time picking his own son out of a lineup, much less me.

Everything is going according to plan.

Ten minutes later, as Bones slowly rolls a rickety restock cart into the aisle behind me, I go to work. Place the copy of *WEST* facedown on the table, concealing its red cover. Hands shaking. *Exhale. Exhale. Execute. Execute.* Close all the books on the table. Stack 'em. Collect the editions of the *Times*. Place my sweatshirt on top of the copy of *WEST*. Unzip my backpack. Pull my cell phone from my pocket, hit *67, then redial.

The phone at the front desk rings. As Bones ambles past, I rise. Stuff my sweatshirt, along with the *WEST*, into my pack. Seize the stack of *Times*, clutch them to my chest and grab the books with my other hand, balance them against my hip, bolt into the stacks. Drop the books onto Bones' cart.

He finally answers the phone. "Hello. Archibald Library. Hello? Hello? Hello. I can't hear you. Hello?"

Take the long way through the shelves, slide the editions of the *Times* in with the current periodicals, under the stack of this week's papers. Confident they won't be discovered for days.

BOOM!BOOM!BOOM! Slow my pace, pull out my phone, hang up on Bones. As I pass the rent-a-security who's reading an issue of *Green Lantern*, I answer a phantom call. "Hi, honey," I whisper. "Yeah, heading home but can't talk right now. Still in the library. Don't want to disturb the patrons."

Through the book detectors, out the front doors, into the sun-drenched day. I smile. Get away scot-free.

My father once told me the perfect crime is one the perp never feels the need to boast about. Ever. Won't be bellying up to any bars in Hollywood, bragging about this little caper, that's for certain. Dad would be proud. On second thought, he'd probably disown me for telling you all this.

west

LOS ANGELES TIMES   May 14, 2006

Meyer Holden
isn't just the
best writer in
Hollywood.
He may be the
best writer of
his generation.
Period.

6

THE GREATEST TRICK A WRITER
EVER PULLED

The article is titled "The Greatest Trick the Writer Ever Pulled." Around the fourth time through it, I wonder if Holden himself might have written it. Maybe he did. Mind you, this is known in the industry as being Meyered in paranoia. It's the belief that everything you're reading might be written by The Man.

Shaking off the phobia, I get back to reality, to business, to learning. The *WEST* piece briefly documents *The Rising Sons of Mourning Park* saga along with a succinct bio of Meyer's career prior to sequestering his work from Hollywood.

Meyer Lloyd Holden, born in a suburb of Philadelphia in 1964, attended Fordham University, studied film and creative writing, moved to San Diego after graduation in 1988.

Would take the world five more years to discover the rest: how seeing *Three Days of the Condor* at the age of ten changed his life, enlightened him to his calling, much as *Star Wars* changed an entire generation currently residing in LA.

He relocated to the City of Lost Angels in 1990 and lived in a dirt-cheap loft in a scary part of downtown. He never held a job, took screenwriting courses, or attended seminars. Never played the game. Instead, he wrote all day every day.

He was once quoted as saying, "I could have lived anywhere, could have written anywhere but chose to move to Los Angeles so I knew what I was up against. Flying in and out for a week or weekend is a vacation. Living here is a vocation."

In 1993, Meyer penned and sold *Fielder's Choice*, a baseball drama depicting the unexpected turnaround of a professional baseball team after they endure a collective near-death experience. Their plane vanishes from radar for over an hour, but everyone on the plane refuses to discuss what happened, which fuels the second-act adventure of the movie. Adding to the mystery is the fact that when the players who were on the plane are on the field together, the team is unbeatable.

Throw in an antihero, the team's narcissistic all-star who was the only player not on the plane. Finding himself locked out of the on-field magic, he spearheads an investigation into what really happened at thirty-five thousand feet. This, in turn, puts the team's winning streak at risk. The conflict culminates as the Magical Mystery Cubs, as they're called, are catapulted into their first World Series appearance in more than one hundred years.

Script was Hollywood gold. A blockbuster that became Hollywood legend. Twelve Oscars, including Best Picture and Best Original Screenplay.

Prior to selling *Fielder's Choice*, Meyer toiled with two other screenplays—*This Time of Night* and *Lennon Bridges*. I read them both along with everything else he's ever written.

He followed up *Fielder's Choice* with *Punching the Clown* and *You and What Army?* Then *Love on the Gun* and *Good Versus Evel Knievel.* All were box office successes, and Meyer was the toast of Tinseltown.

Imagining Images won the rights to Holden's eighth script, *Almost Forgot Myself,* in the greatest bidding war Hollywood has ever seen. They bought it without reading it, thinking they were going to get more of the same from the writer on a roll. Instead, they owned the rights to a pioneering work described by readers as "a script that makes you forget (pun intended) everything you think you know about film structure. The reader is immersed in nonlinear storytelling that breaks ground as compelling scene after compelling scene ultimately weaves into the strongest of narratives. Recommend times ten."

After analyzing the coverage, Imagining Images pushed the project into what Meyer once dubbed eternal-round, an everlasting purgatory of turnaround.[5] In an infamous press release, Imagining Images deemed the script unfilmable— "a film featuring a man searching for a lost love while suffering from Alzheimer's, his vivid memories dulling and disintegrating in every scene is impossible to effectively translate to the big screen."

Tell that to the writers and directors of *Memento* and *Eternal Sunshine of the Spotless Mind.*

Should be noted, *Almost Forgot Myself* went into eternal-round about two years before *Memento* became a cult classic and six years before *Eternal Sunshine* took home the Os-

---

5 In Hollywood-speak, a project put into turnaround is no longer active, has been abandoned by one studio, and may be shopped to another. However, Imagining Images, inept and paranoid, refused to allow the project to be shopped and, to this day, annually renews the rights to a script they have no intention of producing.

car for Best Original Screenplay. During the development process, the big brains at the studio encouraged changing Alzheimer's to amnesia, therefore allowing for a happy ending when the hero recovers his memory and regains the girl in Act Three.

Holden freaked. Then he vanished. Can you blame him?

He skedaddled from the Hollywood scene, not from earth. His address is known. People have tried to contact him in various ways, but he never responds. Not to agents, managers, producers, actors, or groupies begging for his triumphant return. Bold individuals, thinking they are entitled to some quality time with The Man, have accosted him in public and even walked right up and knocked on his door at his ranch outside Denver, Colorado, only to be arrested for stalking and/or trespassing. Basically, he's alive and kicking but not taking any meetings. None whatsoever.

Even before the first Holden Ticket was discovered, people surmised he was writing. Trick is, no one knows how many scripts he's set adrift.

The Rising Sons of Mourning Park was number one.

And then there were two . . .

To my delight, *WEST* eloquently fills in the subsequent blanks in the Holden timeline as it describes the events related to Holden Ticket #2.

Does. Not. Disappoint.

Read the entire article four times already, but the BOOM!BOOM!BOOM! is back. This time it's not fear or adrenaline as much as fervor, a fervor from vocation. My vocation.

The script, called *The Living End*, was penned by Marty Gibb and Cecilia Watts. Of course, these were the pseudonyms tacked onto the cover page of this Holden Ticket.

The 120 pages of nonstop action-adventure followed Mack Fellows, a punch-drunk hit man with a photographic memory who, on the threshold of death, achieves clarity and gains the uncanny ability to defeat adversaries and avoid demise.

Might sound cliché to you, but to Hollywood this is known as high concept. If it's well written, a character like this can develop into a franchise. And studios do love their franchises—enough to drive them into the ground, sequel after sequel, reaping enough profit to build mansions on the sides of hills.

Everyone in the world knows about The Living End, the franchise. I saw the films, but of course that's not what the article is about. It's about the time before we all knew the script existed, before the chain of events that would cease the frenzy and start a Cold War.

The story of the script's discovery is twofold and involves an aspiring actor and a reader working at a major studio. The link? They shared an apartment in Venice Beach, in the less-than-aspirational area below Rose Avenue.

It was on some idle June Gloom Tuesday that the young actor grabbed a copy of the script from his roommate's work pile on his way to take his morning shit. He needed something to read and, liking the title, he chose *The Living End* from a short stack of about twenty.

Seven pages after his cheeks hit the porcelain, the actor's cell phone rang. A playwright casting his latest waste-of-time, off-Santa-Monica-Boulevard tragedy wanted to meet him. They talked on the phone for a few minutes, set up the meet, and after two flushes the actor hurried off to the

Coffee Bean & Tea Leaf on Sunset and Fairfax, *The Living End* under his arm.

The fact the playwright was forty-five minutes late allowed the actor enough time for complete immersion in the screenplay's brilliant second act.

The playwright finally showed, and their meeting ensued. The kid could hardly wait for the conversation to end, though, to find out what happened to the main character, Mack, to the dynamic character/love interest, Lorelei, and to an obstinate villain known only as Rogue.

Atop a pile of neglected screenplays, perched over porcelain filled with excrement, and at the uninspired hut of sham and delusion that is the Coffee Bean on Sunset Boulevard. If we're being precise, this is where *The Living End* was initially read, where Holden Ticket #2 was first discovered. That's not the story often advertised, but it's one I'm confident is true. If you merely read the *WEST* article, the actor might come across as a well-drawn character in a well-written story. Meyered in paranoia? Not this time.

Taking a break from the article, I hit the WWW, dig deep, and uncover an audition video the actor hosted on his long abandoned Myspace page. The three-minute AVI file features the actor talking about how much he loves *The Living End* while recounting the story of how he stumbled upon the screenplay. He then acts out a key scene from the script. Trust me, the actor wasn't acting when he told the story of how he found *The Living End*. Truth told, he wasn't doing much acting in the scene either. Not sure how I'd describe his performance. *Shit sandwich* comes to mind, but I digress.

The kid, bless his heart, thought he might get the

chance to play Mack Fellows. Pretty certain he started day-dreaming about the starring role while he was still sitting at the Coffee Bean that fateful afternoon. As the story goes, upon completing the script at the Bean, he called his room-mate and said something to the effect of, "Dude, I just read the best fucking script on the planet. I shit you not."

This set into motion the chain of events of the well-advertised legend of Holden Ticket #2. All it took was that one phone call.

After his actor roommate praised its virtues, the reader at the studio pulled a copy, started turning the script's pages, and also fell in love with it. That same afternoon, he took it to his boss, a producer, and reiterated its virtues as he handed over the copy. Nevertheless, it remained untouched on that executive's desk for three business days.

Cut to Friday and the studio's weekly status meeting. The readers were being put on the spot by never-satisfied execs, which is an annoying and common occurrence. Trust me, lived there.

When asked why they weren't finding any viable projects, the reader raised his hand and enlightened the room about *The Living End*, much to the chagrin of the producer who had yet to read the work.

"What did you like about it?" a head honcho inquired.

Here's where the legend becomes legendary.

Reader said, "I liked that it's the first thing I ever read I thought might have been written by Meyer Holden."

Buzz in the room resulted in an impromptu conference call to Marty Gibb and Cecilia Watts. At this juncture, as with *The Rising Sons of Mourning Park*, the script's cover page becomes the most important page. In the game the writer plays, the cover page delivers the name and the phone number where you can cash the Holden Ticket and, in turn, contact The Man.

As an intern dialed the ten digits, the energized staff anticipated hearing Meyer Holden's voice on the other end.

To their surprise, Marty and Cecilia picked up on the fourth ring. And much to the room's disappointment, the two sounded like who they said they were: a married couple, both writers, transplants from Baton Rouge currently residing in Calabasas, a suburb of LA.

Rumor has it, when told the company was calling regarding their script, Cecilia exclaimed, "You've made us happier than a couple of clams at high tide."

Of course, this quelled the excitement in the room substantially. This wasn't Meyer Holden. It was Ma and Pa Kettle. Be that as it may, a good script is a viable project, and Moving Picture Films scheduled a meeting with the writers of *The Living End* for Monday morning at ten.

Every executive took a copy of the script home that weekend. This was roughly four years after *The Rising Sons of Mourning Park*, four years of could-be-a-Holden, might-be-a-Holden, and you-have-to-read-this-ASAP. In reality, execs get lazy, hate to read, and after four years legend becomes myth. Add in Marty and Cecilia's southern twang and the first-time writers' seemingly genuine flabbergast and, well, the inevitable happened.

Only one of the six execs read the script that weekend, and he read it Sunday night. He called his immediate boss ten minutes after midnight, apologized for waking the household, and stated he was confident they had indeed found a script written by Meyer Holden.

Monday morning, Marty Gibb, thirty-nine, beer gut, and graying mullet, and Cecilia Watts, thirty-seven, thin, sun-freckled, and sucking a lozenge, arrived at Moving Picture Films. They burst into the offices proclaiming, "This is the first day of the rest of our lives."

The couple met six of the firm's top execs, ate the blueberry muffins provided, and fielded questions about their work. When the interrogation ended, Marty and Cecilia inquired if they could ask the group some questions. By all accounts, the couple expressed only one. Legend has it Ma and Pa Kettle hardly got a response from the beleaguered group.[6]

Marty Gibb and Cecilia Watts departed the Moving Picture offices before the clock struck eleven, and three days later the company quietly passed on *The Living End*. In actuality, they were denied ownership, in part for their "inability to duly impress" the writing duo in that initial meeting and in part for their lowball offer.

End of story? Hardly.

A week later to the day, the reader who brought *The Living End* to his bosses did something that would get any person in his position fired on the spot. Kid picked up the phone and called Marty and Cecilia to tell them how much he and his actor friend loved their script.

Kid said, "It's a crying shame the company passed. I will never understand what the hell we're supposed to be looking for when scripts like yours go to the wayside."

The writers went all aw-shucks and proceeded to ask the reader one question.

The Question.

The reader answered The Question, and that same day

---

6 Article fails to cite what The Question was.

Meyer Holden, Man, Myth, Legend, sauntered into the offices of Moving Picture Films, told the receptionist he was there to see a reader by the name of Ryan Martinez, shook hands with the young man who discovered *The Living End,* and met with him behind the closed doors of the company's conference room for almost two hours.

Finally, the six eager execs were allowed to enter. After handshakes and ass-kissing, they spent five hours hammering out a deal where Ryan and Holden each owned 35 percent of *The Living End*—the script, the subsequent film, any sequels, and all profits from those movies, comics, cartoons, toys, lunch boxes, T-shirts, etc. Moving Picture Films owned the remaining 30 percent.

It was a take-it-or-leave-it offer, and Moving Picture took it in a Hollywood heartbeat.

Bruce Willis was perfect casting for the role of Mack Fellows in what became a blockbuster film. Audiences hated to love Kate Beckinsale as the double agent known only as Lorelei. And John Malkovich set the bar for villains out of reach with his portrayal of Rogue. No awards garnered, just a fuckload of cash.

Happily ever after? Well, gets happier for some, not so happy for others.

Ryan Martinez was shot into the Hollywood stratosphere fast. Way too fast. Head was spinning like tires on an Indy car. All that power and cash inflated his ego to blimp size. He became a staple at every movie premiere, every Playboy Mansion party, every industry event. Kid boned more starlets in a year than Derek Jeter did throughout his MLB career.

Exaggeration? Maybe. You should see the list, though.

Kid also never worked another day in his life. Got lazy. Power, money, and the strange have that effect.

So a year and change after the film's premiere, Moving Picture Films found a loophole in *The Living End* contracts and offered Ryan Martinez an enticing buyout for his 35 percent ownership of the franchise, he accepted and retired from Hollywood at the age of twenty-five with over forty million in the bank. Not bad for a few years of easy labor.

"Needless to say, Meyer Holden was outraged, distanced himself from the franchise,[7] and some believe may have stopped playing the game altogether."

I read that last sentence over and over. If that's true, everything I am doing is for naught. Wasting my time, my life, my father's hard-earned cash—my inheritance and the capital gained from selling his house.

That's right, if you haven't picked up on it by now, I'm cashing in my chips, severing all ties, going underground. Not pondering it, weighing options, or calculating costs. I'm in. All in.

If not now, when?

I'm searching for the one writer in Hollywood who does not want to be found.

Fuck. Me.

Wait! The Question.

You're probably wondering what Marty and Cecilia asked the execs, what they asked Ryan Martinez when he called, and what Holden asked Ryan in that conference room. Was it the same question in all cases?

---

7 Two subsequent *Living End* sequels starring Jason Patric, Lindsay Lohan, and Crispin Glover were considered domestic flops, but both turned a sizeable profit overseas.

Here's the rub. No one knows for certain. Interested parties assume The Question is the shrewd hurdle Holden instituted after the debacle of Holden Ticket #1, but no one except a few Hollywood execs and Ryan Martinez knows what was asked.

That, my friends, is the greatest trick a writer ever pulled.

In a town that runs on dialogue and action, gossip and innuendo, and everything in between, no one's talking. The Question is the best-kept secret in Hollywood. Been three years since it was last asked.

In three years, legend becomes myth.

That's how the Holden Age of Hollywood became a 75-degree Cold War.

Suspicious Minds

I call Share three days after we meet. Been a little too long since I've had some action. Could use one last hurrah before I set sail.

A day later she calls back. "I wanna party," she coos into the cell phone. "You in?"

Going to cost me, but don't care about the money. That I've got. Care about the time and effort. But, "I'm in."

We make plans for the following Friday, which happens to be the day after I'm escorted out of Foster's office.

Pick her up at nine, and she does not disappoint. Sexy dress, heels, looking Hollywood hot.

We leave her apartment, head to my car. My boner, which I like to call Elvis, is already singing in the warm night air.

Dinner at Koi. She eats a lot. I like that. We guzzle champagne, and by her third glass she's rubbing her bare foot all over me under the table, petrifying my evening wood in the process.

Drinks at Skybar. Conversation flows, makes me think we're accelerating toward some naked fun, so I feed her two Red Bull and vodkas to ensure she doesn't fade on me. She's never been to Hyde, so we head there about half past midnight. She gets me to dance. Blame it on the alcohol. We jettison by one thirty.

Smoke a bowl back at my place, make out in between hits, then get to it. She loves to be on top, likes me to pull her hair, spank her, while Elvis slips in and out of the building amid much fanfare. She comes a lot. I like that. I bust a nut at 2:29 with a smoking hot piece of Hollywood ass that only really wanted the Koi and the weed. Both get what we want, though. Way it is. Enjoy her two more times before we slumber, get her to do things I think she won't. She does it all, and it feels really good to be wrong.

We sleep in until ten thirty, fool around until almost noon. When we finally get out of bed, I take her to The Griddle Cafe. It's a popular place in Hollywood for breakfast and the best joint to show off your conquests from the night before, especially at this hour.

Every breakfast has three shifts. First happens from open till about nine and hosts the LA families. By ten, the ambitious Los Angelenos are paying for the most important meal of the day before heading to their industry jobs. Last and definite least comes the parade of delusion, those who rise well after eleven and do nothing until five when it's time to get ready to hit the town and party until the wee hours. That group doesn't eat breakfast as much as they come to be seen, enjoy the beauty contest, and talk about everything they won't end up doing today.

Share and I eat amongst them. I feel so out of place.

"I like it here," she says between spoonfuls of granola and yogurt.

Course you do. "It is entertaining."

When the bill comes, Share makes a reach for it, but I grab it on instinct. "Got it."

"You sure?"

"Yep." I hand my card to the waitress.

"Okay, but I got the next one."

She says it with confidence, as if there will be a next breakfast. I know there won't.

Right now, I look at Share and see a pretty distraction, one I do not need. High maintenance that aspires to the third shift at The Griddle is not on my menu right now, no matter how good it tastes.

We leave.

I drop her off outside her place.

"See you soon," is the last thing she says.

Watch her been-there-done-that ass sway away. Smile, speed off, feel like I've finally arrived, like I can get down to business.

EXTREME WAYS

Where do I begin?

Virtually every movie you have seen in your lifetime follows the same essential formula. First, you are introduced to the main character, the hero, the film's protagonist. A few pages later, somewhere between one and fifteen,[8] this character meets someone.[9] That someone is known as the dynamic character.

The character is dynamic because he or she will serve as the catalyst for the protagonist's change over the next 100 to 120 pages. In the biz, this is referred to as the character arc. Think about *Rain Man* and how much Hoffman's character affected Cruise's Charlie Babbitt. That arc is referred to as the dynamic progression because it is dynamic[10] and because, as mentioned above, the dynamic character is integral in the process.

---

8 Note: every page of a script traditionally equals one minute of screen time. (You can do the math.)

9 Depending on genre, they may be partnered with someone (buddy-cop), united with someone (drama), thrown into a situation with someone (comedy), sequestered with someone (horror).

10 Dynamic (adjective): (1) full of enthusiasm, energy, and purpose; (2) pertaining to effective or forceful action which produces change and development; (3) energetic.

Everything before the appearance of the dynamic character is Act One. It's prologue, mere backstory for the main character. Everything after is the adventure.

Following? Need to slow down? Hope not. If so, take a break and plug your favorite films into the formula above. Mind you, it's a bit like algebra in that you might not see it all at first, but goddamn, when that lightbulb turns on, you've got yourself higher learning, which is nice.[11]

Enjoy.

Wake up tired. Coffee fails to do its job. Be so easy to go back to bed, sleep until noon, fool myself into believing tomorrow will be different. I shake it off, get to work.

My initial move is placing a series of unrelated ads in print and online. Using dummy e-mail addresses via the Hotmails, Gmails, Hushmails of the WorldWideInterWeb, I post a total of forty-six ads on Craigslist requesting scripts. Ten are faux production companies seeking every genre, every size budget, every script anyone's got. Ten are phony agents and managers seeking "new voices," "new talent," "original ideas," "hungry writers," "talented writers." Ten are fabricated screenplay contests, most of which dangle cash money and accolades. Ten offer free script consultation, proofreading, or rewriting services. Five are from actors looking for career-launching vehicles. Final Craigslist ad boasts: "WANTED: a good script that will make me

---

11 Pretty certain there is not a more precise example of this than the motion picture *The Professional*. You might also know it as *LEON*. Depends when you saw it. Hope you saw it. If not, why are we talking? The plot: Leon (Jean Reno) is a reclusive and ruthless hit man, but when the family living next door gets slaughtered by some crooked cops, he chooses to open his door for the family's sole survivor, a little girl named Mathilda (Natalie Portman, age twelve), saving her and, in the process, beginning one of the most compelling dynamic progressions in film.

laugh, cry, become part of me."

I sign that one *Catz*, make myself laugh.

I place the same assortment of ads within the bevy of industry magazines referred to as the trades. *Variety*, the *Hollywood Reporter*, *Script*, *Screenwriter*, *Creative Screenwriting*. Even throw ads in the classifieds of *Los Angeles Times*, *LA Weekly*, Brand X, and the *Canyon News*.

I create sixteen fake websites, five for imaginary screenwriting contests, these also promising cash to the winners. Five other sites are for hungry and honest agents and managers, complete with shots of the individuals, which I purchase from Shutterstock and Corbis. Four sites are production companies, two in LA, one in NYC, one in Chicago, all of them figments of my imagination. One site is for a free script storage service that accepts electronic submissions along with snail-mailed hard copies. The final site is a script coverage and consultation service promising, "We will read, analyze, and fix your script lickety-split!"

Utilize Google Ads to promote all the sites. Always purchase the premium service to ensure maximum exposure. Sites take some time to build, but they look polished, professional, credible. Helps that this is what I did prior to moving to LA. Like my dad, I used to work in an ad agency. Was kind of a jack-of-all-trades—Photoshop, Flash, Dreamweaver, some Geek Squad stuff too. Feels good to put these talents to use again, even though I'm confident it's not what I was meant to do.

Pay for everything via PayPal, which is linked to a cloaked e-mail address and a corporate bank account I opened a few weeks ago. Called the company PaperPenInc. Inside joke.

All the ads and script requests funnel into a post office box I open in Atwater Village. Find a place open twenty-four hours a day, allowing me to make late-night pickups once a week, which is key. Place also allows trojan PO addresses to be used, so my ads feature unique addresses in appearance, but everything gets funneled to one box. They even handle the out-of-town PO box addresses and have shipments periodically forwarded to the Atwater location. All this for a nominal annual fee. Pay for all with cash.

Cast my net wide and it works, to say the least. Takes me three weeks to get everything up and running, but once I do I receive 317 scripts inside a week. By the end of the month, I stockpile close to a thousand from all over the nation. A handful arrive from overseas—five from England, three from Australia, two from Italy, and one that's written in Hindi. Looked that one over several times.

What if The Man had it translated into Hindi? Might need to hire a translator to find out.

After requesting a translation of the title on a University of Delhi message board, I'm told it "loosely translates as either *Lipstick Lesbians Lust Vampires* or *Lipstick Lesbians Suck Vampires*." Suffice to say, I opt to forgo script translation.

Regardless, I'm in business. Drowning in words, though. Most of the scripts are trash—overwritten, cliché-ridden, story-of-my-mundane-life trash.

Begin to abhor my lot in life, but I forge ahead.

Hop onto a different Wi-Fi account every few hours, make no calls from inside the house, in bed by eleven, up by five.

Trust no one, no surprises, smooth sailing.

This is a way it is story.

How to Disappear Completely

The stack of scripts swells. Find comfort in them. They fill the room that used to be the den. Keep the door locked at all times. Shades drawn. Let no one in. Allow no one to know my business. Initial goal was to read every script within two weeks of receipt. Valiant effort but unrealistic. Since launching the plan, I've received exactly 2,106 scripts. Reading seven to ten a day. Not a bad pace, except incoming scripts average fifteen per day. I lock the door, ignore the problem, which for me is a chronic solution.

Every screenplay looks the same, save for a unique title. An average of 120 pages of three-hole paper held together with two shiny clips called brads. All are written in the same font: 12-point Courier. The semblance makes every script begin with the same promise. Any of them could be the one I'm seeking.

Any or none.

Reminds me of Willy Wonka and all those kids searching for a golden ticket in chocolate bar after chocolate bar.

It's exactly like that but not.

Make a withdrawal from the room, sit, open my first script of the day, sip my coffee, fall into the world the writer has created. Everything about it is awful. Know this by page eleven, but I forge ahead. Read every script to at least page fifty, fearful a crap story may turn into gold, paranoid Holden has hidden his latest tome within a shitty first act or slow-building second. So page fifty is my benchmark, and it proves ponderous at times.

Case in point: second script of the day, page one, first line of dialogue:

MAXAMILLION

We gotta get out of hear before all hell breaks lose!

Kill me now. There's a loser on the loose! And the name is Maximilian, you uneducated hack. Fifty pages later *Hell Breaks Lose* hits the To-Be-Shred pile.

Turn off my phone. Stop answering e-mail. No Facebook updates. No Twitter Tweets.

The few friends I had, mostly work friends, stopped calling and sending messages a few weeks ago. Out of sight, out of mind.

What are you in for? Solitary confinement.

It Happened in the Basement by Frank Lambert is a stock horror script that begins with news reports of a police raid on a home where a series of horrendous child murders have taken place. Cut to ten years later. Newlyweds are moving into their first home, the same one seen in the prologue. When the couple pries open a sealed crawl space while renovating, they release an evil spirit that proceeds to haunt the house and torment the couple. Film ends with the disappearance of a neighborhood kid and the reveal of his dead body in the crawl space while the couple sleep soundly. The script plods along and meanders when it should go in for the kill. *Pass.*

t.v. babies by Richard Varga and Philip Bencheck follows a close-knit group of four Generation Y and Z friends, desensitized to a staggering degree by TV, movies, and the Internet, as they are divided by an outsider. It's slowly revealed all their emotions and personalities are not real but instead are a frightening product of the media-driven world and TV-dependent childhoods. Compelling conceit, but there's no conflict whatsoever.

All my days begin the same way. Up before dawn, trek outside for a vat of coffee. Started off this whole venture brewing my own, but by day forty-five the taste was so lost on my palate I might as well have been drinking brown water. Started nodding off before noon, which is when I decided to bring in the experts—Starbucks.

Around the corner from Starbucks is a tiny newsstand, which provides me with the daily trades. I make these essential purchases prior to six a.m. to avoid being spotted. No one in LA gets up this early, which is why I'm comfortable enough to venture outside, to boldly buy copies of *Variety*, the *Hollywood Reporter*, and the *Los Angeles Times*. Guy I buy them from speaks broken English. By day fifteen, I no longer need to ask for the magazines. He has them ready for me, already tucked into a brown paper bag. Look more like the local perv buying the latest copy of *Beaver*

Country, which is the way I want it. I always have the money ready for him. Transaction made sans words, sans attention.

Same with the coffee. Used to say, "Grande, double cup, no room," but my barista has committed my order to memory. She's good like that. Find solace in this. Makes me feel like I'm flying under the radar.

Triple-X Girlfriend by Rupert Hancock is a nonlinear drama that follows Dan Hart, who loses his fiancée, job, and friends in a matter of weeks when he becomes obsessed with an ex-girlfriend after he discovers she's a porn star. Script aims to be *Sex, Lies, and Videotape* but proves inadequate.

Hell of a Birthday by Timothy Del Don is a slasher flick about a kid who hangs himself on his twenty-first birthday after he learns his mom worshipped the devil years ago, slept with him (yep, you read that right), and Beelzebub might be his father. Reunited in hell, Daddy makes him immortal and now he shows up at twenty-first birthday parties everywhere to "have my cake and kill it too." Horny devil even has sex with a few hot chicks. *Pass times ten.*

When the words on the page start to blur, I take a break, shift gears. Move to the computer to maintain the websites, post new ads, refine my plan of action. As I work, I laugh at the poor bastards who think they might win one of my trojan horse contests or receive script consultations free of charge.

Nothing's free here. Ever.

We're All in This Together by Chuck O'Connor, Robert Durango, and Joseph Lowden is a madcap adventure of three slackers who plan a heist of the hotel where they work, only to uncover and foil an ominous plot of terrorism, in turn becoming reluctant heroes to the nation. *Friends shouldn't let friends get high and type.*

Miss March April May by Jennifer Z. Darien is an amusing romantic comedy about a Golightly girl named April May, whose lifelong dream to become Miss March is sabotaged by James Friday, her mother's neurotic political campaign manager. Hilarity ensues when April becomes a media darling, which boosts her mom's campaign, and when Friday falls in love with the centerfold hopeful. If I had a vagina, I'd probably sing the praises of this script. Alas, Elvis and I pass.

Spend all day inside, wait for the night to fall. When everything's dark, I stop reading, start drinking, order take-out most days, relax, then slumber. Venture out three nights a week to one specific location for some undercover reconnaissance. I'd like to tell you more about that, but at this juncture you're still suspect.

Bobby & Clive by Juliet Clarke starts with the bang of a cross-country crime spree executed by two male protagonists who call themselves "the Bonnie and Clyde of the new millennium." We learn they're lovers who went on the lam after Clive discovered he contracted AIDS during a recent prison stint. The duo enjoy CNN infamy and, in the end, go out in a blaze of glory that proves their undying love for one another. Script rips off *Bonnie and Clyde* and *Thelma & Louise*. Bottom line: simply because it's gay doesn't make it original.

Talk to no one. Tell no one where I am, where I'm going, what I'm doing, who I'm looking for, why I'm looking, or how I will find him. Occasionally wonder about the when/

if. Disregard it, focus only on the how.

Head to the script room. Fetch another small bundle from the To-Be-Read pile, stack the ones I've finished in the To-Be-Shred. Everything is going according to plan.

My Date with Minka by Bobby Wickford is an inane comedy about Billy Wackforth's attempt to score a date with TV/film star Minka Kelly with the help of his good friend Sally Crenshaw. In the end, he goes on the date and mind-bogglingly wins the starlet over, then breaks her heart when he realizes he's in "serious like" with good friend Sally. Ugh. Surprised it's not written in crayon.

Chance of Reign by Naomi Wepinski and Elena Nielsen is a taut action-adventure script pairing an undercover cop with a con artist. It all unravels during a meandering third act. The unsatisfactory climax requires four pages of the main character explaining to the dynamic character and, in turn, the audience what happened. First rule of screenwriting: show, don't tell.

After three months and more than 780 scripts, I realize I've disappeared completely.

Think Radiohead said it best: "I'm not here. This isn't happening."

Ten-Digit Fun

WHOOSH!SLAP!BANG!

I fling the bound pages across the room. The bundle caroms off the white wall and falls to the floor, coming to rest wedged between the wall and my TV stand. Cover page is still visible, title branded along its center, contact info of the "writer" in the lower right-hand corner mocking me.

Bad day. Fistful, generous pour, bubbles.

In the beginning, had a rule to never drink and read. Fourth month in, that philosophy went out the window. Usually start drinking between five and six. Despite the booze, I'd rather read a few more screenplays than watch already produced scripts on TV or DVD.

Let's call it overtime.

I'm numb, but I can still smell a shitty script. The bundle of joy that moments ago went WHOOSH!SLAP!BANG! was a waste of paper. Waste of ink. Waste of two brads. Waste of postage.

Contact information taunts.

Contact information.

I get up, retrieve the script, scan the writer's vital information. Area code 215. Philly. Almost ten here, one in the morn there. I pick up the phone, punch *67, dial the digits, listen to the rings.

"Hello?"

"Yes, hello. Michael Lee Barton, please."

"Speaking."

"Michael, Alan Smithee here. Not sure if you know who I am, but feel free to call me Mr. Smithee. Listen, I recently finished your script and, well, I felt compelled to call."

"Really? That's great."

"It is. A call from me is like a call from someone you don't know who you should know because they can get you where you want to be faster than you could ever get if I didn't call, you know?"

"Mr. Smithee, what company do you work with?"

"You ever hear of Fox Searchlight?"

"Of course."

"Well, I work for a company much like them. Now this screenplay of yours."

"Yes?"

"What made you write such a thing?"

"Well, I thought it would be great to see the horror genre combined with a buddy action flick."

"Sounds great. Can you send me that?"

"That's *Dead & Barry*. That's the script you called about."

"It is? Fuck me if I didn't get that from what I read."

"You didn't?"

"I didn't. In fact, I was wondering a few things about

the script. A few things we have to maybe change in the course of development of the concept. You with me? I'm sure you know all about development, right?"

"Yes, yes."

"Good, good. Then can you tell me why your second act spends sixteen pages away from the dynamic progression by delving into a subplot with no horror or action or humor, while avoiding all conflict and ignoring the opponent?"

"I'm not sure I understand the question."

"You can fucking bet you don't fucking understand the fucking question, you fucking hack. Worse thing that ever happened to you was the word processor. Without it you wouldn't take the time to churn out the crap you sent to me neatly bound with gold-plated brads. None of you would. Might as well fucking blame Gates and Jobs for this shit you called *Dead & Barry*."

"What company did you say you were with?"

"Listen, we got off on the wrong foot. Let me connect you with my secretary, and she'll schedule lunch."

"Okay."

"Hold on one sec. I'll transfer you." Click!

Adrenaline rush. Feeling good. Damn good.

Have to do that again sometime.

I pick up another script.

Soon.

HOLD FOR BABY JESUS

Partner & Crime by Mike Hilgenberg and Sven Doodle is a buddy cop action–comedy that's not funny and has little action. It's about a retiring cop who reluctantly takes on a young partner. When that young buck convinces the old codger that cops like them would make the best criminals, the duo perpetrate a series of absurd bank robberies they're assigned to stop. It's like *Dexter* meets the short bus. In the end, they get away with it all and are hailed by the city for stopping the crime wave by vaporizing the nonexistent criminals with the brand-new P9000 vapor guns we conveniently see being tested in the first act. *F-ugh-k me.*

I pick up the phone, *67, dial.

"Hello, this is Foster Films. Hold for Justin Lackey, please." I put the phone down, hit the head, G&T myself, check to see if the Twins won tonight, and finally pick up the phone. "Justin Lackey here."

"Hello, sir."

"With whom am I speaking?"

"This is Mike Hilgenberg."

"Ah, wunderbar. Read your screenplay and, well, I must say it is 111 pages . . ."

There's a pause, then, "Of . . . ?"

"Of course. Now what was your role in the process? I see two monikers on the cover page here."

"Ah yes. Well, I came up with the story and acted as lead writer. Sven was a story consultant and punched up the dialogue here and there."

"So you'd say you're mostly to blame?"

"S'cuse me?"

I exhale dramatically. "Look, I am not going to butter your bacon here. On a scale of one to ten, I would give it a D minus."

"That's not good."

"No, it's not. Neither is your script. For the life of me, I didn't get it. Didn't laugh either. And I'll have you know I'm a laugh-easy kind of chap."

"I'm sorry to hear that. That you, um, didn't like it. The good news is we have recently completed a rewrite . . ."

"Of course you have."

"Would you maybe consider reading the revisions?"

"No."

"Oh."

"Look, you seem like a nice man who wants to be a talented writer."

Silence.

"Do this and I'll reconsider. On notebook paper, write one thousand times, 'I will not write screenplays without a clear conceit because it wastes the time and effort of everyone who reads them.' One thousand times. Written. Not done on one of those fancy computer processing machines. Send the work to Jon Foster's office in Culver City, California, care of Justin Lackey. I expect it by the a.m. on Wednesday." Click!

4Play by Sunny Malone is a drama that follows a stripper with a golden heart as she works the pole in order to put herself through cosmetology school, while fending off an abusive boyfriend, a sugar daddy, a drug lord, a pimp, and the sexual advances of her best friend, who the writer insists must be played by Megan Fox (character's name is Megan Foxy). Writer also cites every single song that must be used in the film when the main character dances. Going out on a limb by saying Sunny hopes to play the lead, maybe also direct this sure-to-crash vehicle. Not certain why, but I read every page, right up to its—what's the word I'm looking for?—*flaccid* climax.

```
EXT. SUNSET BOULEVARD -- MORNING


Sunny exits the strip club carrying her
heels. There's a smile on her lovely
face and newfound hope in her heart.
She's going to make it after all.


                SUNNY (V.O.)
     I left that morning and I never
     looked back. I defeated everyone
     that tried to hold me down and I
     literally soared like a phoenix
     from the wreckage that was my
     horrible childhood.
```

Sunny begins to run. Where is she headed? She doesn't know. It doesn't matter, though, because she's free. She's finally free!

SUNNY (V.O.)
Sunny Daze rose that morning and let me tell you all, she rose higher than the biggest star there is—the sun!

FREEZE FRAME on Sunny's happy ending.

THE END

Need to distance myself from this script, and pronto. Hurl the script into the To-Be-Shred pile, but since I'm reclining on the couch and the pile is behind the locked door of my den, the pages crash against wood. The brads that bind give way, sending 8½ x 11s in all directions. Happy ending indeed.

I get off the couch, head to the bathroom cursing Sunny Malone. Stop bedamning her when I realize my pee smells like I had asparagus. *Did I eat asparagus?* For the life of me, cannot recall what I had for dinner last night. By the flush, I stop trying to remember. That's when I spy my reflection, my Chia Pet face.

I run a hand across my Hemingwayesque beard, wondering if the look suits me. I'm nowhere near as tough as the old man. Certainly not as terse. "A man can be destroyed but not defeated," I whisper, scratching at my chin. I grab the crop of hair, deem it more Melville than Hemingway. Regardless, it should not be on a face of my age. I start clipping the excess, get to ratty beard status, and run the tap till the water steams and fills the sink.

Foam. Apply. Lather.

Razor. Soak. Shave.

Sunny. Cocktease. Malone.

Razor. Soak. Shave.

4Play. Lap dance that goes nowhere. I want my money back.

Staring at the murky water and hair I've set adrift, I resolve to give Sunny a call to brighten up her day. Wiping my face with a towel, I approach the disintegrated script, search for the vital page, the cover with the scribe's contact info. *Thar she blows*. Find it trying in vain to get away, halfway under the door of the den. Reel it in, scan the phone number printed on it.

Dial *67, her digits, rings.

"Hello?"

"Hi! I am wishing to speak to *4Play* scribe Sunny Malone."

"This is her."

"I think you mean she."

"What?"

"This is she."

"Okay."

"Sorry, I'm a stickler for grammar. Comes with the job."

"I see."

"Sunny Malone, I read your autobiographic screenplay and, well, what can I say?"

"It is autobiographical. How did you know?"

"Well, how do I put this?" I pause and "hmm" for about a minute. Then, "I didn't see anything creative enough in your script to make me think it was fiction."

"You didn't like it?"

"No. I did not. Look. I'm going to be frank. You couldn't pay me to see this movie if you paid me."

She's silent for a sec. "Then why did you call?"

"To tell you that. Criticism builds character, and I thought maybe you could use some character. Your script sure could."

"Look, a lot of people have read it and loved it."

"I see. Maybe I read it wrong."

"You're an asshole."

"Now that's not fiction."

"Look, I don't need to prove anything to you, but I'll have you know the *Suburban Star* did an article on me, declaring me the next Diablo Cody."

I have a laugh. "Hearing you say that, I'm reminded of the girl who told me she was a virgin, but her baby's name was not Jesus." Click!

"You missed a spot."

It's 6:11 Monday morning and my barista is speaking to me. My barista never speaks to me. Thought we had an unwritten agreement.

"Excuse me?"

"You missed a spot." She laughs and gives me a you-got-something-on-your-face gesture.

My fingers slide across my smooth chin until they encounter roughness. Half my face sports the hacked-up

Hemingway beard. Or was it Melville? Been walking around like this since yesterday. Good thing I don't get out much.

"Coffee's on the house. Anybody that can make me laugh at this hour deserves it. Enjoy."

I grab my coffee and exit, head down, chin to my chest. *Show's over. Move along. Nothing to see here.*

Head home, shave the other half of my mug as my coffee cools. Fresh-faced, I get busy living by perusing the trades as I caffeinate. Start in on the pile by ten to seven.

In a Pickle by Jerry Kucharczyk is a dark comedy with zero structure, no dynamic character, no villain. Simply a story about a kid who falls down a well, detailing his 132-page struggle to survive . . . until his mom calls him for dinner and it's revealed the kid was merely playing in his room and we, the audience, were privy to his imagination. Fact: twists are for schlock writers.

I call Jerry Kucharczyk to tell him that.

He pleads with me for ten minutes. His excuses end with, "Come on. I wrote it in two weeks. Imagine what I could do if I had a couple of months and a plot. My next script—"

I cut him off. "Right now, you remind me of that boy who murdered his parents and begged the judge for mercy because he was an orphan."

"What?"

Click!

Ten after four. Cannot sleep. Been like this six nights in a row. Eyes wide open. Stare at the ceiling for an hour or more. I do what they tell you to: I get out of bed. Head to the computer to research insomnia. Discover there are three types: transient, acute, chronic. Praying it's transient, which typically lasts about a week.

Some cited causes for insomnia:

1. Serious illness. *Let's hope not.*
2. Changes in the sleep environment. *Nope.*
3. Changes in sleep time. *Negative.*
4. Severe depression. *The word* severe *seriously depresses me.*
5. Stress. *Was more stressed working for Foster and Lackey.*

So what's up? I back up to number four, conduct some quick research on depression, discover a myriad of scary kinds. One stands out.

Melancholic depression, which Wikipedia defines as a loss of pleasure in most activities, a failure of reactivity to pleasurable stimuli, a quality of depressed mood more pronounced than grief or loss, a slowing down of thought, and a reduction of physical movements in an individual.

Gulp. I need a drink. Then again, might already be drunk if I'm trusting Wiki to help solve this issue.

Definitely getting somewhere, though. I take pleasure in nothing these days. And since the most active I am is reading scripts, I'm forced to point at the sea of piss-poor writing. But am I depressed over it?

Think. When did the insomnia begin? Six nights ago. Tuesday. What did I do that day? I read all day, of course. What did I read?

Sod, a funny horror film parody about mutant carnivorous grass that's terrorizing a small town. *If the Shoe Fits*, an awful rom-com I bailed on after twenty-one pages. *Under the Cottonwood Tree*, an interesting fantasy about two siblings and their perilous journey into an enchanted forest. *déjà vu* . . .

Not talking about the psychological sensation. I'm talking about a script. *déjà vu déjà vu* by Kip Watson was a futuristic sci-fi action epic about a race of humans whose DNA is stored aboard a massive spaceship scouring the universe the last two hundred years for a habitable planet. The ship is controlled by AI. Through the years, the computers got bored and started utilizing the DNA to play a heart-stopping game of cat and mouse with the humans—over and over again. In a brilliant déjà vu moment, our cloned heroes realize they've been here, done that before, quite possibly dozens of times, and it motivates them to give the machines a fight unlike any they've ever seen.

Project had merit. Even thought it Holdenesque for the first fifteen pages. However, it began to crumble late in the second act and collapsed amid an insulting happy-ending third act. Had Kip Watson gone for doom and gloom, he would've had a masterpiece on his hands. I recall finishing it and being disappointed, but enough to keep me up nights? Not sure about that. Tried to read another script that afternoon but couldn't concentrate. Around four o'clock, gave up, called it a day, turned to the fistful, pour, bubbles. Talk about déjà vu.

What I couldn't comprehend was why the writer of this conceit-filled screenplay chose to go down the yellow brick road with the ending, especially because the influence of *Blade Runner* and *Alien* is apparent.

Philip K. Dick's grim science fiction classic *Do Androids Dream of Electric Sheep?* acted as the source material for *Blade Runner*. The original screenplay embraced Dick's somber ending with one of its own. That's what got it sold.

Ridley Scott, the director of the film, tried to keep that version intact but lost the battle in the end.[12]

Similar story with *Alien*, also directed by Ridley Scott. The original screenplay featured a shockingly dark ending until the studio forced a change.[13] Yet that scripted shock is what got Hollywood's attention in the first place.

Ironic. And infuriating.

Here's one to grow on. If you're writing a script, you don't need to Hollywoodize it. This town will do that for you if you're fortunate enough to have your work optioned. Trust me, they'll deep-fry it in a vat of happily ever after. Nevertheless, what gets noticed is a compelling story that grips until the climax, not one that T-bags the reader when they're not suspecting it so the writer can conveniently put a happy face emoticon after the words **The End.**

I glance at the clock—4:31. Cover page of *déjà vu déjà vu* sports a 323 area code. Los Angeles. Decide to *67 my dear Watson despite the time. It rings seven times before going to voice mail. I hang up, redial. Voice mail again. Redial.

Five rings later, a groggy, "Yeah?"

"Kip, I don't know you. You don't know me. And I don't know how much you know about crafting screenplays, first acts, main character intro, dynamic characters, dynamic progression, conflict, second-act adventures, second-act complications, low points, third-act resolutions, blah, blah, blah. Blah. You can obviously tell I know a lot, right?"

---

12 Early screenplay versions of *Blade Runner* (and Ridley Scott's 2007 final cut DVD) feature an ending radically different from the version seen in theaters. They end with Deckard realizing he's a replicant. Because test audiences did not like the bleak ending, changes were made prior to the film's release.

13 Ridley Scott has reportedly said that in the original ending for *Alien*, the alien would bite off Ripley's head in the escape shuttle, sit in her chair, and then start speaking with her voice in a message to earth. Apparently, 20th Century Fox wasn't too pleased and ordered changes.

"I guess."

"Well, you either know a lot or you got plum lucky with *déjà vu*. This your first script?"

"It is. How did you know?"

"There were a few subtle indicators that led me to that conclusion. Look, your script is good. Your conceit is compelling as all hell. But your third act—"

He cuts me off with, "The end kicks ass."

Don't take too kindly to being cut off. "Hey, Dungeon Master. Are you versed in the material that clearly influenced your homage to the genre and Ridley Scott's work in it? Or did you CliffsNotes your way? Are you aware of the original ending intended for *Blade Runner*? What about *Alien*? Or did thousands of hours watching Hollywood's version of science fiction lead you to conclude your story required a happy ending and your heroes needed to defeat the machines no matter how much of an imbalanced battle they faced?"

"Oh, come on. You can't tell me you didn't like the end."

"Yes. I can. Oh, and one more thing. Yes, I can. How's that for déjà vu?" Click.

Back to bed. Sleep like a baby the rest of the night. Dream aplenty amid the REM.

The following night, an encore presentation. Insomnia cured. Thank you, AT&T, for that.

FATHER'S OFFICE

Fifth month in. Approximately twelve hundred scripts read. And look what I have to show for it: I'm lethargic, a tad pasty, about twenty pounds heavier. Not helping the last issue by being here, at Father's Office, a bar in Santa Monica. I like it here. Reminds me of a few places back in San Fran. Decadent burger and a stellar selection of beers, including one I've adopted and want to include in my will, given all the happiness it's brought me.

"Another Racer 5?" my best friend tonight inquires.

"Please," I say, my seventh vocalized word today.

Drone of the crowd deafens. Place is small and packed. Always is around dinnertime. Opens at five. Quiet until six thirty, when the parade of young Hollywood takes over. At times it's too much to bear. Despite that, I come here three times a week—Tuesday, Thursday, Saturday—for a reason.

Meyer Holden was a regular here back in the day, before the Office Burger debuted, back when a pool table compromised the limited seating. Holden resided nearby and came here to drink with colleagues he called friends. It was their place. Took me about ten minutes my first visit to understand why.

Beneath the polished wood, dressed-up menu, and annoying cologne of LA attitude—things I assume were ushered in as the pool table was ushered out—stands a place of nostalgia, reminiscent of the watering holes journalists hung out in when they still wore fedoras. Holden and his friends were screenwriters and novelists, but they were Hollywood's inner circle, an elite group in LA who loved to write and were paid handsomely for their efforts. After long days spent with their craft, they met here to unwind, bounce ideas, and share Hollywood war stories.

A few of his friends still hang here. Mind you, they don't come for the burger or the scene. From what I gather, they simply refuse to leave. They still consider the place home and huddle in the corner near the bathrooms. It's obvious they loathe the delusion, which endears them to me.

So here I sit, a tourist with an agenda but one I can conceal. Good at that. Three days a week, I walk in shortly after five, belly up to the bar. Ass cheeks do their suffocating, fingerprints tattoo glass. I read the paper, wait for the locals to talk to me one day.

Sure, I peek from the *Times* whenever one of them says, "Well, look who's here," wishing in vain it's Holden's silhouette framed in the passageway between setting sun and dim bar. Never is. Not sure why I look. Have no idea what I'd even say to him. Chasing the words he Couriers is different from stalking The Man, right? Hope so.

Around ten visits in, I have to laugh. A regular calls to

the bartender, this extremely hot blonde, even by LA standards. Thought her name was Christine.

"Christmas," he exclaims.

"Another Arrogant Bastard, Ron?"

"You know me all too well."

My eyes glaze over the Dodgers commentary I'm reading. Someone else asks, "Did you just say Christmas?"

He laughs. "The gal behind the bar. Her name is Christmas Noel. She goes by Christine, but I do not know why. Such a great name."

"You're shitting me."

"I shit you not."

I laugh. Not out loud, mind you, lest I blow my cover.

Never take a script to Father's Office. Never utter Holden's name. It's my clandestine attempt to reap intel on The Man from those in the know. Three times a week, I perch myself at the bar, gaining weight as I wait in the hope of gaining ground. And wouldn't you know it, the ground buys me a beer fifth month in. Today. Happens while I'm chowing on a burger and fries, sipping my second 5, watching highlights of my Twins against the Royals on the TV. I cringe, offended by a lousy call against my team. Slap a hand on the bar as Sal Burton sits down right next to me.

Sal Burton. Writer of four esteemed films—*A Walk Across the Rooftops*, *Hats*, *Peace at Last*, and *High*. His work is revered by Hollywood, film buffs around the globe, and me. Problem is those four scripts were delivered within a seventeen-year span, none less than five years apart. Legend has it Burton, a notorious perfectionist, set fire to more words than he sold in a series of infamous bonfires over the years.[14] Adding to the mythos, he allegedly hasn't written a thing in eleven years. Beginning with the pioneering *Rooftops*, a refined and heartrending drama set in Los Angeles that helped usher in an era of quiet film,[15] Burton became an overnight success—albeit after a decade of, in his words, "writing for an audience of none."

His follow-up, *Hats*, which many refer to as his masterpiece, is a melodic love letter to an unidentified city. It follows a never-named protagonist in a heartbreaking quest to find an "ordinary girl who can make everything all right." Many call it Hollywood's most sobering love story. Funny words if you ever find yourself face-to-face with the writer.

"Minnesota and KC?" Sal says. "You care about either of these crap teams, or was there money involved?"

I glance over and swallow the holy-shit-Sal-Burton-just-sat-down-next-to-me feeling. Sal's thin, graying, and has tired-looking eyes. In a better light, they might look beaten.

"Unfortunately, I was born in Minneapolis. Twins fan my whole life." I play it cool, but I'm already cursing the fact I pulled my eyes out of the *Times* to enjoy some ESPN. The less you project, the more advantage you have. Learned that rule a while ago. Bad time to break it.

"Sorry to hear that, but at least you'll always have '87

---

14 James Lipton once said, "Sal Burton is old school personified. The accomplished writer hunts and pecks on a Smith Corona typewriter and distills his work with a No. 2 pencil. Only then does he invite trusted individuals for evenings in which he generously pours spirits as they gratifyingly pore over his words. Through the years, those privileged enough to take pleasure in these works also cringe when informed Burton deemed them unworthy and allegedly set the sole copies ablaze."

15 John Black of *Queue Magazine* coined the term "quiet film" in a five-star review of Sal Burton's 1983 debut. Black applauded the scaled-down story, writing, "In a day and age of unrelenting action, tits, and periodic explosions, *A Walk Across the Rooftops* is a one-off, a film like nothing else we've ever encountered. Sal Burton's haunting voice carries fragile strands of story that melt into the backdrop before you've quite grasped them. It's as if he spent years deciding how much he could leave out and still have enough meat and bones to allow the narrative to stand up." Seven years later Black apologized for the "one-off" comment in light of Burton's sophomore achievement.

and '91," Sal remarks as Christmas gives him a nod indicating that she'll be right over. "What brings you west?"

"Career."

"Actor?"

"Writer."

Christmas arrives.

"Sorry to hear that too." Sal chuckles. "Chimay, Christine. And another for the young scribe here. Put it on my tab."

Christmas eyes Sal. "Tabs are supposed to be paid one day, Sal."

Sal winks at her. "Well, that's not the spirit of Christmas we've all come to love."

She rolls her eyes, turns her attention to me. "Another Racer?"

I nod. It's my third of the night. I never drink three. Then again, this is what I'm here for. So I gain a little more weight, notice the Twins lost by one, make small talk with Sal. He never lets on who he is. I never give him any more than I did when I told him where I grew up, who I root for.

He drinks, spews advice. "Write what you know." Leaning in close, he whispers, "And write what you know will get you laid." He laughs at his own funny, then sobers up to add, "Seriously, though, make it unique. Don't be bothered if some people don't like it. Simply find the one person who loves it."

That's beautiful. Hallmark needs writing like that. "Thanks for the advice."

Sal wants to buy me another. That's four. Think I just cracked the case of Sal Burton. For years it's been rumored his career is over because he's a drunk. Might be he's a drunk because his career is over.

"What kind of stuff you write?"

"Well, I'm working on a horror script where the hero-ine is haunted by her aborted baby boy who chokes victims with his umbilical cord, and in the climax she tells him she's pregnant with his baby sister, tricking him to crawl back in her vagina, imprisoning him in her uterus. Until the sequel!" I say this because I know Sal isn't listening.

He's checking out the two lost angels to his right who are trying to get the bartender's attention. His drunk head bobs from their tits to his beer to mine. "You gotta keep writing. Every day. No matter what. Christine!"

She glances over at us.

He points to the women.

She gives another nod.

"I do. I do," I say.

"What's your script called?"

"*After Birth.*"

He smiles, loses eye contact again. Before he looks back to the treasure chests next door, he says, "I'll keep a lookout for it at my local movie theater."

Yeah. You do that.

The chicks take off twenty minutes later, which brings Sal's attention back to me as I'm contemplating an exit strategy.

"One more?"

"Sure." Mistake.

Sal buys another, my fifth in under two hours. He starts to pontificate about the East Coast versus the West Coast, apparently forgetting I'm from the Midwest. Pint half empty, he says, "Los Angeles is New York resting on its laurels."

I smile. Such a great quote. One that made me laugh when I was eighteen sitting in a movie theater watching *A Walk Across the Rooftops* for the first time. "Great line. One of your fucking best."

Tired eyes come alive, giving me a glimpse of the intensity that undoubtedly fueled his writing back in the day. "Thought you didn't know who I was."

Busted. Loss for words. I stare at the remaining amber imprisoned within my glass.

"Thought there was something off with you. Who roots for the fucking Twins? So my guess is you're an agent wondering if I'm for hire these days or maybe you're fishing for Holden. Which is it? Shark or fisherman? Aw, who the fuck cares?"

He's genuinely pissed. Apparently the look on my face answers some outstanding questions.

"You're chasing a ghost, kiddo. Ain't a chance in hell you'll win that lottery."

Better off chasing a ghost than thinking I could get anything out of a has-been who thinks his muse is at the bottom of that glass.

Wait. Did I say that out loud?

Look on Sal Burton's face confirms I did indeed. He blinks twice. Loss for words here and now—and for the last decade.

Should get up and leave. Drunk. Tired. Fed up. Ass kisses barstool one minute too long.

"Attention, everyone," Sal bellows. "We got a bona fide ghost chaser in our presence tonight. Minnesota here is hunting for my dear friend Meyer Holden."

"Sal," Christmas calls out from across the bar. "Sit. Keep it down."

80

Patrons turn their heads, crane their necks to catch a glimpse of Sal or of me, not certain which.

"In a second, Christine. I want you all to take one long look at a man wasting his time, playing Dick Tracy in the Technicolor of his imagination, where he dreams of being a lottery winner for finding a golden ticket in someone else's trash."

Pretty good line. Should have ended it at *imagination,* though.

Bouncer approaches Sal, makes him sit down, shut up.

I throw more than enough cash on the bar, wobble from my seat. "Thanks for the beers, Sal. Luck with the writing."

And we leave it at that.

I depart, stumble out of the bar into a dark and chilly Santa Monica.

Fucked up back there. Fat, lazy, stupid, drunk. Fucked up back there. Fuck.

"It's like little kids coloring," I sermonize, groggy, drained, discouraged.

Talking to a machine. Have been for a few minutes. Two o'clock here, four in the morn there.

"When you're a kid, you color without abandon. You color outside the lines. You color however you feel. Blue elephants, red bears, purple trees, green oceans. It's all good. As you get older, though, everyone tells you to stay inside the lines, to color everything just like you see it. Why? Where's the fun and intrigue in that? Writers care too much about coloring within the lines. They all seem to be painting by numbers, everyone wanting their stuff to look and sound exactly like what they see up on the big screen. It's a shame. A few write what they want. A few make their mark, but then everybody copies them and they ultimately wax and wane into the masses. Damn shame. Should write what you feel. Write outside the lines. We need more green oceans, blue elephants. I want to read blue elephants."

There's a rumble as someone picks up the phone.

I stop talking.

Sobering silence is broken by, "What did you say your name was?"

"I didn't. I called to say your script sucks," I slur. "Like all the rest." Click.

ROUTINE FUCKUP

Phew, for a minute there, I lost myself.

Sort of went off the deep end. Week after my encounter with Sal, I realized the extremes were not working, made some changes.

New rules. No more late-night calls. No more Father's Office. Focus on the prize, remain strong, get into shape, exercise, eat right, drink less. New schedule: wake before five, head to Runyon Canyon for a run before anyone in their right mind even gets up, secure trades and coffee by six, home, shower, get to work. Two mornings a week, Tuesday and Thursday, I grab breakfast at The Griddle, get in when they open at seven, out before eight, gone before the LA families are done spooning fruit and yogurt into their babies' mouths. Also eat dinner out three nights a week. Quality food, no fast food.

Feels good to be out and about, to decompress after the day's work, though I can't say I'm not looking over my shoulder every five minutes. Doesn't take long for the new routine to produce results. Mood is better, shed some pounds, have more energy throughout the day.

They say if you do anything for twenty-one days, it becomes a habit. After twenty-one days of seeing the same ten apparent insomniacs at Runyon, the same handful of people in and around Starbucks, the same fussy babies at breakfast, and the same early birds at dinner, it all becomes routine.

Thing is, routine breeds complacency. Complacency breeds mistakes. More mistakes.

"Bateman," a voice interrupts my morning read.

I'm at The Griddle, head in a script—*Sheer Evidence*—and it's good. Too good. Sucked me in despite its flaws. As I suddenly tune back in to reality, the decibel level in the joint tells me I've been here too long.

Gaze darts to the number on the upper right corner of the page: 103. BOOM!BOOM!BOOM! *Shit.* Started the script after ordering. I do the math. Must be almost nine. Bled into ambitious LA time. Even before I look up, I smell his cologne, know I'm busted.

Justin Lackey stands before me, all suited up, every hair locked in place. "Well, well, well. If it isn't Mr. Savant himself. Or can I call you Idiot?" He's grinning Cheshire-like.

Looking over his shoulder, I notice his breakfast date as she bends to collect her belongings from their booth.

"Long time, no blurb," he adds.

He means my name hasn't been in the trades since I was tossed from Foster's office. "No shit, Sherlock. That's because I'm done. No interest in blurbs anymore."

He laughs. "Right. So whatcha reading there? More

importantly, who you reading for?"

Deliver an emphatic, "No one."

He laughs. "Oh, come on. I caught you. You can't pretend you're not caught."

Tequila Sunrise. I nail the quote but have zero interest in his game.

He grins, pokes between his teeth with a toothpick. "So where did you land?"

I put down the script, lean back, and stretch. "Didn't. I'm in advertising now. Have the day off and was reading this as a favor for a neighbor. It's her brother's work."

"Sure." His gaze dips to his chiming Treo.

"No. Really," I lie through my coffee-stained teeth. "Not part of the chase anymore."

"Sure," he says again. "That's why you're still living here. Because everyone loves LA." He puts up a finger and turns away to answer the call.

Stupid, stupid, stupid. He knows. I'm being careless, and now he knows. Stupidity.

He's still standing in front of me. Apparently he wants to continue our conversation after his call.

Jaw clenched, I scan the crowd. The place is packed. Why did this fucking script have to be so good? My eyes land on Lackey's breakfast mate at the register, a sexy young thing wearing a knit cap and denim skirt. Shoulder-length hair hangs past the knit, miracle mile legs extend from the denim. Her back's to me and her ass captivates. I chuckle at the fact she's paying. Lackey doesn't even buy his broads eats the morning after. *Stay classy, Lackey.*

"Will do," Lackey says into his phone as he turns to me. "Be there in fifteen. Late." He hangs up, and I have to look at that fucking smile of his once again.

"So for someone who quit the biz months ago, you sure read a lot of scripts."

"Like I said, I'm reading this one for old times' sake."

Lackey picks his teeth, admires the steady stream of on-my-way-to-an-audition actresses lining up at the register. "Bateman, I saw you in the parking lot last week as I was pulling in. You had a script under your arm. I don't know, maybe you keep reading the same one over and over for your neighbor's brother." He smirks. "For old times' sake."

I laugh, but I'm a bad actor.

"You're fishing for Holden, aren't you?"

"No idea what you're talking about."

"Bateman," he says, finally looking my way, "I'm about to branch off from Foster and want to prepare for that transition so I can hit the ground midsprint. I could use a good man to help me get my project on wheels. Come work for me. Besides, you're wasting your time fishing by your lonesome."

"Nah. It's advertising now, and it's peaceful in this boat."

"It's stupid. I'll pay you to go fish."

"And you'll fuck me if and when I bag the elephant."

He grins. "Hey, my boy is back. And you're right. Greed, for lack of a better word, is good. But there ain't no Moby Dick out there. It's a myth. You're wasting your time."

"At least my time belongs to me and not Foster."

"Fuck you. Call me when you change your mind."

"Fuck that. Have a nice life."

"Always a pleasure, Bateman." He laughs as he walks toward the back exit, joins his chick who's leaning against the wall, two-thumbing her BlackBerry. They leave.

Pound my fist on the counter, startling the couple next to me. Disgusted and fuming, I wave the waitress over, ask for my bill.

"It's been taken care of."

"He paid for my meal?"

"No. She did."

She did?

I glance at the register.

Share.

FIELDER'S CHOICE

by
Meyer Holden

Meyer Holden
323-898-1 80
WGAw: 904037

Maybe True Hollywood Story

When things seem bleak, when the weight of what's in my den starts to bully my motivation, I pull a copy of one of the ten Meyer Holden scripts the industry already knows about, park myself on the couch, and enjoy the read. Doesn't matter which one. I own all ten. Accrued the impressive collection of original copies in the months after I drank in The Legend.

Found the first one by chance at a Hollywood flea market, a mere eight days after Kevin slurred, "Meyer the writer Holden," at the Culver Hotel bar during happy hour. Passing a table of books at the swap meet, I was suddenly caught in the tractor beam of a small stack of scripts in the corner. Atop the pile, a weathered copy of Meyer Holden's dark thriller *Punching the Clown*—109 wrinkly pages of three-hole paper bound by two dull brads, cover page branded with The Man's name. Held it in my hands, felt like fate. Took it as a definite sign. Destiny. A stirring BOOM!BOOM!BOOM! provided the soundtrack as my little adventure commenced. Purchased that copy of *Punching the Clown* for a mere five bucks. Read it twice that night. I was hooked.

So began my extensive study in everything Holden. So began my quest.

Utilizing eBay, Craigslist, hollywoodcollectibles.com, and a few other resources, I procured the rest of Holden's works. Bid, bought, and acquired via an anonymous e-mail linked to my PayPal, a live.com account I created. Username: VerbalKint. Was relentless in these furtive efforts until I ultimately possessed all ten. Only took me three weeks.

Hardest to find, most cherished in the collection, is what I'm reading today—an original spec copy[16] of *Fielder's Choice*, the script that put Holden on Hollywood's speed dial.

EXT. CLARK & ADDISON -- MORNING

Heels clicking on pavement, reveal Harriet passing, noticing a paperboy sitting on a stack.

                    HARRIET
      You know, you'd sell a lot more
      papers if you'd shout out the
      headlines.

                   PAPERBOY
      You think?

---

16 At any bookstore in any city, you can purchase a copy of the shooting script for *Fielder's Choice*. However, a shooting script is just a translation of the final film, while a spec script is the version the writer initially wrote and sold. *Major* difference. This spec copy of *Choice* contains the original vision of the story/characters/world that Holden sent to anyone and everyone when he was just another writer striving to be discovered.

                    HARRIET
     I know. It worked for ages.

Harriet walks on. The boy scans the
paper, calls out:

                   PAPERBOY
     No comment from vanishing Cubs.

Harriet stops, returns to the boy, whispers, points to the paper.

As she walks away, we hear:

                   PAPERBOY
     Dale Wennington, major league
     prick!

Harriet smirks. Pedestrians approach
the boy, coins in hand.

I laugh out loud, even though I'm reading it for about
the fiftieth time.

"What's so funny?" Share inquires. She's at the other
end of the couch, wearing one of my dress shirts, painting
her nails Bubblicious Pink.

"Nothing." Trust no one.

"You never tell me anything," she huffs on her way to
the bathroom. My bathroom.

We've been seeing a lot of each other lately.

If you're looking for rationale in all this, here it is. After running into Share and Lackey that morning at The Griddle, I came home, tried to work. Finished *Sheer Evidence*, hated the ending, which, in turn, immediately revealed to me the inherent flaw in the script. Wondered why the writer didn't see it, so I *67'd him to find out. It was my first call to a writer in almost a month. Promised myself I would refrain from the charitable act of telling writers what I felt they needed to hear. Fell off the wagon—and hard.

Conversation did not go well. Imagine that.

"Conrad, Conrad, Conrad, how do I sum this up nicely? Aw, you know what? Fuck nice. Nice is overrated. Now listen up. Next time you take the time to write a film noir, you might not want to shoot yourself in the head by typing a bunch of stuff between the words *fade in* and *the end* that you haven't completely thought through."

"What? Mister, who in the hell do you think you are?"

"Me? I'm Hollywood's number one belligerent savant. And a not-so-private dick that's about to hang up on your amateur ass." Click!

In the wake of the call, I questioned everything—my quest, this lifestyle, my den, the To-Be-Read, the To-Be-Shred. Needless to say, it was not a good morning. Blamed it all on *Sheer Evidence*. Sheer crap in my book. Regardless, it was no Holden, so I moved on. Rest of the day was a wash. Couldn't concentrate. Found myself rereading mind-numbing, exposition-filled dialogue, and there's nothing worse.

Called it a day before noon.

Called Share just after two.

"Hey," was her greeting.

Caller ID had betrayed me, meaning I was still programmed in her cell. "Thanks for breakfast."

"Told you I had next time."

"You cut your hair."

"I did. Change is good."

Suddenly did not know what to say, why I called, what I was doing.

"Pregnant pause," Share whispered.

Rule of thumb: Never say *pregnant* around a single guy. Especially if he's going through some heavy-duty shit at the time.

"I thought you were going to call. I actually thought we had a good time."

"We did," I responded, believing the words. "I should have called. Let me make it up to you."

Fell into bed that night, didn't want her to leave the next morning. Ain't the genre of romance grand?

My trip down memory lane is disrupted as Share returns from the bathroom, stomping a bit, nails on her fingers and toes still shiny-wet. She gathers the script pages she's been practicing all morning.

"I'm sorry for whatever it is I did. Sincerely."

She laughs. "You can tell me things, you know?"

"I know I can, baby. But I choose not to."

"Whatever. Are you staying home to read more scripts today?"

She knows too much, might-wind-up-in-someone's-trunk too much.

She kisses me before heading to the bedroom to get dressed.

I watch her sway. Maybe she'll keep quiet. Maybe I'll spare her.

If you're *still* looking for rationale in all this, well, here's more.

The morning after we got together again, we stayed in bed until noon. Took her to Ammo for lunch. She was telling me her Maybe True Hollywood Story while I was weighing my options.

I liked her, enjoyed being with her, but could ill afford distractions. Sex was fantastic, but the fact she was with Lackey honestly made me never want to touch her again. She was sweet, but we seemed to be on different pages at times.

Case in point, we were finishing our meal when David Spade walked in with Heather Locklear. The hum in the room waned for a pay-homage moment, and for that suspended second I hated everything about Hollywood—including Share, who leaned in to whisper, "Wow. She's with him? He's so come and gone."

Made my decision then and there. Better off going it alone.

So what the fuck? Why is she here getting ready for her audition in my bedroom?

Well, she took a picture. Yeah. Read that right. A fucking picture.

We bolted Ammo, and I almost ran smack into two tourists with their starstruck eyes to the sky, gawking at something off in the distance. I crossed the street, in a hurry to get back to my reading, but then I noticed the clicking of Share's heels ceased.

Turned to see the touristy dude about to digitize his

wayfarer wife, Hollywood sign over her shoulder.

That's when Share offered, "Want me to take a picture of both of you?"

They gushed, handed her the camera, huddled together, smiled.

As she counted down, Share beamed.

Her smile made me smile.

Standing there on Highland, blocks below Sunset, I honestly could not recall the last time this face of mine had done this.

Click.

Was the kindest, most midwestern gesture I've seen while doing time. Watched her scamper to catch up, amidst a distinctive BOOM!BOOM!BOOM!

Why'd she have to take that damn picture?

That was a month and a half ago. Been together ever since.

Early on, she kept asking all these questions about what I did, until I did something about it. In between the third degree, she often took time to complain about her current agent, whom she mentioned Lackey helped her obtain. Mere mention of his name made me throw up in my mouth a little. Also stirred my competitive nature—*for old times' sake.*

Somewhere between the third or thirtieth complaint, I decided to call up Curtis Landon, a retired manager who never paid much attention to detail but was the most dependable guy I've ever worked with. Knew the former trait would mean he most likely thought I was still working with Foster, while the latter had made him the success he was. Asked him to take a look at this girl who came across my desk—figuratively, not literally. Sent over Share's head shot/reel.

He took a look-see and called an agent he felt would be good for her.

Agent was impressed and signed Share on the spot.

That led to a string of auditions for choice TV shows—*CSI, Criminal Minds, Grey's Anatomy.* The potential parts on these episodic shows tended to be guest-star roles, which sounds like when some established star shows up, but it's not. It's when any actor who's not a regular appears in an episode. These one-off actors play everything from lawyers and doctors to victims and killers. They can also appear briefly as the girlfriend of the guy that turns out to be the killer or waiter with a bit of vital information for the detectives.

All this got Share so excited she stopped asking so many questions. Also kept her busy and at bay. Mission accomplished.

I might sound like an ingrate, an asshole who might not know a good thing if it saved his life. Not true. I've become fond of Share in our time together. Behind determined eyes is an insecure girl looking for affirmation. Sure, that's maybe true for much of Hollywood, but what makes it endearing is most of the time it seems my affirmation is all she needs. Appears I am on the list after all.

I recognized this one night about three weeks into our dynamic relationship.

"Bateman, play that music. The band I like." Share whispered this as I hovered above her, tugging at her jeans, exposing her forever-and-a-day legs.

The requested album was Roxy Music's *Avalon.* She'd never heard it before I made it the soundtrack to us. Most her age haven't. It's one of my favorite CDs, a piece of incriminating evidence of my slightly-past-the-expiration-date status as far as Hollywood is concerned.

Backstory. I attended Whitman, a small college in the state of Washington. Upon arrival, I learned there was a long-standing, unwritten rule that if you really liked a girl, you played *Avalon* for her when you got her back to your room. Always loved that. Carried the tradition into my postcollegiate life.

Since graduation, I have enjoyed the album with a mere three, Share being the third and the sole one while doing time. I didn't tell her about the tradition. Didn't have to. The music says it all. I watched her body react to track one, "More Than This." Took her face in my hands, kissed her like they do in the movies. She smiled, wrapped herself around me. Together we enjoyed *Avalon*.

But wait-wait-wait. I was explaining my rationale. I realized something after Share sang a duet with Elvis in the reverse cowgirl position. I came, and it was one of those good-God-this-chick-is-so-smoking-hot-I-wish-my-high-school-buddies-could-see-me-now moments. Seem to have them a lot with this girl. Way it is.

However, that wasn't the moment of realization. After the naked fun, I was finishing a less-than-stellar script when Share interrupted.

"You know," she said in a manner that told me she wasn't going to continue until I stopped doing what I was doing and looked her way.

I stopped reading, pulled the script to my chest.

"You throw yourself into your work with a determination that can only come from trying to find a replacement for love."

"What? Where did you hear that?"

"I don't know. I read it somewhere. But it's pretty spot-on, no?"

"Yeah. No. I don't know. What the hell? Who are you?"

She laughed. "I'm your girl, dummy. And you're like that guy. That guy in that script you read last week."

"I'm not like that guy," I said, knowing precisely which traits of which character in which script she was referring to.

Been telling her way too much.

She smiled at me with her eyes, these chestnut-colored windows, and there, then, simultaneously I thought, *Why'd she go and take that fucking picture of those fucking tourists thank God she took that fucking picture of those fucking tourists.*

That enough rationale for you? It is for me.

Just like that, we became boyfriend/girlfriend. Our Act Two commenced. We made love again, under the covers this time. Come to think of it, might have been the first time.

BACHMAN TARANTINO OVERDRIVE

Morning. Rise. Runyon. Coffee. Trades. Pull from room. Couch. Assume the position. Read.

Share is off filming a spot on *CSI: NY*, third role she's garnered since gaining representation.

This is good for business. My business. As much as I might like the girl, I've got work to do.

Sink into the cushions.

Immerse myself in the writer's world.

Do what I do.

All day.

Put it in overdrive.

Productive day.

Believe the secret to this search—my advantage, if there can be one—comes from reading Holden. Those who have seen his movies yet talk like they've read his scripts are fooling themselves. Check that. They're simply fools.

Lost in translation from script to screen is the level to which Holden paints in written word. The Man knows

99

his craft and puts that knowledge onto born-blank pages bound by brads.

Dare I say I'm addicted to the heights his words take me? May be why I resent all scripts that fall short. Maybe.

The acquired articles and gathered research were informative, but his body of work tells the real story, adds first-hand knowledge to my studies, my education in Holden.

While growing pains are apparent within his first two spec scripts, *This Time of Night* and *Lennon Bridges*, Holden hit his stride with *Fielder's Choice*. Something clicked in his writing, and from then on, we entered the Holden Age of Hollywood. The ten scripts that are his oeuvre, masterpieces in my opinion, rival the work of any artist in any field—composer, novelist, sculptor—and in any period of time—Renaissance, Romantic, Modern. Take your pick. Bring it on.

If you're balking, I probably know why.

Screenplays are not given the credit they deserve and often are viewed as mere blueprints for films. That's hogwash. How can anyone think that when the entire world, characters, actions, and dialogue are contained within those pages? Scripts are the soul of a film. Take that soul away, and you're left with something lifeless.

Might argue a well-written script is as enjoyable as a novel, song, or painting. Might argue, but alas, no one's here to challenge me.

Also have the advantage of knowing how to read a script, what to look for, the essential ingredients, vital beats, effective structure, and most of all, uniqueness of the idea.[17]

---

17 Original ideas are often referred to as the *conceits* of a script. Conceit-filled scripts should be the number one goal for every writer, yet when Hollywood is delivered the gift of a conceit-filled script, they fuck it up every time.

Holden fills all criteria to a T. Each time. Times ten.

And even though each one of his scripts is unique—distinct genres, settings, time periods—Holden's style jumps off the page, at least to me. Then again, I'm well versed in his work, studied it at length, dissected it page by page. Can detect Holden's nuances, much as art experts can identify painters from the palettes, brushstrokes, compositions, or subjects of their work. Holden's well-drawn characters have distinct voices, and he often uses clever devices to achieve variation. Each character in his work debuts with unique cause-and-effect descriptions, which is a trademark of sorts.

```
MACK FELLOWS, 35, punch-drunk but
threatening, never looks anyone in
the eye, making all he meets imme-
diately uncomfortable.[18]
```

```
LORELEI, 27, petite, alert, body
dripping with sex, causing eyes of
all genders to cascade over her,
nose to toes.[19]
```

Action sequences, always triggered at the precipice of conflict, are multipage, vivid symphonies that somehow advance the characters and story while providing edge-of-your-seat entertainment. You finish these scenes, realize what felt like five pages was in fact twenty, then can't wait to reread them. Mind you, the action isn't always of the guns-blazing, blood-splattering variety. Holden's conquered that

---

18 Mack Fellows, main character/hero as introduced by Meyer Holden in *The Living End*.

19 Lorelei, dynamic character/love interest as introduced by Meyer Holden in *The Living End*.

but also had his way with psychological thrillers, drama, mystery, and even a dark comedy.

Finally, while he'll never blatantly infringe upon a director's job, Holden will at times paint one into a corner with descriptions of specific and brilliant action that can only be filmed one possible way: his.

Detailing all this might lead you to believe finding a Holden is a cakewalk. Not so. See, success in this town leads to imitation. Case in point, in the wake of Quentin Tarantino's *Reservoir Dogs* and *Pulp Fiction*, Hollywood was flooded with screenplays with pop culture–riddled dialogue, nonlinear storytelling, and ruthless hit men whose characters arc and suddenly gain a conscience. Flood got so bad Tarantino himself didn't pen another original screenplay until four years after *Pulp Fiction*.[20]

Having said that, I have hope. I trust Holden's talent will be as evident to me as Stephen King's was to avid fans when he released *The Bachman Books*.[21]

Can only hope.

---

20 *Jackie Brown* (1997). Note: between *Reservoir Dogs* (1992), *Pulp Fiction* (1994), and *Jackie Brown*, Tarantino did have his name on *True Romance* (1993) and *Natural Born Killers* (1994). However, those scripts were penned prior to *Reservoir Dogs*, and Quentin was just cashing in on his newfound success with what was sitting in his desk drawer. Wasn't until *Jackie Brown* that the world got a taste of post-*Fiction* Tarantino.

21 *The Bachman Books* is a collection of short novels by Stephen King, published under the pseudonym Richard Bachman between 1977 and 1982. Some say the already celebrated author wanted to see if his books were successful because of the writing or because they simply had his name on the cover. In "Why I Was Bachman," an introduction added to later printings of the *Bachman Books*, King wrote, "I did five books under [the pseudonym] and I've been getting letters asking me if I was Richard Bachman from the very beginning."

SHARE EVIDENCE

déjà vu déjà vu - Kip Watson (DreamWorks SKG)
DreamWorks SKG has made a preemptive six-figure
acquisition of *déjà vu déjà vu*, a sci-fi action script
by Kip Watson. Deal marks the first sale for Watson.
DreamWorks also made a blind commitment for a
future Watson script. **8/13**

Blurb appears in *Variety* this morning, makes my coffee
taste all the more bitter. Pretty certain the writer didn't
take my advice. Sold it despite the ending. I'm livid. Not
sure why.

Might be because I don't take too kindly to being proved
wrong. Read *déjà vu déjà vu* months ago, enjoyed it despite
its minor flaws, detested it when the author delivered a preposterous heroes-defeat-the-opponents happy ending. Yet
here Kip Watson is having the last laugh via a blurb.

Might be my lot in life. The script, despite its flaws, had
merit. It simply needed to be developed. That's what we do.

Check that. What I did. Past life. No going back.

Might be due to my current state. Tired, bleeding money, submerged in stacks and stacks of non-Holdens, struggling to remain afloat, weighted down by all this cruelty to the English language, bastardization of screenplay structure and execution. Every day I read and read, think, *Syd Field is turning over in his grave—and he's not even dead yet.*[22]

Also might be all of the above. Or none. That uncertainty puts me in a foul mood all day, culminates with me taking it out on the wrong person.

"Bates. Can I ask you a question?"

Don't want to look up, shouldn't, wish I hadn't.

"Do you read all these scripts only because you're looking for one guy? Don't you get anything else out of it?"

I look back into the pages of the script in my hands. "Don't ask me about my business, Share." Quote is from *The Godfather*. Was supposed to make her laugh, forget the question, leave me alone, none of which happens.

Few seconds of silence.

"You think you're funny, Bateman, but you're not. God, it pisses me off when you act like this. You're this bitter, selfish, son of a bitch sometimes, and in a town full of 'em, well, that makes you a fuckin' cliché."

"Thanks."

My sarcasm does not go over well.

She gets up from the couch, looks me in the eye. "I like you, Bateman. You're smart. You're funny. You're the most determined person I've met while doing time." She breathes deep, looks to the ceiling, shakes her head. "I like you. I like

---

22 Syd Field wrote the book *Screenplay: The Foundation of Screenwriting.* If you haven't read it, well, you are not a screenwriter. Basically, it's to screenwriting what the textbook *Gray's Anatomy* is to medicine.

being around all that. It's why I'm here."

She reaches down, grabs the script from my hands, holds it up.

"Despite all this, I like you." She tosses the bundle to the floor. "But you're angry, Bateman. I'm not sure at what or who because you won't talk to me, and that's fine for now. But when you turn that anger on me after what I've given you, after what I've given to us . . ." She exhales, doesn't finish the thought. Instead, she looks back down, her gaze delivering an ultimatum. She turns, walks away.

"Where are you going?"

"To bed."

"I'll be there in an hour or so."

"No, you're sleeping on the couch tonight."

"But that's my bed."

Share stops, turns. One look confirms I'll be sleeping on the couch tonight.

"See you in the morning," I say.

No more words. Bedroom door shuts.

I brood, ponder my actions, Share's words. After a few minutes, I lock out the thoughts, ignore the problem, which for me is a chronic solution. I pick up the script from the floor, continue reading. Takes a lot of effort to finish this less-than-stellar yarn but finally do. Get up, head to the den, introduce the just-read to the To-Be-Shred, grab the top script from the stack, plop down on the couch, immerse myself in something called *Ghost Man on Third*.

Sixty-six pages later, I give up on that one, head back to the den, toss the pages you know where. Reaching to grab another, I watch the just-tossed script slide off the pile and ski down a slope of 8½ x 11s until it comes to rest near the bottom, on top of a memorable bundle, spine tattooed in black Sharpie with the title *Sheer Evidence*. The one that accompanied me to The Griddle the morn I was confronted by Lackey and unexpectedly treated to breakfast.

And here we are . . .

Stare at the title, let the thoughts in.

Bitter.

Selfish.

Son of a bitch.

Nailed me.

Cliché to boot.

Twenty-five after midnight.

Tired.

Pull *Sheer* from the bottom of the pile, dial *67 before adding the digits on the script's cover page. Five rings.

"Hello?"

"Hey, Conrad. Wake you up?"

"Who is this? It's three thirty."

"Same guy who called you several weeks ago about your script. The belligerent savant."

Crickets.

"Don't hang up. Hear me out. Want to apologize. Was an asshole to you. Was off base. I liked your script until its second-act woes, and—"

"I don't care to hear all this again."

"I care. That's why I got mad. At you. At your script. But that's also why I was off base. Listen, not going to take too much of your time. Sorry to wake you, but I was wondering if you ever considered something. Ever consider combining your dynamic character and your opponent into one character? Dynamic obviously needs to perish for your main character's destiny to be fulfilled—for her arc to be complete. That's the conceit of your story. Applaud that, but combining the supporting characters also resolves all conflict simultaneously. Makes for one effective climax instead of the deferred domino effect that handicaps the script."

The honesty of his silence deafens.

"Conrad?"

"Why are you doing this?"

"Because your script is good. But needs to be great. Or it doesn't stand a chance." Click.

Slip into the bedroom, bend to kiss Share on the forehead.

She stirs. "Asshole," she whispers, eyes closed.

"I know. I'm sorry."

"I know. Now come to bed."

Quantum Mañana

Out of my element. Away from my cave. Feeling claustrophobic.

Share puts a cold glass in my hands, pats my chest on her way to the couch. Her couch, her place, her friends. Her episode of *CSI: NY* debuts tonight, and she wants me here for moral support.

Why'd she go and take that picture of those fucking tourists?

I sip the drink. G&T, coldasfuck, limed, sans the fruit's carcass. *Perfection.* Taste the Hendricks within, glance at Share.

She grins, raises an eyebrow.

I raise the drink. *Cheers!*

Her place is nice, a spacious and well-decorated condo in Burbank. Eight of her friends are buzzing about, grabbing drinks, presenting their potluck dishes on the coffee table for all to see and consume. Six are girlfriends. There's a gay guy and one other dude, boyfriend to one of the six.

Don't really want to talk to anyone but know that won't go over well, so, "Hey, you're UGG girl."

Girl that Share was with when I met her shuffles into my zone. She's typing with both thumbs on her Sidekick, shoots me a quizzical look. "Did you just call me ugly?"

"No. No. I said UGG. You were wearing UGGs at Lackey's party."

Her face morphs, resulting in another bewildered look.

"The big place in the Hills. Back in January."

"Justin's."

"Yeah. Where I met Share." She's about to say something else, but I unintentionally cut her off. "What do you do?"

"Makeup artist," she replies as she glances at the TV. "Ooh. Show's about to start." With that she walks away.

Good talking to you.

Dude walks over, clutching a Heineken to his chest. "Kill me now," he whispers as he grabs some chips from a bowl. Looks up, widens his eyes before he stuffs his face.

I laugh. "I'm in touch with that emotion."

The entire room suddenly goes, "Shhh-shhh-shhh-shhh."

I move behind the couch, grab a stool, and take a seat.

Dude follows suit after quickly filling a plate with eats.

I've been to shindigs like this one before. Too many, prior to falling off the grid. They're impossible to avoid if you work in the industry, especially when you have a habit of dating up-and-coming actresses. Can't say I've missed them—these parties I mean, not the actresses. This same scene must play out countless times every week in this town: groups of friends gathering to watch one of their own enjoy a prime-time moment. While some of these guest-star roles might consist of juicy parts with multiple scenes, others can be single scene quickies featuring a handful of lines or less. Then there are the extras who will gather their friends in order to shout, "There I am!" when they merely appear in the background of a scene. And in my book, you can't really call Hollywood home until you've been to a party that gets derailed when it becomes apparent the star of the night was edited out of the show. *Good times.*

Hoping tonight provides quality *and* quantity. Hoping Share's role isn't an embarrassment.

It's obvious she's nervous.

Show begins. Share is in the opening scene. Her character is jogging early morning when another woman unexpectedly attacks her. She looks great, and the scene is good. Easy to play fear, in my opinion, but Share captivates.

Opening chords to "Baba O'Riley" by The Who kicks in, and the room gets giddy. Share is one big smile. It's fun to see her like this. Her friends congratulate her, comment on the scene. I watch her juggle all the attention. Two friends jump off the couch, make a beeline for the bathroom. Share leans back, rests her head on the cushions. She looks up at me, motorboats her lips into a smile.

I lean in for a kiss. She tastes like wine.

"Thanks for coming. Means a lot," she whispers before I lean back. She looks away, laughs at something UGG girl says.

"You're with Share?" the dude asks, jealousy detectable in his question.

"Yeah."

"Nice." He nods, wipes chip grease on his jeans, in the process showing me precisely why he's not with her.

The show blows. Its meandering, packed-to-the-gills story gives me a headache, and the reveal at the end that helps solve the case is absurd. I almost laugh out loud, which would definitely perturb the could-hear-a-pin-drop room. Thing is, Share shines in all four of her scenes, especially during her interrogation by Gary Sinise. Maybe I'm biased, but there's calmness to her acting. Draws you in, makes you believe her character, her dialogue 100 percent.

"Bravo," I tell her in the aftermath when we finally have a moment alone.

"Really?"

"Really. Loved how you mouthed Sinise's questions back to yourself."

"You liked that?"

"I did. Made sense for the character, given the reveal."

"That was actually my idea. Director was impressed, liked my choices a lot."

"Oh, he did, did he?"

"She did." Share grins, gets pulled away by two of her friends.

I mingle.

"How did you and Share meet?"

"She stalked me for two years. Did you know your friend was a reformed stalker?"

"Where are you from?"

"Sydney."

"Ah, thought that's the accent I heard."

"Have you ever been?"

"Nope, but it is on my list."

"Share is fabulous. And gorgeous."

"What do you do?"

"Costume designer extraordinaire."

"How's that working out for you?"

"Well, fashion is my life, so it never feels like work, even when I'm busting my balls and working twelve-hour days, seven days a week. I definitely found my calling. How about you?"

"I'm a mechanic."

"You, mister, don't have the hands of a mechanic."

"Oh. Not cars. Quantum mechanics."

"Shut. Up!"

As I socialize, I observe the party and how the group interacts. Compliments for Share abound, yet I sense restrained resentment in their words and actions.

UGG girl says, "Awesome job, Share. Wish my agent could work some magic like yours does."

The babe from Australia remarks, "Cheers, love. I used to do roles like that back home. They're fun little gigs."

Chip grease says, "I didn't really get the end. Who was the killer?"

And the designer extraordinaire chimes in, "You're like Tuesday Weld back in the day. Before she mucked up her career with bad choices in roles and men."

Reminds me of those weekly support groups where addicts meet and lie to each other over baked goods and bad coffee. Only difference here is the drug is affirmation, something those doing time cannot buy, cannot quit, cannot get enough of.

I stay two drinks after the show ends, bow out when the group decides to Wii Karaoke.

"That cool?" I ask as Share walks me to the door.

"Of course. Glad you came. Good to see you out, about."

During a lengthy kiss, my hands venture into her jeans, squeeze her cheeks. No underwear. Nice touch.

"Coming by later?"

"Probably not. You could stay. I'm sure we won't karaoke for more than a few hours."

"Mmm. Tempting as that ass of yours is, I will have to pass."

"I understand."

Head home, ignore the pile. Put some work in on the ads and sites but feeling uninspired. Move to shredding some really bad scripts. You'd think the action would be therapeutic. Instead, it's always glum. After disposing of four garbage bags in the apartment complex next door, I fall into bed with a script. Bed feels large. Been months since The Griddle, and in that time nights with Share far outnumber nights without. Time flies.

She texts me around midnight.

"U told Gil ur in quantum mechanics?"

"Guilty."

"ha! everyone liked u & thought u were funny"

Still reading that one when another pops up.

"don't worry - told them u were an editor"

"Editor? Great. Now I pass for a pot-smoking/slacker editor."

"LOL – mañana"

18

MTHRFCKR

Days go by. Most are uneventful. Most.

After Runyon and a shower, I'm enjoying some b-fast, perusing the trades. A blurb in *Variety* catches my eye.

SuperVillain – Brian Sweeney (New Line)

It's the first deal for part-time teacher Sweeney, whose script gained the attention of executive Justin Lackey. It's also the latest deal to emerge from Lackey's development company, Establishing Shot Productions, and their first-look pact with New Line. **10/23**

Read it three times, all the while flashbacking to that day in the conference room when Foster asked me how to fix Sweeney's script, Lackey said it wasn't worth our time, and the project vanished. Until now.

Through clenched teeth, the word "motherfucker" is spewed sans vowels. It's Lackey's new name in my world.

Don't have to read the version New Line purchased to

know Lackey ripped my notes on the project months ago and ran with them. Not sure how he got the script out of Foster's office after their apparent breakup, but I don't care about that as much as I care about being screwed over by this "Mthrfckr."

Throw half-eaten cereal in the sink along with most of my coffee. The white and black make brown, a mess I'll clean up later. Head to the bedroom where Share's still asleep. Try not to wake her while I get dressed, but in my present mood it's like Fred Flintstone trying not to rouse the baby.

"Bateman. It's fucking six thirty."

I look over. Her face is imbedded in the pillow, eyes still shut.

"Sorry."

"What the hell are you doing?"

"Getting dressed. Going out."

Pretty sure she opens her eyes. "You're going out? In the daylight?"

I don't respond.

"Careful not to burn up from the sun."

Funny. Not in the mood. "Have to meet someone."

"You have a meeting? At six thirty in the morning?"

"Whtvr."

Memories of the day I was escorted out of Foster's office arrest my thoughts as I drive, play in my head like a pivotal flashback in some film.

Plan was to get fired. Wanted to be let go versus quitting to avoid all the where-are-you headed-what-will-you-be-doing.

Plan was to pull a copy of *SuperVillain*, which was

purgatoried by Foster a week before. Was going to call Sweeney, leave the writer a few messages asking him to call me at
Foster's at a time I knew only Lackey would be there. Lackey
went out of his way to spend time in the office alone. Used
to say he needed solitude to prepare his brain for us new fish.

I aimed to have Sweeney call back then, asking for me.
Lame plan but an infallible one. Junior executives are not
supposed to contact writers. Ever. Or at least ever since
Meyer Holden Version 2.0 debuted with *The Rising Sons of
Mourning Park* and *The Living End*. No exec of sound mind
was going to allow the discovery of another Holden Ticket
to launch anybody else into the stratosphere.

So my plan was obvious, at least to me. My actions were
sure to get me fired, setting me free to do my thing, no
questions asked. Thing is, I didn't even need to make the
call. Pulling the script was enough.

"What are you doing with that?"

"What?" I feign dumb.

"With the script. Project was shelved."

"I . . ." Voice trails off. Lack of any acting skills works
in my favor. I look like a guy busted for doing something
wrong. Works like a charm.

Lackey picks up the copy of *SuperVillain*. "Bateman.
Coffee run. Now. Go."

I look up. Lackey's already walking away.

I leave the office. Return fifteen minutes later with coffee, am greeted by two security guards and a swearing Foster.

"Cunthole thief. Do you know who I am?"

I survey the scene. My desk has been cleaned out.
Security guard number two is holding a box. Number one

grabs my arm, turns me around, and starts to march me out.

So this is how it's going to go down. Okay.

Tempted to answer Foster. Thing is, tell a dinosaur he's dying and he stomps you out, but walk away and he's still heading toward extinction. I stifle a smile, turn to look at Lackey.

Foster says, "Never liked your cockfuck attitude. Never trusted your ass."

Lackey salutes with two fingers.

Also tempted to go all Tricky Dick with, *You won't have Bateman to kick around anymore*, but I refrain from the refrain. Still holding the tray of four venti coffees, I raise them, flip the holder as I slam it down and into a box on the ground containing over a hundred unread screenplays, this week's to-do box.

I'm escorted out of their lives, knowing they will be reminded of me all week as they turn those stained brown pages.

Last thing I hear is Foster: "Fucktwat!"

Flashback over.

"Mthrfckr!"

Lackey is almost to his Audi when I spring from my Explorer, march his way. Looks like a guilty dealer during a drug bust, head darting, eyes scanning to see if I brought reinforcements.

"Bateman? What the fuck?"

Fists for hands, I bellow, "Let's talk."

"Settle the fuck down, loser. This is my home. If you want to talk, make an appointment."

"We talk. Now."

Element of surprise gone, the fear drains from Lackey's face and he turns into the snide son of a bitch I loathe. "Five minutes. But inside."

Before Lackey closes the front door, he's already on the offensive. "So how is it a guy with a swell career in advertising has already read *Variety* this morning?"

"Did you use my ideas in the revision that sold?"

Lackey laughs. "That's why you barreled into Beverly Hills? To find out if you were cheated a credit?"

"Fuck you. Answer the question."

"Fuck you. Grow up and learn shit happens in this biz."

"Answer the question."

"I don't know. I don't care. I don't even remember your input."

"Bullshit."

"I don't have time for this. Go back to your advertising gig or whatever it is you do with your time these days. I have a meeting."

"Answer the question."

"I did. I. Don't. Know."

"Think you do."

"What are you going to do? Kick my ass in the school yard during recess? Fucking grow up, grow a set, get out of my way."

"Get out of my way," I repeat his words. "That's it, isn't it? You always feared I was in your way."

Lackey smirks.

"Never understood you," I say, checking out his place. "You got all this."

"Hey, I worked for this. Took my entire trust fund and invested it in the distribution of a little project called *Blair Witch*. Ever hear of it? Could have went down the toilet on that ugly bitch, but instead I hit the jackpot."

"You invested your trust fund," I mumble.

Lackey doesn't hear me. He's still in his own little story world. "Sucker grossed two hundred fifty million worldwide. Sizable chunk of that was mine."

"Yeah, you really worked your fingers to the bone there. Like digging coal, I imagine."

Slow claps. "Funny man. Here all week. Try the waitress."

Stare him down until he stops clapping. "Obviously got enough money to do anything, but you're here and stepping on bodies to get to the top. Why?"

"Bateman. I gotta go. Been a pleasure."

It dawns on me that Lackey was already in contact with Sweeney by the time I was escorted out of Foster's. It's why he knee-jerked when he saw the copy of *Villain*. He turns to the door, but my words spin him back. "How did you get the script out of Foster's office?"

"You asking for a lesson in how to do business? That's what this is all about?"

"How did you get it out?"

Lackey grins, shakes his head. "He gave it to me. He had to. The day I was promoted to VP, I made him sign a deal that let me walk with twenty projects if he ever let me go. But only scripts he'd already passed on. And he passed on *Villain*. You were there."

"But you lied to him. Project had merit."

"Lied to him? Which lie did I tell? And what the fuck color is the sky in your Hollywood? That fucker never said an honest thing to me in two years' time. He'd skullfuck my grandma if it garnered him a blurb in the trades. Again, you were there."

I'm exhausted. Seven in the morning and I'm exhausted.

Hate this coldfuckcold town.

"Look at you, Bateman. You're lost. You're a mess. Get it together. Heard you're with Share. That's great. But how long is she going to stay with this?" He waves a hand my way.

Curb a desire to snap his fingers off. "Don't fucking even mention her name."

"Ah, so you like her that much. Good for you. All the more reason to come work for me. I'm on my own now. Starting up something big. Big. I'll let you in, but I need to know you're in. Now."

"Fuck you."

"I'm big enough to admit it. I need a man like you. A smart guy. One with pent-up anger who can run my readers. Think it over."

"Fuck you."

"What are you accomplishing on your own? Zilch. And don't tell me you're an ad man. Fuck born yesterday. I know you're on your own, dude." He shakes his head. "You're in a galaxy so far away from where you need to be. No lifeline to any information."

"Found out about *Villain*."

Lackey chuckles. "*Villain* happened two weeks ago. I celebrated that shit a Hollywood lifetime ago."

"I have no interest in this shit anymore."

"Wait. Found out about *Villain*. Have no interest anymore," he mimics. "Found out. No interest. Which is it, Bateman? Encyclopedia Brown of the industry or Meyer Holden of assistant development execs? You want us to think you vanished, but here you are." He starts putting on a show. "Come out, come out, wherever you are."

Watch him laugh at his own joke. Coming here was a

mistake. "Way it is," I whisper.

Split second is all it takes for his laughing face to maniacally morph into something scary. "There's that patented 'way it is' of yours. Never got that. Way it is, is you're stubborn. Way it is, is you think you know something I don't. You think you have a better chance at success than me when in reality you're alone, lost, a loser." He pauses, like he's debating whether to say something. "You don't even know there's a third."

"What are you talking about?"

"There was a third."

I say nothing.

He grins. "Holden Number," he boasts as he holds up three fingers. "After your unfortunate departure, we were a man down, so we had to employ some additional readers. One morning one of them enters the office and hands me a script, its pages stained brown all over from coffee."

I look up.

Lackey smiles. "He hands it to me, tells me he thinks it's a Holden, tells me I need to read it ASAP. I send him home, study his coverage on the screenplay, and agree with his assessment. So I make a few copies of it, keep the original for myself." He pauses. He's in the moment. "Make the mistake of taking it to Foster. Of course I debate trying to screw him out of it, but I know it's already logged in the system and I can't sneak it out of the office without that reader or someone else talking about it in one of those fucking status meetings. That's the mistake I made. I should have called the"—he air-quotes like a drama queen—"*writer* myself."

Sick to my stomach, I keep listening.

"We set a day and time for the meeting, but the fucker

screwed me over, met with the writer on his own." Lackey pauses again, exhales. "Foster upped the meeting day. Didn't tell me. Day before our scheduled meet, I'm busy trying to get a hold of Ryan Martinez to bribe him for info on The Question when some scrawny, zit-faced kid marches into the place. Foster corrals him in his office. Less than ten minutes later the kid exits, leaves the offices. Foster doesn't come out. I go in. He's poured himself a scotch. It's ten a.m. He looks up. 'I think I fucked it up,' he whispers. I do the math, lose it, rip that assfuck a new cockhole."

Lackey almost makes me laugh there. Almost.

"He throws me out of his office, fires me."

"He fires you? Knowing you can walk with twenty projects? He wouldn't do that. You're all he's got."

"You'd be surprised what a man does when you throw a glass of twenty-five-year-old scotch in his face. He has me escorted from the building. It's humiliating, and I have to take the edge off. So I go get fucking drunk, which is stupid because when I get home, I see the Holden on my desk, contact information right there on the cover page. I call the number, but it's disconnected already. I try the e-mail address, and it bounces back. Kid up and disappears, Shawshanks like a fart in the wind."

"Along with any way of contacting Holden," I whisper.

Lackey looks up at me. "Exactly. I'm sure you can figure out the rest. Foster was asked The Question. But he obviously blew it. Guessing once Holden was informed he blew it, the script was pulled off the table."

I process the intel. "Without a way to get a hold of the writer, no one is able to buy it."

Lackey breathes a laugh. "There you go. The third

Holden is a lame duck, thanks to the late-great Jon Foster."

"Jesus."

"Yeah, Jesus." Story time over, he goes back to being the mthrfckr he is. "And you didn't even know. You're living on an island, thinking you have a shot at finding him. You need me. Come work for me. When you see what I got planned . . ."

I'm done listening, done arguing. Done. "Well, you're right about one thing, Lackey. I am with Share. And you aren't."

Turn, head to the door, but he won't let me have the last word.

"What the fuck did you just say? She tell you I saw her last night?"

Grab the doorknob, pull, walk out.

"She tell you we had dinner?"

SLAM!

TORPEDO THE SHIP

SLAM!
"Bateman? That you? What the fuck?" Share exits the bathroom, wet hair, towel wrapped around her body.

BOOM!BOOM!BOOM! "Get out. Now."

"What the hell is wrong?"

"Just go."

"No."

"Yes." I grab her arm.

She immediately yanks it away, pushes me. "What the hell is wrong with you?"

"Me? What's wrong with me?" A laugh spews from within, and I can tell it startles Share.

She flinches when I raise my hand to speak.

"Get out. Now."

"I'm not going anywhere until you tell me why you're acting this way."

I steam. Erupt. Grab her arm again. She squirms, but this time I don't let her get away. I march her down the stairs.

"Bateman. Tell me . . ."

I push her outside, slam the door, hear her sobbing as I take the stairs back up, two at a time.

"Bateman. This is embarrassing."

She's in a towel. Fuck. *I don't care. I don't care. I don't care.* I wish she wasn't here. I wish this wasn't happening.

"Bateman."

I head to the bedroom, slide open the closet door. Aim to grab something for her to throw on so I can rid her from the doorstep and my life. I find more than two dozen of her dresses and outfits hanging inside. Pull open the drawer I bestowed to her about a month ago. It's overstuffed with a catalogue and a half of Victoria's Secret. Slam it shut, slide open the drawer below. That one's also filled with frilly perfumed clothing. When did this happen? How did I let this happen?

Heart races, head throbs. "Fuck." Walk to the window, see Share sitting on the stoop, arms wrapped around her bared legs, face buried in her knees. Tempted to throw all her shit out the window. Tempted, but unwilling to be trite.

She stops crying as I unlock and open the front door. Leave it ajar and travel back up the stairs. Wait until she climbs the flight and enters the living room before I say, "Grab all your shit and go. All of it." Make eye contact. "It's over."

Share stands there, trembles, wet haired, wet faced. My last two words seem to sting, maybe even piss her off.

She walks across the room and sits on the edge of the couch. "I'm not going anywhere until you tell me what's wrong."

Resilient, this one.

I take the high road, aim to remain calm. "Do us both a favor. Go."

"Tell me. What happened? You at least owe me that."

"You really need me to say it?" Composure goes out the window. I shout, "You fucking lied to me." Trite after all.

"When did I lie?"

"When did you not?" I'm still standing, and I fight the urge to punch something. Not certain what's boiling my blood most—Lackey with Share, Lackey's intel regarding Holden #3, Lackey gearing up for a run at The Man, or that trifecta coming together to blindside me this fine morning. Clench my fist, scowl at the wall.

"Calm down and tell me what's wrong. Please."

Jaw clenched, teeth grinding, I seethe. "You saw Lackey last night. You fucking had dinner with him."

Share's face crumbles in an avalanche of guilt. "Bateman . . ."

"You lied. Fucking lied. Fucking liar." I point to the door. "Get out."

"I didn't lie to you. Ever. I just didn't tell you the whole truth."

"Did you. Have dinner. With him?"

She starts to weep.

I pace. Want her gone. "Hard enough to think you ever slept with that fucking guy before, much less that you're cheating on me with him now. Get. Fuck. Out."

"Bateman, there's something you need to know." She stops.

I pace.

She waits.

I inhale, exhale.

Resilient, she waits. "There's something I need to tell you."

Know she won't disappear completely until I acknowledge her. I stop pacing, want it over with, make eye contact.

"A few months ago, when you saw me and Justin at The Griddle, you assumed we were dating. Well, we weren't."

I process the info, but it doesn't resonate.

"Bateman, he's my brother."

What. The. Fuck? "What the fuck?"

"Bateman, don't freak out. He and I are not even that close, and I'd never tell him anything. About you. Ever. I'm on your side."

I think of my father. Then and there. It'd be poetic to say I don't know why, but I do.

The woman he loved betrayed him. It's how and why he ended up raising me on his own. I grew up watching him patch the heart she fractured, tend to the life she blind-sided. Along the way, I learned this: There are moments in every relationship that can torpedo the ship. All depends on the collateral damage, reaction to it, and recovery from it. I stare at Share, heart echoing in my chest as nonlinear memories are sorted, edited in this new light.

Lackey's party in the Hills. She asked me how I knew Justin but never divulged her connection to him. I called him a son of a bitch that night. Might be why she remained tight-lipped when we met.

On our first date, I went on a tirade at Koi when she asked about work. Having been escorted out of Foster's office the day before, my bile for Lackey was spoiling the mood until she seductively changed the subject with some under-the-table hijinks.

In bed, I told her I was jealous when I saw them together at breakfast. She said, "Trust me—no grounds for jealousy whatsoever."

I am with Share. And you aren't. The words I baited

Lackey with. *What the fuck did you just say?* What the fuck did I just say? He must take me for a buffoon.

Time and silence unite the room. I contemplate. My head hurts. I cover my face with my hands, rub the tension out of my eyes.

Share's huddled in the corner of the couch, legs drawn to her chest, arms wrapped around them. Her chin rests on her knees. An abundance of tears make her cheeks shine.

I speak through clenched teeth. "I came here almost two years ago with a purpose. Vowed no distractions." Raise my volume. "No distractions. Knew my enemies. Kept them at a distance. Had a plan." I correct myself. "Have a plan."

Share shuts her eyes, but the flood persists.

"Share . . ."

She shakes her head. Refuses to look my way.

"Look at me."

She does not.

Could ask her why she didn't tell me this from the get-go, but I already know the answer. Could ask why she waited so long, but I get it. Could be a prick and jettison her to teach her a lesson, but I opt for what's behind Curtain Number Honesty.

"I'm not going anywhere. Don't want you to go anywhere. It's not over." For good measure, I add, "I trust you."

Her head stops shaking, her eyes open. They shimmer. In an instant, those tears for fears turn to a gleeful cry. How do women do that? I'll never know.

She rushes to me, arms outstretched, enveloping me, holding me.

I hold her, smell her Neutrogenaed hair, feel her curves against my body, her BOOM!BOOM!BOOM! alongside mine. Tell her something I might not have been aware of prior to the here, the now. "I'm falling for you."

"Good." She blubbers. "Because you've got some catching up to do."

That's my girl.

Psycho Writer

When I first moved here and started working for Foster, I'll admit, I was sipping the Kool-Aid. A calendar of premieres, rubbing elbows with the stars, nailing a few just-off-the-bus, out-of-my-league actresses, and yeah, my lips were stained red. Happens. Town can change you, blur your vision, cloud your judgment. You start to use knowledge and experience to your advantage, to impress fucks you shouldn't care about.

Case in point, used to play this game in bars where I'd slap a hundred-dollar bill on the table and announce, "Franklin goes home with you if you can answer one question."

No matter the zip code of the industry folk I was drinking with, the cash money on the table got their attention. "Phones on the table, though. Can't Google it," I'd instruct. BlackBerrys, Treos, iPhones all lined up, I'd ask, "Who wrote the movie *Psycho*?"

No matter the area of expertise—development exec, casting agent, actor, director, editor, writer, agent, or manager—the look on their faces was always the same: *This must be a trick question.*

Everyone wanted to say, "Hitchcock." Most did.

Must have slapped that hundred down more than fifty times in front of over three hundred of the industry's most determined. Franklin never left my wallet.

Know you're saying, *Nice story, Bateman. Why should we care?*

Origin of the *Psycho* writer game is as follows.

My dad's obituary appeared in the San Fran papers the morning after Kirby was put to sleep. Same day it ran, same page, center stage, an article ran—a celebrity obit picked up from the *Los Angeles Times*. Was for a man named Joseph Stefano. Surprised even me, but he wrote *Psycho*. The script was based on a book, but the article stated it was Stefano who came up with the plot twist of killing the main character twenty minutes into the film.

Hundred out of a hundred people, any walk of life, would give that credit to Hitchcock. The Franklin in my wallet proves that, and I was polling experts in the category. *Motion Pictures for one hundred, Alex.*

The rub is no one knows Stefano's name. Why is that? How is that possible? *Psycho* is one of the most noted films of all time, in large part because Janet Leigh's character shockingly perishes in the second act. Yet the man who contrived this clever bombshell isn't celebrated. What the fuck? Irked me then, irks me now.

I know, *Touching story, Bateman. But, again, why should we care?*

My dad was fighting an uphill battle, aspiring to be a writer for this fucking hell-on-earth town. Moment I opened the newspaper that day and read the two obituaries, I decided to move to LA.

Started driving toward a clear destination, uncertain where I was headed. Remember driving along the Pacific Coast Highway, en route to Coldfuckcold, thinking it odd the two obits ran on the same day. Obsessed over it a long while. Never arrived at any sort of hypothesis other than I guess I came here to try and change things.

Talk about an uphill battle.

The kid who arrived on some sunny/75 day didn't stand a chance. So I buried him, became someone who blended in rather than sticking out. Became this belligerent self-anointed savant.

Talk about killing the main character at the top of Act Two.

Along the way, lips stained red, I also buried the lead, which is that writers deserve more credit than given. Along the way, turned this anomaly into a drinking game no one could win and one that most failed to recall the next morning.

Regret that. Now.

If you're asking what sparked the trip down memory lane, it's something I hear Lackey say. Not to me directly but to a room of impressionable new fish dying to swim in his Kool-Aid.

Positioned in the back of a big conference room at Establishing Shot Productions, Lackey's newborn development firm, I run a finger across my moustache. Check that. Fake mustache. Risky move but glad I'm here. Helps to have a girlfriend who whispered me the intel regarding this little meeting, which she overheard Lackey discussing on the phone before their dinner a few nights prior.

Meeting is supposed to be starting but no sign of the man of the hour. Volume in the room goes from eleven to pin-drop and Lackey walks right by me en route to the head of the class. Doesn't notice me. Not even close.

Didn't even recognize myself in the mirror before heading here. Helps to have a girlfriend who's adept with make-up and wardrobe. Hair combed across my forehead, hanging into my eyes. Glasses, plus the fake lip tickler. Look ten years younger, ten times more geek. Sad to say, but I fit right in.

Lackey smiles at the room. Nerd herd applauds. Half expect him to raise his arms and spout, "Can you dig it?" What he does spew is way more entertaining.

"Here's the thing about writers. They're a cantankerous lot. I'm not a fan of them, but I am a fan of their end result. They write scripts. Scripts are the blueprints for movies. Movies are my trade. I avoid hearing the live version of any writer at all cost, instead opting for the Courier 12 version of them. If you've ever heard them talk, you probably do the same. If you fancy yourself a writer, well, then I refuse to apologize for being honest."

He laughs at his own joke. "Writers. They're borderline grating and always want to tell you about every idea they ever thought of putting on paper. Writers think you care about a character's backstory and their own backstory, for that matter. Writers think you care to know the exact day and time they conceived the idea that brought you together, along with what they were wearing and who they were jerking off to at the time. Writers. They're a bunch of fucking cunts, if you ask me. There, I said it."

I look around. The room is riveted.

"I don't care about any of the aforementioned. I only want to know what they're working on and when it will be delivered to my doorstep. Look, I'm not antisocial, but tell me, what's compelling about a writer's ability to craft a thought, a concept, and a sentence into an entertaining story? It's a lonely and maddening process, which turns the lot of them into desperate, socially retarded lepers. Giving them an audience is like sending them to a strip club with an endless amount of funny money. They suddenly think everyone loves being around them. Doesn't take a moron to know the love comes from the sharks when the smell of profit prevails. Most are morons, though. Which is why I find it ironic I am chasing a writer. Stalking one, if you will. A writer I cannot wait to meet, sit down with, and talk with."

BOOM!BOOM!BOOM!

"There, I said it. I'm searching for the one writer in Hollywood who does not want to be found."

Mthrfckr stole my line.

"Which is why you are all here today. Not going to hide it, deny it, dip it in chocolate, or spread penicillin on it. I am here today to announce that I am putting an all-points bulletin out on Meyer Holden . . ."

The crowd cheers.

They actually cheer.

Arms outstretched, Lackey bellows, "Y'all know me. Know how I earn a livin'."

Told you. Way more entertaining.

When the room settles, he continues. "I am putting an all-points bulletin out on Meyer Holden or his next script, I should say. And you, the valued readers of this unappreciative city, have gathered to hear my pitch. Well, here it is. I appreciate you. I value you. I want you to work for me. I want these offices to be your home. All of you, if I'm so lucky to convince each and every one of you."

I look around. Must be more than 120 here.

Lackey continues, throwing his weight into the words, "I'll pay you more than anyone else. You will never take your work home with you. Meals are on the house."

Murmurs permeate the room. Not sure which of the three is sparking the discussions, but together they set the room abuzz, which spreads a smile on Lackey's face.

Starting to get what's up his sleeve, but I'm smarter than the average nerd. Never take work home, free in-house meals—he's opening a sweatshop for readers. To ensure a Holden doesn't escape his grasp, no work leaves the place. The pay, while it will seem like more, robs them of their lives, waters down the net-net. Most probably won't realize that, though. They'll fixate on a larger bottom line for doing what they already do. Have to say, Lackey surprises me with the strategy. Didn't think he had it in him.

My thoughts retreat, regroup. Tune out Lackey as he repeats himself, which he does often. He's building an army of me. I'm averaging around six and a half scripts a day these days, maybe two hundred a month. With fifty readers on staff, he'll average around ten thousand. One hundred on staff doubles that. Odds are on this psycho executive's side for sure.

Pretty certain this isn't going to end well. For me.

OBITUARIES

Joseph Stefano ☆ 1922-2006

Writer of the screenplay for Alfred Hitchcock's "Psycho"

*"Killing the leading lady in the first 20 minutes
had never been done before," he said.*

LOS ANGELES--Joseph Stefano, the writer of the screenplay for Alfred Hitchcock's esteemed motion picture thriller "Psycho" and part-owner of the science-fiction anthology TV series "The Outer Limits," has died at the age of 84.

Stefano, who endured surgery for lung cancer in 2001, died of heart failure Friday at Los Robles Hospital & Medical Center in Thousand Oaks, California, according to Marilyn Stefano, his wife of 52 years.

A former composer and lyricist, turned screenwriter and playwright, Stefano's earliest credits included "The Black Orchid," a 1958 movie drama starring Sophia Loren and Anthony Quinn; and "Made in Japan," a *Playhouse 90* production about racial prejudice.

However, his best-known work was the movie "Psycho." It was Alfred Hitchcock who optioned Robert Bloch's 1959 novel "Psycho" and delivered Stefano a copy of the book the night prior to meeting with him to discuss adapting it for the screen.

In a 1990 interview in "Media Scene Prevue Magazine," Stefano commented that, with the exception of the ending, he felt the story was "weak in writing and characterization." The novel begins with Norman Bates, the mother-dominated motel owner, and, according to Stefano, "focuses

on him too much. I was sure that no audience was going to like Norman enough to stay with him throughout an entire movie."

However, as Stefano was driving to Paramount Pictures for his meeting with Hitchcock, he came up with a solution to the problem. He decided to begin the story with a character that steals $40,000 from her Phoenix employer in order to begin a new life with her lover. However, after stopping at the Bates Motel, she is murdered.

"With so much early emphasis on the character known as Marion Crane, no one dreams she'll get killed," Stefano was often quoted as saying. "Killing the leading lady in the first 20 minutes had never been done before. When it happens, people are blown away . . ."

Hitchcock loved the idea and hired Stefano on the spot. The rest is history.

"Hitch suggested a name actress to play Marion because the bigger the star the more unbelievable it would be that we would kill her."

"Psycho," starring Janet Leigh and Anthony Perkins, became a phenomenon when it hit theaters, mostly because of the infamous shower scene where Leigh's character is stabbed to death.

HENRY BATEMAN -1944-2006

Henry Samuel Bateman April 15, 1944 - August 24, 2006

Henry was born and grew up in Minneapolis, MN where he graduated high school in 1962. He then served with the US Navy from 1962 to 1965. He went on to obtain a degree in communications from the University of Minnesota in 1969.

Minnesota and later in San Francisco, where he was a Senior Copywriter at Goodby, Silverstein & Partners until retirement in 2003. Henry enjoyed traveling, collecting wine and enhancing his much loved home. He is survived by his son, Sammy. Henry often used a hearty handshake to pull

CUT THE KIDS IN HALF

Immersed in fantasy when reality injects itself. Again. "Bateman?"

I keep reading, try to appease the pretty little distraction sitting next to me with a halfhearted, "Hmm?"

"Why do you do it?"

Fantasy interruptus. "What?"

"This. All this reading. Why do you do it? I want to know."

I take my eyes off the Courier, drop the script into my lap. "You're looking for motivation?"

Share furrows her brow. "I want to know you."

"Insight into character. I get it. Character is motivation. Motivation is character."

"Stop. Stop it. Don't do that. How many times do I have to tell you I hate when you do that? I ask you a question, and you get smarmy and patronizing."

She's pissed and rightfully so. I do that. Often. Pause to ponder what she's asking. Pause too long. This is hard for me. Think she senses that.

She slides her foot across the couch, touches my leg with her toes.

I exhale and start at the beginning.

"If you're looking for motivation in all this, here it is. Decided to move to Los Angeles fifteen days after I buried my father, seven days after I discovered a drawer filled with his writing—six screenplays, eleven short films, one play, a few short stories, and one unfinished book abandoned after less than four chapters. . . ."

By the time I finish, Share's mouth is agape. She's in tears. She opens her eyes wide for a sec in an attempt to stop the flow.

"Blah," I whisper. "Hey, don't look at me like that. You asked."

"I know. I'm sorry."

"Don't cry for me, Burbank. Don't say you're sorry for asking either. Should have told you a long time ago."

"Glad you told me now." She contemplates, wipes away some tears. "I don't want to cry again, but where did the kid in that story go?"

My turn to mull things over. "I don't know. Still here, I guess. But doing time changes people. You know that."

Share chews on the corner of her lip.

"There's more. You asked about motivation. Well, the rejection letters that bothered me most were all from Foster. My dad sent him every script he wrote, and I know why. He loved his films. But I'm certain Foster never read one word my father wrote. The letters were filled with blatant discrepancies. Every one. Signed on paper, with a pen, in ink with the name Jon fucking Foster. That's why I called him the day I arrived in LA, why I campaigned for a job I didn't really want, and why I stayed there so long. Guess you could say I was seeking revenge."

I close my eyes. Not fond of this subject. Hate thinking about it. Harder to talk about it. Glad it's over.

"Bateman?"

Jinxed it. "Yeah?"

"What about Holden? Where does he fit?"

I think about her question. "My first year in Cold-fuckcold had an effect on me. One I didn't like. Came here with conviction and lost sight of my intent all too quickly. I became someone I didn't like. Bought into the charade. Blinded by the glitz. Kool-Aid tasted fuckin' good."

"Like you said, that kind of happens to us all."

"I guess. By the time I regained my senses, a year had passed and I was right where I started, at Foster's office, a lemming in the scheme of things. So much for revenge. So much for conviction."

"You're too hard on yourself."

"No. Back then I was too lax. Came here to make a difference. To make my mark."

"To make your dad proud."

I force a smile, nod. "When I heard about Holden, it all fell into place. Believed . . ." I catch myself, correct myself. "Believe finding him would allow me to make a difference but without losing myself along the way. Doing time changes people. That's a fact. Finding Holden puts me where I need to be, conviction and intent intact."

I stop talking, look up at Share.

She inflates her cheeks, slowly lets the air out, says,

"Wow. Now I get it." Her gaze darts away from mine for a sec as she thinks. She looks back at me, whispers, "Bateman?"

"Yeah?"

"You're an only child, right?"

Shake my head.

A crease forms at Share's brow.

"Have a younger sister."

"What? Where is she?"

"No idea. We never talk."

"What? Why?"

"It's a long story. Not a happy one either. Whatsoever."

"I don't care. Tell me."

Look down at the script open on the table, mini stack next to it. Fixate on it for a second, can't recall what I was reading. "What's to tell? Parents got divorced when I was seven, cut the kids in half. My dad and I moved in the left direction until we hit the coast. Haven't seen my mother or my sister since. Way it is."

"What? Way it is? What does that mean? How could you do that?"

Close my eyes again. Open them, but I'm still here. "Because she had an affair. My mother. With my uncle. With my dad's brother. For over ten years."

"No way."

"Yeah. My dad never recovered. Never talked to her, his brother, his family again. I chose to go with him. And we disappeared."

"So she never tried to contact you?"

"Well, it's not like we left a forwarding address. So I honestly have no idea if she ever tried because my dad was pretty intent on disappearing."

"Like father, like son," Share says to lighten the mood.

"Like father, like son."

Share grabs my hand, squeezes it, whispers, "When did your dad die?"

"Almost two years ago."

"Then you saw your family at the funeral, right?"

I shake my head. "You're not listening. I was his family. And he would have wanted it that way. Positive of that."

Share starts to cry.

I laugh. "Burbank. More tears?"

"It's so sad."

"Well, make it better."

"How?" She wipes away the wet from her face.

I watch her, frankly still a bit unsure at times where the actor ends and my girlfriend begins. "Tell me something about you I don't know."

"What do I have to tell?"

"Could start with your real name. Love to know that."

Share looks at me, big brown eyes subtly changing, perhaps finally trusting me as much as I trust her.

That night, Sherilyn Marie Lackey and I stay up till three telling each other who we really are, who we were before recasting ourselves in novel backstory and Hollywood facades. After, in bed, we merge, no longer trying to impress each other.

Two Ships Passing in the Fight

ScriptGirl is the Internet persona of an unidentified producer's assistant who regularly presents a Hollywood script sales report via a YouTube blog.[23] Each witty and partially animated report delivers the vital info on who sold what to whom and for how much. She provides all in an entertaining and cleavage-enhanced manner.

She's a gimmick, albeit a popular one on the InterTubes, and even has a catchphrase. At the end of each video, she signs off with her encouraging words, "You can't sell it if you don't write it."

It's American Greetings meets Robert McKee.

ScriptGirl is on my mind because of a headline/link on DoneDealPro.com that caught my eye.

ScriptGirl Debuts All Establishing Shot Webisode

---

23 Story goes she used to provide weekly sales reports to the producer, but he was too lazy to even read that, so one day she decided to videotape it so he could watch it at his leisure. After a few weeks, friends suggested she put the videos online at YouTube (youtube.com/user/scriptgirl411), which is when she became an overnight sensation.

Clicking on the link surfs me to ScriptGirl's YouTube page. Pressing play on the featured video makes a strip club's version of a naughty librarian appear on my computer screen.

"Hi. This is ScriptGirl in Hollywood with your weekly script sales report for Friday, November 2. It's a very special webisode for me, as it's my first time"—she pauses to wink at the camera—"documenting the exploits of a single company. It seems Executive Producer Justin Lackey and his newly formed Establishing Shot Productions have been busy, busy, busy acquiring and acquiring and acquiring. Could the purposely leaked reports that Lackey has assembled a staff of readers ten times larger than any studio be true? From the accelerated rate of script sales, I think there might be a lot of truth to those rumors.

"First up, Establishing Shot made the highest bid on Christopher Schulman's action script *Days Never Ending.* This was a preemptive sale, which means simply that Establishing Shot paid a premium to purchase the script before any competitors had a chance to see it. The script features a female protagonist in an enticing tale about a cop who toils as an off-duty vigilante who enjoys making life difficult for a powerful mafia family. When she meets a mysterious woman sent by the mob to kill her, they unexpectedly fall in love and team up in order to wage war on the bad guys. Rumor is Jessica Alba and Jessica Biel are attached. Schulman is repped by Jake Lofton of Original Artists."

ScriptGirl hardly takes a second to breathe before she forges ahead.

"Next up, Trey and Marsha Kirkman have optioned their ensemble drama *The Big Blind* to Establishing Shot.

Big Blind is described as a compelling look at the competitive world of professional poker as seen through the eyes of an unexpected underdog. Establishing Shot is going all in on the project in hopes to develop it and flip it to a major studio."

With another wink and a sexy smile, ScriptGirl continues. "And finally, Taryn Southern's *Match Dot Net* was purchased for low to mid six figures. It's a romantic comedy where matches are made, you guessed it, on the World Wide Web. When the main characters meet and fall for one another, conflict arises when one discovers the other may be a serial Internet datist. Ooh . . . say that one five times fast. Is it love, Web sight unseen? Or is he an e-male chauvinist pig? Ha! Taryn Southern is repped by UA.

"Yes, that's three major sales, all in one week's time. So what's next for the high-flying Establishing Shot? It seems the sky's the limit for this well-oiled machine . . ."

Close the browser's window before ScriptGirl reaches her signature sign-off. Heard enough. Already read two of the three scripts the video blog mentioned. Liked *Days Never Ending* a lot but felt it needed a component rewrite[24] addressing the dynamic relationship and the dynamic character. Most dynamics are simply a story device, but when the characters and their relationship to the main character aren't seamlessly intertwined, the device becomes painfully apparent, as it was in *Days*. Truth told, I never believed they fell in love, never saw it on the page. Nothing that can't be fixed in development, though.

Hated *Match Dot Net*. Thought it was a cliché-filled romantic comedy. Not certain what the reader at Establishing

---

24 A component rewrite focuses on one ineffective or lacking aspect (component) of a script and aims to fix, improve, polish, and implement that facet throughout.

Shot saw in it. Then again, Hollywood churns out a baker's dozen of these cookie-cutter rom-coms a year, so what do I know? Suffice to say, not my genre.

These days, I'm averaging eight and a half scripts a day, more than two hundred fifty a month. Picked up the pace a bit, but at the expense of a normal day's sanity. Been pulling twelve- to fifteen-hour shifts.

All work and no play makes me Jack's inflamed sense of dejection.

The drama continues the next morning. In *Variety*, the blurbs announce:

The Outer Banks - Gary Burg (Establishing Shot)

Establishing Shot has bought the rights to Gary Burg's family drama *The Outer Banks*. Burg is a seasoned writer, having penned six seasons of the ABC drama *Be Home for Dinner*. Scott Allen Perry is attached to direct. **11/9**

And . . . Scene! - Laurel Wickliffe (Establishing Shot)

Establishing Shot has purchased and will develop *And . . . Scene!* a screwball comedy written by Laurel Wickliffe. While working as a makeup artist in the industry, Wickliffe penned this story of a mother and daughter tandem of aspiring actresses in Hollywood. **11/9**

And . . . Scene! was in my To-Be-Read pile. Not anymore. A sale means it ain't a Holden. While that should be enough for me to dispose of it and forge on, I'm compelled to give it a read before it hits the To-Be-Shred pile. It's good, not great. Funny, not hilarious. However, it's the kind of work Hollywood loves to develop, hiring dozens of writers to punch up for whatever bankable stars are attached to it at the moment.

You Die - Anthony Richards (Establishing Shot)

Anthony Richards, a part-time wine maker, has sold his horror script *You Die* to Establishing Shot for an undisclosed amount. The script is about a demented Boy Scout leader with the eerie ability to bring campfire horror stories to life as he tells them. Reports are *You Die* has the makings of a franchise. Rumors are New Line Entertainment has already inquired about the availability of the project. **11/9**

Finish something I approve of, a screenplay called *Palindrome Is a Racecar*. Head to the den, add it to my Projects-With-Potential pile, a new stack within the room. It's a short stack of scripts, six deep, currently avoiding death row. Check that, five deep. Forgot to dispose of *Days Never Ending*.

Pull it, toss it into the To-Be-Shred pile, check the time, do the math, grab another three scripts, which will take this fine workday to its fourteenth hour.

Turn, leave, shut the door, forge on.

Four days from now, I will pull *Palindrome Is a Racecar* from the Projects-With-Potential pile when, over coffee and bile, I read in *Variety* it's now owned by Lackey.

Four deep and dwindling. Vicious cycle.

Couch. Full immersion.

Share enters, throws her keys into the bowl near the door.

"Did you get it?" I inquire.

"Yes. Can't believe you have me chasing scripts now. What have you done to me?"

"It'll be worth it. You'll see."

She throws herself onto the couch. "Could use your help later tonight."

"Can't until around nine. Working until then. That work for you?"

She nods, gaze already deep in her script.

My focus dips into mine.

Two peas. Couch, our pod.

Calling All Cops will never be owned by anyone in this town, including Lackey. First of all, the title screams cop drama or maybe cop dramedy, yet it's not about the police. It's about a welfare family, led by Mama Crenshaw, who turn to a life of crime after Papa Crenshaw lands in jail for selling drugs. When Mama Crenshaw proves to be adept as the kingpin of her neighborhood, the real crime families of Atlanta take note and threaten the family's livelihood. While it's well-written prose, the story meanders and falls flat in the end. Might be good fodder for an hour-long episode of TV drama, but it does not fly as a motion picture.

Nine o'clock. Punch out for the night.

Enter the den, which I have come to call my Den of Banality. Toss *Calling All Cops* and *Brimley* and *Hip-Hip Hooray* into the To-Be-Shred pile. One by one they meet their fate, deservedly so.

Prepare for tomorrow by pulling the morning reads, the first four, from the pile. Glance down, read the top script's title. My day will begin with something called *Light of My Life*, written by a Lydia Depasqualli.

See you in the morning.

Pretty certain *Light of My Life* will suck a bag of dicks, but I'm too tired to care.

Until tomorrow.

Unbeknownst to me there, then, the third script in the pile is one that'll change my mood, my day, my ultimate course of action.

Third script in the pile.

Mood.

Day.

Ultimate course of action.

Click off the light in the den, shut the door, help Share with an audition, slumber until tomorrow.

CHANNEL 5UPER4ERO

S it back, relax, and enjoy the show. Or the pitch, as they call it in Hollywoodland . . .

The script we're analyzing today is titled *Channel 5uper-4ero*.

The premise. Twenty years after the fall of superheroes at the hands of a powerful villain named Omni, a new generation of heroes arises to battle the tyrant. When their exploits are recorded and broadcast to the world, they become celebrities overnight, which leads to the world's first group of corporate-sponsored superheroes and the birth of Channel 5uper4ero.

The year is 2040. Twenty-some years ago, superheroes suffered a fatal blow. The Sentry, guardian of Capital City and the most powerful superhero of them all, met his demise at the hands of Omni, an alien villain the likes of which the world has never seen.

Omni then aligned an army of villains and waged war

against all heroes. The wrong side won. Superheroes as we know them were wiped out. Those who survived went into hiding—but not without a plan. They coupled, procreated, and reared a new generation of superheroes they hoped might rise when the time was right.

Enter Nathan Webb, billionaire, media mogul, owner of Channel 54, a once powerful superstation struggling to survive in this day and age. At the outset of the war, he was a young producer, brave enough to grab a high-def cam and point it at The Sentry and Omni as they waged their bloody and infamous battle. The Zapruder-like clip[25] was watched millions of times through the years and helped make Webb a fortune, which is the sole reason Channel 54 exists today. Most importantly, Nathan Webb is the reason The Sentry still *lives* today—a compelling reveal in the script. Twenty-some years ago, Nathan risked his life and pulled the thought-dead Sentry from the battlefield, transported him to safety, found him medical attention, and hid him from the world. The Sentry, now an amputee and shell of the hero he once was, went underground, fearing his reappearance might threaten the family he left behind.

Now, two decades later, the new generation of superheroes is ready and Nathan Webb has a plan. Over the years, he utilized his fortune to build a base for them along with a new superstation that will broadcast their exploits to the world on what he's dubbed Channel 5uper4ero. Requiring The Sentry's help to recruit and train Capital City's new heroes, Nathan lures him out of seclusion by enlisting the one person on earth The Sentry cares about—his daughter

---

25 Abraham Zapruder shot the silent color film of President John F. Kennedy's assassination as his motorcade passed through Dealey Plaza in Dallas, Texas, on November 22, 1963.

and, unbeknownst to all, heir to the throne of Capital City's most powerful superhero.

The script is good. Too good.

The characters fall into place on the story's chessboard. The action is jump-off-the-page riveting. Add in a dozen new-gen heroes with irresistible personalities and names like Bunny, Gale, Wits, Kamikaze, Gnat, Elixir, and Rift. Insert an equal number of compelling villains plus one lethargic and overweight Omni, who must whip himself back into shape after he learns reports of The Sentry's demise were greatly exaggerated.

I've never seen, nor read such a dramatic arc in a villain. For multiple pages, as he goes through a brilliant, Rocky-like transformation, I find myself rooting for Omni. That displaced emotion ends with a perfectly placed movie quote homage.

OMNI

I have come here to chew bubble gum and kick ass . . . and, folks, I'm all out of bubble gum.[26]

That quote precedes a gruesome mass execution, which sets off a 32-page battle between good and evil that reads like 10. All of the above flows together into a 103-page don't-ever-want-to-get-off ride.

Don't want to jinx it, but BOOM!BOOM!BOOM!

This, my friends and enemies, is what Hollywood calls high concept. A tent pole motion picture. Franchise in the making. Chock-full of conceits, this script written by one Finn McMillan has me so jazzed I cannot read it fast

26 An homage to the sci-fi/dark comedy classic *They Live*, written and directed by John Carpenter.

enough. Third script I pulled today and, most imperative, the first in nine months I suspect might have been written by Holden.

These are my initial thoughts.

Problems arise as I continue to read. Uncertainty sets in when I finish. Doesn't get any better my second time through. Read it two additional times, four in total, dissecting it, analyzing it, judging it. Characters, while well drawn, lack Holden's cause-and-effect initial descriptions, his trademark.

Is he testing me?

Dynamic progression, while compelling and quite brilliant, misses the mark with a can-see-it-coming-for-ten-pages complication yet redeems itself with an impressive estrangement and low point.

Holden would have polished those stains away.

Finally, and I cannot believe I am saying this, but the ending, while satisfying, overlooks a beg-for-a-sequel moment. Omni is obviously defeated, but the audience sees him die. Believe the writer missed a déjà vu moment where media mogul Nathan Webb should have pulled the thought-dead Omni from the battlefield, transported him to safety, found him medical attention. After all, every good story requires a great villain.

I'm no writer, but those changes would make this good script great. *Sofa-king great.*

Alas, back to reality.

Conclusion, Meyer Holden did not pen *Channel 5uper-4ero.* Some bloke named Finn McMillan did. Script has mad potential, but it needs to be developed.

If I were still at Foster's office, it might move up the

chain of command, and in the process credit for finding it and championing it would get lost, like a penny in a wish-me-luck fountain. Had I stayed by Foster's side another two or three years, maybe I'd be far enough along to merit a producer credit on the project, but I'd be far enough along to likely miss the script altogether. Too busy to read, too occupied to hunt, too unavailable for mere spec.

On my own, sans pot to piss in, I have nothing to offer a writer. No connections, no funding, no stars to attach. That's what a Holden can net you. Playing a proverbial board game here. Holden takes you up-up-away to the top, do not look back, get out of doing time, collect your hard-earned dollars.

Way it can be.

More than 2,200 scripts read, but who's counting? Who am I kidding? Been 2,261. Nine months. Nothing to show. Nothing whatsoever. No closer to Meyer Holden than the lazy fuck sitting at the Fairfax/Sunset Coffee Bean & Tea Leaf right now proclaiming to his buddies, "Know what we should fucking do? Find the next Minor Holden script and make that shit starring all of us." High five.

Toss *Super4ero* on the coffee table, rub my brow, tired, depressed, defeated, glance at the clock. Supposed to meet Share for happy hour.

Poetic.

THE GOOD LUCK CLUB

"'N other round?"

Share and I are enjoying cocktails at the Good Luck Bar. Truth told, we're enjoying the alcohol much more than each other's company. Call it unhappy hour. Way it is. Both had shitty days. Both nod to the bartender. Might as well be a split screen. I kick back my Tanqueray and tonic, hating the fact I think this way: split screens, exteriors, interiors, dynamic progression. Find comfort knowing in two more drinks I won't.

Share's fondling her tonic, thoughts adrift in her own loss. She had a callback today. About a week ago, I helped her practice her lines for a supporting role in an independent film. The character was damaged and unforgettable. Together, we combed through the sides—the few pages of a script actors are provided with for auditions—looking for nuances for this peculiar yet engaging love interest. When she learned she got a callback, she felt obtaining the entire screenplay would allow her to delve further into the role.

I concurred. So she called in a favor to her brother, and Lackey came through.

Set in a rehab clinic, the full-length script titled *Cold Turkey* tells this cynical yet uplifting tale of lost hope and found love. Sounds hokey, but it wasn't. It was right on.

Share coveted the part. That was obvious from the moment she told me about the project, even before she asked me to run lines with her. She has this way about her when she falls in love with something, this little-girl-seeing-the-world-for-the-first-time quality that's virtually extinct in this town.

After reading the script last night, her enthusiasm for the role soared, which is how and why I stayed up well past my bedtime helping her run lines.

Character's name was Abby.

ABBY, 30s, clean and sober but clearly weathered.

She didn't look the part. Nonetheless, if you've never been witness to a talented actor transforming into character, well, let me tell you it's something to behold.

Abby, thirties, clean and sober but clearly weathered, recited line after line for two hours last night. We moved beyond the sides and fleshed out some character traits we uncovered amid the other scenes in the full-length script.

I headed off to bed close to one.

Share put in another two hours.

She didn't get the part. The honesty of her silence as she kissed her first glass of vodka told me that. Been here almost an hour, growing closer amid the speechlessness. It's nice. Really is. Show me a couple who can enjoy the quiet, a couple who don't feel the need to fill every hush with another verbal dear-diary-guess-what-I-did-today homily, and I'll show you a script that does not suck. Guess what? They all suck. That's what I'm drinking to this evening.

"'Nother round?"

I don't budge. Taxiing on the runway of numb, find solace knowing Share's got this round. She's there when I need her. That's what I love about her, what I love about us. We're a project with merit. One that deserves an agent and a manager. Sold to the highest bidder, high six figures over a low seven.

As the bartender concocts a cure for what ails us, Share whispers, "Bateman . . . ?" She pauses, as if I'm going to encourage her slurred disclosure.

Oh, baby, c'mon. Don't ruin this. Was going so well.

She continues without me. "Bateman, the first time we met . . ."

I watch her fingernail scratch at the Revlon stain tattooed to her glass, pray my numb is not about to be disturbed.

". . . you called me Ass Eyes. You called me Ass Eyes the first time we met."

She makes her point. She makes me laugh. I look her way, and her ass eyes go wide for an instant, before an unexpected appearance of her pearly whites.

Hands down, best thing I read today.

An hour later we're still drinking, but melancholy has hightailed it out of here. We've moved to a cozy booth, and our conversation has evolved.

"Most embarrassing thing you've ever done in LA," I

say, and it's a perfect escalation to the game of twenty questions we've been playing for the last half hour.

Share thinks. "Hmm, I stood outside of Koi once."

"What? I was there. We stood outside waiting for the valet."

"No. I went there once before that."

"You told me it was the first time you ate there."

"It was."

"Baby, are we going to fight?"

"No. That's why it's embarrassing. Maggie and I went there some Friday night, months earlier. The place was still new and a total scene. We stood outside for like forty minutes talking on our cells, waiting on a car that was never coming, trying to act cool. We thought we'd be seen, make an impression, meet people."

"That's so sad. So LA. Did you?"

"What?"

"Meet anyone?"

"Hell no. Not one person. Everyone else was too busy talking on their cells, looking cool. So Maggie and I headed to The Dime and told everyone we just came from Koi."

"Jesus, baby, I don't know what to say. I cannot top that."

Share points my way. "Exactly. Embarrassing, right? We were like addicts getting our fix of Hollywood methadone. As you would say, sofa-king lame."

"Holy shit!"

"What? Bateman, you look like you saw a ghost."

"You just made me think of something. A script."

Share groans. "Are we really going to ruin a good night and talk about work?"

"No, this is different. It's a play my dad wrote. It's called *methODone*, spelled with an *OD* in the middle."

She laughs. "Love it."

"Share, you will love it. I think it will resonate with you. Always thought it could be workshopped, maybe turned into a great script. It's better than *Cold Turkey*, and there's this supporting role you'd die for."

"Really?"

"Yeah."

"I want to read it."

"I want you to read it. Tonight."

"Smashing," she says, smacking the table for effect. "Ooh! And if it is good, maybe we can find a theater and mount a production of it."

"I like that idea. Maybe I can even call a writer to work on a script version with us."

"You actually talk to some writers?"

"Been known to pick up the phone every now and then."

"Maybe I want to try my hand at writing it."

"Maybe I need to see your résumé."

She shoots me her mean face. "You serious about doing this? What about that thing? That thing you focus on all day every day?"

"I can do both."

"Hell yeah. Good answer. I'm game."

"Let's get out of here."

And just like that, we're off.

SECOND-HALF ADVENTURE

Page ninety-seven. Main character is hauling ass to catch a train he thinks is carrying the young girl he's been protecting the entire second act. He'll hop the wrong train. I know before I read it. Why? Because in three pages or less the writer needs to get to the low point, which often takes the form of a dynamic estrangement, the stage in every effective film when the main character and the dynamic character spend a few scenes apart.

In horror films it's where the main character finally goes it alone after losing a close friend due to confusion or death.[27] In love stories it's where the couple fight or cheat or think something/someone better is out there.[28] In action movies it's usually the hero losing the one he or she is chasing/protecting.[29]

---

27 *Friday the 13th*: Group of kids sequester themselves for a weekend or longer. One by one, they get picked off until the hero is revealed. The hero/main character always gets separated from his or her last remaining friend before somehow defeating Jason.

28 *When Harry Met Sally*: After Harry and Sally sleep together, for the first time in years they spend New Year's apart. Harry then runs all over NYC to get to Sally, which leads to the climax.

29 *The Terminator*: On-the-run Sarah Connor and Kyle Reese are arrested and separated in a police station. Kyle is questioned by a psychologist, who deems him nuts and almost convinces Sarah of this. However, the Terminator's arrival proves he's not crazy and gets the duo together again.

EXT. TRAIN — CONTINUOUS

Tanner reaches out as he sprints,
as the train pulls away. He somehow
finds the strength and the momentum
to grab the handrail. Quite suddenly,
he's tugged out of frame, his legs
flailing until they land on metal.
He's aboard!

I jump off.

"Share?"

"Baby, I'm reading."

Ironic.

"Well, the fact you're chewing on your hair like you do when you're bored, I'm going to go out on a limb and say what you're reading isn't so great."

She has to spit out a strand to say, "I don't do that." She kicks me with a bare foot. "Well, the fact you stopped reading tells me that ain't a golden ticket in your hands."

"This is a true story."

"You're hungry, aren't you?"

"Is it obvious?"

"Well, it's almost five thirty, which means your stomach is beckoning. It's like clockwork. God forbid we don't feed you by seven."

"So I'm predictable, huh?"

"No, you're geriatric. The elderly like to eat around five."

"Thanks. I needed that."

"Aw, bad day?"

"Same as all the rest." I catch my faux pas before Share

pounces on it. "I mean this part is always the same." I raise the script. "The rest is grand."

"Nice catch. So what's wrong with it?"

"What?"

"The script."

"It's lame."

"How so?"

"It's a hundred pages of mundane. That's all."

"Why? What's it lacking? I know with you it's all 'don't ask me about my business,'" she says, imitating me or maybe Pacino.

Women forget nothing.

She adds, "But, well, how do I put this? Sometimes you're always wrong."

The line makes me laugh. "You're proud of that, aren't you?"

Share grins. "A little."

"You should be. It's effective dialogue."

"Regardless, that rule of yours is dumb. And besides, I can handle things. I'm smart. Not like everybody says." She trumps my quote from *The Godfather* with one from *Part II*.

Well played, but I still balk.

She raises an eyebrow.

I'm tired, hungry, and not in the mood to teach my girlfriend about the craft of screenwriting. However, she asked and I don't want to fight, so I tread lightly. "In this script, the second-act adventure . . ." I start over. "The second part of the movie, where the story really kicks in and the main characters spend time together, is yawn-inspiring. In fact, there isn't one. There's a first act and I'm guessing an adequate ending, but without a middle you really have nothing."

Share stares, listens.

I continue, "The middle is the bulk of a movie, but most ideas lack a second act. And in that act, the characters need to be moving toward a goal, which is usually stated by the main character early on. There's an opponent, of course, who's tied to that goal in that they want the same thing or maybe want the opposite. That's conflict. You also need a complication, which usually happens right in the middle and raises the stakes for all involved. Finally, you need a low point, which usually ends the second act. That's when it appears all hope is lost for the main character or characters."

Share stares me down. Think I lost her somewhere back there.

She grins, almost laughs. "I know what a second-half adventure is, Bateman. You don't have to be so goddamn condescending."

"You know what a second-half adventure is?"

"Yeah, I do. Remember? I'm smart."

"Give me an example."

"Name me a film."

Like her gumption, like the fire in her eyes. I go easy on her, give her a simple one. "*Wizard of Oz.*"

She rolls her eyes, kicks me with that foot again. "Oh, come on. That's 101." She sings, "'We're off to see the Wizard, the wonderful Wizard of Oz.'" Performance over, she adds, "Second-half adventure is that journey. Her goal is to go home."

I'm impressed but chuckle to hide it. I raise the stakes. "*Star Wars.*"

Takes her but a moment. "It started when Luke asked the old guy to teach him about the Force. Oh . . . he said, 'I want to be a Jedi Knight like my father.'"

"What? Who are you?"

She gloats, giggles. "I have a big brother that's a tad obsessed with everything *Star Wars*. Remember?"

"Don't remind me. How about *King Kong*?"

"Um, main guy wants to save the girl, but bad guy wants to capture Kong."

"*E.T.*"

"Geez, way to throw a meatball right down the middle. 'E.T. phone home.'"

"Hands down, worst E.T. impression ever."

"Oh, Bateman, wait." She reaches into a pocket in her jeans. "I have something for you." She pulls out her middle finger. Sticks out her tongue for added effect.

"All right. You're freaking me out. How the hell do you know all this?"

"Ever hear of Writers Boot Camp?"

"Of course."

"Well, I took classes there a few years ago."

"Share, why would you take writing classes?"

"Why wouldn't I?"

"Because you're an actor, not a writer."

"But that's why I did it."

"Care to elaborate?"

"It's just a theory of mine. I don't want to bore you."

"Share. What's up with that? Tell me."

She bites her thumbnail, inspects it for a sec, finally says, "I just think most people move here with big dreams. They want fame, but they aren't willing to work at it. They think they're going to be discovered sipping their Red Bull in some impossible-to-get-into club or buying overpriced caffeine at the Bean on some lazy weekday. They treat LA like it's a party, like it's spring break. It's stupid."

"Instead of treating it like . . . ?"

"Like school. Look, if you want to be a lawyer, it takes four years for a bachelor's degree and three years of law school. Seven years total. Doctor, eight years. Plus residency. You have to work your ass off to succeed. Yet people pull up to Hollywood with their mattress tied to the roof of their car and think they'll be making movies by the weekend. They think they're entitled to it for some reason. That's pretty daft, if you ask me. I think the work begins when you arrive. You have to study, learn, be a sponge. Every audition is a class, every script a textbook. At least that's how I approach it. I don't care if it takes four or six or eight years—I'm going to graduate. And studying screenwriting was part of that. I wanted to know what I should be looking for in scripts. I thought it might help me choose roles. Plus, understanding story arcs helps me build my characters."

"How do I not know this?"

"Because you don't ever want to talk about things, especially work. I probably kept my mouth shut at first because, well, in the beginning you were a little paranoid. Plus, bitter-selfish-son-of-a-bitch guy."

"*Were*. Past tense, right?"

"Yes."

"Good. But wow, that's so refreshing," I mull over what she's divulged. "So fucking impressive."

"Think so?"

"No. I know so."

"Hmm, I think maybe it was the disdain in my voice when I was talking about Hollywood that's turning you on in some way."

"Oh, that too."

She laughs.

For someone I thought I had pegged when we first met, first went out, first fucked, second fucked, started dating, began falling for each other, man, was I off. Way off.

Hour and a half later, we're still on the couch. We ordered from California Chicken Cafe, chowed while we explored second-half adventures. We've upped the ante, added in second-half complications.

Share thinks of one. "Hey, how about *Kill Bill*?"

"One or two?"

"Stupid question. You have to look at it like one big movie."

"Well, the adventure is killing everyone on the death list, including, of course, Bill."

"It's the title of the film. That was too easy," Share says. "Complication?"

"Complication. Hmm. Even though Tarantino uses nonlinear storytelling, it's 'Bill, it's your baby.'"

"Right before Bill shoots her. Bam."

"Yep."

"Very nice," Share says.

"How about *Titanic*?"

"Oh my God. I saw it so many times. Let's see . . . Leonardo wants to win over Kate."

"And the complication?"

"Um," she says, twirling some locks. "I'm not sure."

I laugh. "Pretty sure the complication is the boat hits the iceberg."

"Duh. That's embarrassing. How about *When Harry*

Met Sally?"

"Adventure is becoming friends. Complication is when they sleep together, of course." I serve up, "*Tootsie.*"

"Ooh, I like, I like. Hoffman wants to be a successful actor, dresses like a woman. Complication is . . . the father. When the father falls in love with Tootsie."

"Nice."

Share does a little victory dance on the couch. "Hey, if we were a movie, what would our complication be?"

"Um, maybe when you told me my enemy was your brother."

"Oh yeah," Share whispers. "Spot on."

Share shifts, props her head up with her hand, elbow anchored in the cushions of the couch. "Ooh, I got a good complication. Maybe the best one yet."

She's got my attention.

Her eyes go wide. She whispers, "*Jaws.*"

I ponder. Stumped.

Share laughs. "Gotcha!"

"Wait. Let me think it through. The sheriff obviously wants to kill the shark and save the town, but what's the complication?"

"Five seconds," she teases. "Four. Three. Two. One. Bzzzzzzz! Oh, I'm sorry. You've run out of time. Thanks for playing."

"What is it?"

Share beams. "I remember this one from Boot Camp. The shark starts hunting the hunters."

Takes a moment, but it registers . . . resonates. "What did you say?"

"The shark begins to hunt the hunters."

I can feel the blood draining from my face. BOOM!BOOM!BOOM! My God. That's it. Can't believe I didn't think of it sooner.

"Bateman? You all right? You got that just-saw-a-ghost look again."

"Been hunting him all this time," I whisper. "Need Holden to start hunting me."

NEED A BIGGER BOAT

Monday.

On the back of a postcard with a picture of Sam Spade, I print:

> *Always wondered why you chose to let the opponent live in your second spec. Lennon Bridges could have been great, but Turick needed to die. Way it is. SB*

I put a stamp on it, mail it two minutes after the post office opens at nine.

Tuesday.

On the back of a postcard with a picture of the old Hollywoodland sign, I print:

> *Was the sex scene with Lorelei coldcocking Mack with the gun in The Living End ever shot? Always felt something was missing in the development of their relationship. Never knew that scene existed until I read the script. Just curious. SB*

Put a stamp on it, mail it at a quarter after nine.

Wednesday.

On the back of a postcard of the neon Father's Office sign, print:

> *Sal Burton sort of says hello. What a killjoy he can be.*
> *Told me I was chasing a ghost when I got too drunk.*
> *Blew my cover. Damn Racer 5. SB*

Stamp it, mail it at 9:05.

Thursday.

On the back of a postcard of Bruce Willis as Mack Fellows in the film *The Living End*, print three words:

> *Fuck Jason Patric.*

Stamp it, wait five minutes for the post office to open.

Friday.

On the back of a postcard of a hideous clown, print:

> *To this day, think Punching the Clown is your most*
> *underrated work. Film is also an amazing adaptation*
> *of your words. Only thing that sucks in it is your cameo.*
> *Way it is. SB*

Drop it in the mail at a quarter after nine.

Saturday.

On the back of a postcard with a pic of Redford in *Three Days of the Condor*, print:

> *They do not make 'em like they used to. SB*

Mail it at nine sharp.

Sunday.

On the back of a black-and-white postcard of an old-fashioned typewriter:

Q: How many writers does it take to change a lightbulb?
A: Change? What needs to be changed?

Stamp it, drop it in a mailbox on my way to Runyon.

This is merely the first week of postcards. Vow to send one every single day, never miss a day. Let's call it the chum I toss into the ocean to bait The Man.

Day after Share played the *Jaws* card in our game of second-half adventures/complications, I ventured to an Internet café in Venice to pull Holden's vital information from the long-defunct message boards at meyerholdenisaneffinggenius.com.

Fan sites such as this had begun to pop up around the release of Meyer Holden's first film, *Fielder's Choice*. However, after he vanished and, more precisely, after *The Rising Sons of Mourning Park* was discovered, a wave of paranoia tsunamied Hollywood. Sites like this were quickly acquired, seized, and shut down in order to limit the intel on The Man. This was essentially the "shot heard round the Internet" that began the 75-degree Cold War.[30]

Now, anyone who knows a thing or two about the WorldWideInterWeb knows the Internet is like Vegas in that what happens there stays there. Soldiers in the Tera-Byte Army don't take too kindly when terrorists invade their homeland and attempt to eradicate content. So they mirrored said info, including the above mentioned meyerholdenisaneffinggenius.com, and found a well-hidden and well-protected online home for it.

Took some time and some skill, but I uncovered a portal

---

30 Many speculate it was the studios that acquired and/or forced the cease and desist on the Holden sites in order to gain an upper hand in the Cold War. Others point the finger at individuals like CEO of Shot/Cut Productions, Billy Wise, the one who found/benefited from *The Rising Sons of Mourning Park* and someone plenty motivated to keep all the Holden hunters at bay. And, of course, some conspiracy theorists believe it was Holden himself who erased the intel in order to make his little Houdini act all the more impressive.

into Holden's little online library, which is where I garnered his vital info. Site was actually mirrored and stored on a total of three private servers before being shut down. The mirror sites are suspect, most likely riddled with an insane amount of spyware, malware, trojans, dialers, and cookies, hence my trek to Venice. Definitely worth the trip.

I plugged the address for Holden into Google maps, and it pointed to ten acres of land outside of Denver with an impressive ranch-style home at its center point. B-I-N-G-O.

In addition to his address, I acquired an e-mail address, two telephone numbers, and a list of preferred locales in Denver, amassed from a series of Holden sightings over the years. Information is more than four years old. Assume the residential address might be the only valid intel. Regardless, it's all I needed. I hightail it out of the Internet café before anyone can be dispatched to the location to identify who's poking around in Holden's vitals. Mission accomplished.

Now every day my postcards will be delivered to The Man's doorstep, his home outside of Denver, Colorado. Not sure if his mail is filtered. Have to hope it's not. Have to hope my cards reach his hands, pray they resonate.

Shot in the fucking dark.

Decide not to stop there. Can't put all my eggs in one basket.

On the way home from my morning run, trying to hatch more plans when I pass a construction site, notice a bunch of wild postings on a temporary wall, some for movies coming soon and some for albums about to drop. Turn the corner, pass a row of eight Andre the Giant OBEY posters on the same wall. Also spot a Post No Bills sign, which makes me laugh.

I stop, turn back to the OBEY wheatpaste posters. Contemplate for a moment, allow a stroke of genius to have its way. Start walking again. With purpose.

En route, I turn an idea into an elaborate strategy.

Back at the homestead, I mask my IP and surf the InterTubes until I locate a high-quality photo of Holden clutching a screenplay as he walks. His face is turned to the camera, and the shot captures the moment he's become aware he's being photographed. It's perfect. The pic is from INF.com, a digital photo agency specializing in celebrity candids. I PayPal the licensing fee from a trojan account I have registered under the name Randall Stevens.

After downloading the photo, I work on it in Photoshop. An hour forty-five later, I achieve the desired result. Via another anonymous e-mail account, I send the file to California Poster in Van Nuys and place a print order for five hundred three-by-five posters, specifying they need to be bundled in ten stacks of fifty. Requires a 30 percent down payment and eight hours to complete the job. Take care of the 30 percent via a prepaid credit card. Then wait all day for night to come.

That evening, I'm pulling up to the print shop when I spot a teenager with an Efron haircut skateboarding toward me.

I jump out of the car and call, "Yo. Want to make a quick twenty bucks?"

Kid looks at me like I'm a recurring character on *To Catch a Predator.*

"No, no. I need you to pick up a print job for me. All you need to do is run into the shop, pay them, and carry it out to my car. Twenty bucks for you. Cash money."

The kid rolls up, flips his board in the air, catching it with one hand and landing on his feet directly in front of me. "Why can't you pick it up?"

"Bad back."

"Hmm. Sounds pretty shady." He pushes the hair out of his eyes, only to have it fall back a moment later. "And Xander doesn't work for less than fifty."

"You Xander?"

Kid gives a thumbs-up.

"Xander. Here's three hundred. Outstanding balance on the job comes to two-sixty-seven. Rest is yours. Deal?"

He pulls out an iPhone and brings up the calculator app.

As he figures out his take, I add, "And don't even think about bolting. I'm nimbler than I look and will catch your ass pronto if you try anything."

"Xander always plays it legit."

He stretches out a hand, so I assume we have a deal. I slap the money into his palm. "Job is under the name Thomas A. Anderson. If they ask any questions, you don't know me."

He laughs. Skates to the store, dismounts, heads inside. Ten minutes later, he comes out carrying the posters.

We load them in the back of my Explorer.

"Pleasure doing business with you, Xander." I close the hatch, but he's already skating away.

He raises a hand before he accelerates with some kicks.

Kid of few words. Gonna go far in life.

Get in my car, hightail it with the goods.

Like a kid on Christmas Eve, I hardly sleep a wink that night.

Next morning, I'm pulling into Home Depot on Sunset as they open their doors at five.

Inside, I grab a cart and fill it with ten five-gallon buckets, ten horsehair brushes, and ten one-gallon jugs of wheatpaste.

As I'm loading the last few jugs into my cart, I hear, "Señor, do you need labor today?"

"Yes," I respond before looking up.

When I do, I spy an eager day laborer smiling and clutching a Dodgers cap to his chest.

"But I need ten of you."

He stares at me.

"Do you speak English?"

His head bobs.

"What's your name?"

"Miguel."

"Miguel. Can you round up nine more dependable men and meet me outside?"

"Si, señor. Yes."

"All ten must have their own vehicles."

More head bobs.

"Very well. I'll be outside in about ten minutes."

"Big job?"

"Big job. Good pay. Not difficult."

Miguel smiles, then walks away.

On my way to the register, I grab ten LA County maps along with a Sharpie. Purchase everything with cash.

Outside, I see Miguel organizing the team. He looks at me, and I point to the far corner of the parking lot. "Blue Ford Explorer. When you have the nine men, meet me there."

Miguel nods. So do the seven day laborers behind him. At my truck, I organize the materials into kits of a

174

bucket, brush, paste, and map. My party of ten arrives as I'm completing the last one.

"Ten?" I say, conducting a head count.

"Sí, señor."

"Okay. Each of you will grab one of these buckets and fifty posters." I point to the open hatch of my truck. "You will hang the posters on walls in the area I assign for you." I look around and spot a wall across the street covered in art. "Hang them like that," I say, pointing. They all look, and most nod. "It should take you each about one hour of labor. I will pay you fifty dollars each."

Half the group smiles. I assume the other half needs to be brought up to speed.

"Miguel, can you translate?"

He does. When he's done, everyone starts to grab supplies.

"After you have a kit and fifty posters, see me." Head to the hood of the car. Line forms. Call the first worker. Grab his map, unfold it, and circle an area with the Sharpie. "You will go here and look for places to hang the posters. Construction walls, bus stops, abandoned buildings."

He nods. So do half of the others.

"Miguel. Make sure everyone understands."

"Sí, señor."

Fifteen minutes later, I'm watching my workforce head to their trucks and cars and venture off to complete my plan.

I glance at my watch. It's 5:35 a.m., and I find myself laughing. Someone I know once said, "Anybody that can make me laugh at this hour deserves it." So I head to Starbucks, treat myself to a venti.

A few hours later while I'm immersed in scripts, Cold-fuckcold, California, wakes up to five hundred posters strategically wheatpasted across town, near and en route to all the major studios. The posters depict a black-and-white, Banksy-esque version of Holden, script in hand, looking at the camera. Added to the artwork is a Photoshopped milk mustache and the tagline:

got holden?

By noon, the story and pics of the wild postings begin popping up on blogs, Twitter, and Facebook. Online editions of major publications including *USA Today*, *Los Angeles Times*, *Variety*, and *Entertainment Weekly* run the story—and not by chance, mind you. I had the foresight to *67 and alert all of them to the potential breaking story. Midafternoon, the news is everywhere.

Popular theory is Holden's trying to send Hollywood a message. Lazy theory, in my opinion, but why would I expect more from Coldfuckcold? Regardless, my plan enjoys a conspicuous snowball effect.

Come out, come out, wherever you are.

More chum. Same day, late afternoon, take a reading break, get busy creating a website for a new screenwriting competition—anonymously, of course.

Two hours later, the first annual So You Think You Can Write Like Meyer Holden Contest goes live.

1st Prize: You get to call yourself "the *new* Meyer Holden" *PLUS*
you'll receive 250 professional business cards
proving to all you're "the *new* Meyer Holden"!
2nd Place: There is no second place.

3ʳᵈ Place: Third place is you're fired.

Add the tagline:

> Be the *new* Meyer Holden—
> because the original has faded.

Tomorrow, ads for the contest will appear in *Variety*, *Hollywood Reporter*, *Los Angeles Times*, *New York Times*, *Chicago Tribune*, and *Denver Post*. Also e-mail press releases to fifteen online scriptwriting blogs.

Brazen chum.

End of day, still on the couch, I surf away from the latest news stories about my wildly intriguing posters and head to Hotmail. I create an account, screen name SBinLA@hotmail.com. To Holden's last who-knows-if-it-is-still-active e-mail address, I send the following.

> Struggling to find a common bond with his teenage son, my dad took me to a revival theater downtown one afternoon to see one of his favorite films—*Three Days of the Condor.* Suffice to say, I was blown away by it. Walking out of the theater, I asked him if we could see it again sometime. He said, "Sure. How about right now?" Will never forget that day, and from that moment on our love for movies—and I'm talking real motion pictures, like the ones you gave Hollywood—became our thing. TMI? Hope not. SB

I hear a key slide in the lock and the front door open. Share's heels click up the stairs.

I close my laptop.

"Hey." She swoops in to deliver a welcomed kiss. She click-click-clicks to the bedroom. "So what have you been up to today, Ishmael?"

"Same old same old." Unable to stifle a grin, I stop talking.

Sans heels, Share turns the corner, busts me beaming.

"I knew it."

"What?"

"You've been up to no good."

"What? What are you talking about? And why am I Ishmael?"

"Well." She falls into the couch, sweeps her legs up to her side. "I figure my older brother would be Ahab in this novel battle you two have going on."

"I see." I contemplate the roles. "Pretty clever."

"As far as what's going on, I had an audition today. For a pilot. A good pilot. This courtroom drama with *CSI*-type stuff peppered in. I like the part. I like it a whole hell of a lot. And I don't say this often, but I think I nailed it. After I read, everyone in the room was smiling and exchanging glances. It was kind of weird but in a good way."

"Share, that's great. Think you'll get it?"

"I don't know. I hope so. But this ain't my first rodeo, you know?"

I laugh.

"But that's not why I bring it up, actually." Share fondles her cell phone. "I ask again, did you do anything noteworthy today?"

"Same old," I deadpan. "Little of this, little of that."

"You're such a bad liar."

"What are you talking about?"

"Bateman, Bateman, Bateman." Share raises her Black-Berry and two-thumbs with purpose. "Did you have any-thing to do with this? Everyone in my audition was buzzing about it when I walked in the room."

She hands me her BlackBerry. On its screen is a pixi-lated image of one of the wheatpastes.

Try to stifle my grin but fail miserably.

"I knew it." She snatches the phone from my hands. "I just knew it."

"You didn't let on to anyone, did you?"

Arms outstretched to strangle me, she leans forward. "Yes, I told them everything I know. There's a SWAT team surrounding the place as we kiss."

Her lips press against mine, and for an instant I'm like, *Holden who?* Then she twists, turns, until she's on her back, head in my lap.

She studies the photo on her phone some more. "How in the hell do you think of this stuff, much less make it happen?"

"There is no try. Only do."

She shakes her head, laughs as she gets up.

"Anything going on tonight?"

"I have to be at play practice in about an hour."

"Need me?"

Share heads into the kitchen. "No. Not really. Still blocking Act Two. Unless you want to come."

"Next time. Actually thinking about going to see an old friend tonight."

Silence. She rounds the corner again, folds her arms, leans in the doorway. "Old friend? You've changed, Bateman. You definitely have changed."

That night, I don the disguise I wore to Lackey's little coming out party with his readers. Grab a stash of cash money, head to Father's Office, belly up to the bar, enjoy a Racer 5.

Sal is there. Oddly, feels good to see him.

Enjoy my India Pale Ale, watch the staring contest Sal's having with the stout in front of him. Listen as he pontificates to an older woman sitting next to him.

Hear him say, "There's nothing sadder in this world than a pawnshop in Hollywood."

Makes me smile. Good old Sal, bitter as my beer. Drain my glass the fun way, motion to Christmas.

"Another?"

"No, but I'd like to pay Sal's tab if I could."

She eyes me, my moustache, my glasses.

"As a favor," I add.

"Tonight's tab? Or the whole shebang?"

Without hesitation, "The whole shebang."

Christmas walks to the till, glances at Sal as she passes. He owes nearly a grand, but it doesn't matter. Luckily, brought enough cash.

"Awful nice of you . . ." Her voice trails off as she counts. After the tenth Franklin, she adds, "I didn't catch your name."

"Just make sure he gets this." Hand her a business card. Made it earlier, just one copy, reads:

S.B.
Holden Hunter

Christmas glances at it as I get up, walk away.
"You people are weird. You know that?"
"This is a true story."

FLOWERS IN THE ADDICT

Flowers in the Addict enjoys a successful three-night run at the Tres Stage Theatre in Hollywood. The play is the polished and renamed version of my dad's *methODone*.

Share and I decide on the new name after a long discussion about what the old title says. *methODone* emphasizes the drug and its detriments, while *Flowers* underscores the characters and the hope springing eternal within. It's tough to part with my father's title, but things happen in development and title changes are often one of them. Altered very little else. We only updated some references and gave the female role an additional monologue we felt was missing.

Credit where credit is due, Share does most of the heavy lifting to get the production up and running, handling the casting and directing. Jack-of-all-trades that I am, I man the tech booth.

The two-act play is unique in that it follows a recovering heroin addict named Benji Wiggins as he meets and interacts with two dissimilar but linked dynamic characters, Howard and Mindy Crumb. Suffice to say, they have opposite effects on Benji. With Howard, he tumbles further into his addiction, while Mindy pulls him out of it. Howard fills the first act, Mindy the second. They never share the stage because, in the story, Howard checks himself into the clinic, striving to get clean for his wife, Mindy. The first act ends with him failing, fatally. The second act sees Mindy being admitted, having relapsed after her husband's death. Benji and Mindy quite unexpectedly fall in love, despite a secret Benji harbors—the fact he played a key role in Howard's fate.

BENJI
(whispering)

I think I might be in love with
you.

Mindy hardly misses a beat, jumps on
Benji's sincerity with:

MINDY

Well, just because you feel it
doesn't mean it's love.

The words sober his mood.

BENJI

That's . . . my God, that's the
most cynical thing I've ever heard
anyone say.

MINDY

What? I'm not cynical.

BENJI

You're not cynical? You're not cynical? Then prove it. Please, by all means, say something positive.

Mindy searches for words, finds none, instead rushes forward, kisses Benji.

The contact gets them high.

By the time handfuls of plastic spoons rain down on the stage, a symbolic gesture of the couple's attempt to make a sober go of it, the audience has been through the wringer. Somehow they find the strength to get out of their seats for a standing ovation all three nights.

The response affirms my dad's writing. Being wrapped up in his words each of those three nights makes me miss him. Wish he could have been there.

In addition to directing, Share plays Mindy and she shines. Steals the show with subtle character nuances like scratching a different patch of skin during each performance until it bleeds, which pulls each audience uncomfortably close. Girl's got talent. And drive.

As *Flowers* was being rehearsed, she started toiling with a screenplay version of the story. It's a challenge, given the two different dynamic characters, but she makes it work.

Blue elephants, I think as I read it for the first time. *Blue fucking elephants.*

One night, after showing me some reworked pages, Share asks, "Bateman, why don't you write?"

"Can't."

"Can't? Or don't want to?"

"I can't. Can read a script or see a film and tell you what's wrong with it, what's missing, what's not working, but if you put a blank canvas in front of me, I'm crippled. Wasn't born with that gene. I don't know, maybe it skips a generation or something."

In all, 246 people see the play. Not bad for three nights in a 100-seat theater. All of Share's friends and her agent come out in support, while Justin cancels on opening night via a text: "Work has me by the balls -- will see show Sun." He's a no-show/no-text closing night.

"Motherfucker," Share remarks at the wrap party.

Stole my nickname for him. "You know, I've been there, and the job clouds your judgment, can make you forget what's really important."

"You defending him?"

"Not really. I was trying to make you feel better."

"Hmm. Thanks, but no thanks. I like when you're hating on him. Seems more sincere."

"Note taken."

Theater Review: "Flowers in the Addict"

A A A

By **Stanley Brown -- L.A. Weekly Theater Critics** *Friday, October 14, 2008 Click here for comprehensive theater listings, new reviews, and stage news.*

FLOWERS IN THE ADDICT There's more to this two-act play written by Henry Bateman than its clever title. What could have been an offbeat melodrama of lost souls doing time in a methadone clinic is in fact a bulldozing narrative that draws you in with flowing scenes and kaleidoscopic characters. Divided by a startling turn of events, the acts play as two

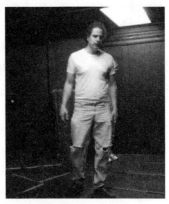

Gianopulos as methadone patient Benji Wiggins. Photo by Kirk Dauer.

unique narratives. Each act features a dependent character to the mainstay Benji Wiggins, an amusing motormouth junkie ingeniously brought to life by Ted Gianopulos. It intrigued me how Wiggins' addiction, while never forgotten, ultimately does not come to define Gianopulos' interpretation. Instead, it's his codependence on his two supporting actors that allows all three characters to shine and makes the production stand out. Initially, we meet the amiable Howard Crumb, whose subtle passive-aggressiveness (distinctively brought to life by former Chicagoan Ben Shields) sets the main character on a path of self-destruction. With hopelessness coursing through the veins of the story, the aggressive and damaged Mindy Crumb stumbles onto the stage, arresting the hearts of the audience and impacting Benji in unexpected ways. Mindy's savage wit and broken disposition are portrayed in a spine-tingling manner by a gifted actress known only as "Share." I cringe as I type that, but I cannot let her inane namesake overshadow her achievement as an actor and as director of this must-see black-box production.

Tres Stage 1523 N. La Brea Ave., Los Angeles, today through Sunday, October 19. (323) 850-7827 or http://www.berubians.com

Version2PointZero

Monday morning, having breakfast, perusing the trades. Blurb in *Variety* catches my eye.

Sheer Evidence -- Conrad Stevens (Columbia)

Columbia scooped up Conrad Stevens' noir spec titled *Sheer Evidence*. The deal is pegged at mid six figures and marks the first sale for Stevens, a onetime journalist. **3/19**

"Fucker sold it."

"Hmm, I don't recall ordering a side of profanity with my breakfast," Share says as she spins, slides off a stool, carries her plate and cup to the sink.

"My bad. Letting this stuff get to me. Don't know why."

"Because it's your job. It's your world."

"I guess."

"Gotta get dressed. Heading to the gym before my auditions. Then I'm meeting Maggie to help with her new place."

"Okay."

"I'll be home for dinner. I can pick up some sushi and wine. Sound good?" When I don't reply, she invades my space, makes eye contact. "Sound good?"

"Yes. It does."

She smiles, stares at my lips for a beat before pinching both my cheeks and delivering an air kiss.

"Luck on the auditions."

Her bare soles slap on hardwood en route to the bedroom. When she's out of sight, my gaze darts back to *Variety*, the blurb.

Sheer Evidence. We meet once again. Why do you keep coming back from the dead? Took you to The Griddle one morn, and you altered the course of my keep-it-on-the-hush-hush quest.

Been months since I called Conrad—the second time—to share my vision of how to fix the script. I do the math. More than enough time for a component rewrite, and if he got it to the right people, it could have sold this quick.

Wonder if he took my advice. He had to take my advice. Wouldn't have sold without it. Need to know. Need to get my hands on a current copy of the script. Need someone on the inside.

"Share? Baby, I need a favor."

Three days later, Share hands me a copy of *Sheer Evidence*, the cover branded with a Columbia Pictures Entertainment logo. Over breakfast with Lackey on Tuesday, she mentioned a script she heard about while auditioning for a TV show on the Sony lot. Sony owns Columbia, which owns *Sheer Evidence*. She told him her agent was working on getting her an audition for the film so she wanted to read the whole script in preparation. Share said he never looked up from his Treo but replied, "I'll put in a call."

The request flew under Lackey's radar, as it should have. He has no ties to *Sheer*. Nor would he suspect I do. Script's already sold, which makes it irrelevant to Lackey. He thought he was just doing a favor for his ambitious little sis, a task he most likely passed to his assistant via an impersonal e-mail. Today before noon, a messenger delivered an envelope containing the script to her apartment. This is how Share came to deliver it to me—along with some unexpected collateral damage.

"Thank you," I say.

She smiles, but I sense distress.

"Something the matter?"

She shakes her head.

"Talk to me."

"It's just . . ." She bites her lower lip, glances down, then back up at me. "I just feel weird lying to him. I think I need to clarify something. I've mentioned a few times we're not that close, and that's true. He's seven years older than me. I mean, he was graduating college when I was entering high school, and that made it hard for us to connect."

"Share . . ."

"Wait. Let me finish. I know he can be a self-serving prick, but I love him. He's my big brother, warts and all. And while I'm on your side 100 percent, getting the script for you felt like too much deception on my end."

"Share. Of course. I'm sorry it made you feel that way, but I don't really get where this is coming from."

"I'd do anything for you, Bateman. But don't ask me to betray him. He's my family. And your . . ."

Voice trails off again.

I reach out to grab her hand, snag a few fingers, rub them lightly, wait, listen.

"Your uncle lied to your dad, and that affected your life so much. I don't want you to ever think I'm like that."

The father/uncle mention catches me off guard. I look down at our hands. Back up, I ponder her words, try to decipher her logic. "What are you talking about?"

"I'd do anything for you, Bateman, but I don't want lying to my brother to maybe make you think I'm not honest. Or loyal."

I get it. Family betrayal is part of my backstory, and asking Share to do the same, despite mitigating circumstances, does not make it right. Whatsoever. Lightly squeeze the fingers I'm still holding once more before I let go.

"You're absolutely right. I apologize. I will never ask you to do anything like that again. Ever. I promise."

She purses her lips, rubs a hand through her hair. "I gotta get going, but there's something else."

"Good news or bad news?"

"Not sure. My birthday is next week . . ."

"I know," I whisper.

"Justin says he wants to make it up to me for missing the play. He wants to take us to dinner."

Rather dip my ball sack in a hornet's nest. "Okay," I deadpan. "Where's he taking us?"

Eleven pages into *Sheer Evidence* v2.0, I see the changes. My suggested changes.

Evidence is a modern film noir that effectively shuffles the formulas within the genre. It's so easy to fall into cliché with these kinds of stories, but a set of well-drawn characters lay claim to the tale and arrest your attention. Happened to me ten months ago sitting in The Griddle. Happens to me again, here, now.

Version 1.0 of the script featured a recently divorced beauty taking over the one asset of her husband's estate her lawyers could get their hands on, a modest detective agency. First day on the job, two clients knock on her door, a down-and-out private eye looking for a muse and a sleek high roller desperately seeking a set of fresh eyes on his case. The former has a job that requires a lady's touch and helps her learn the trade. The latter is accused of butchering his ex-wife and puts the main character center stage in an infamous murder case. True to noir, she falls for both men, picks the wrong one, which results in the death of the former, forcing her to shoot and kill the latter.

Don't want to say any more, lest I ruin the movie for you, even though you'll never see that version of the film. You'll see the version I'm now reading. My suggestion was to combine the latter and former into one character, make the dynamic and opponent one person, which not only makes the story aerodynamic but makes the main character's arc all the more dramatic and turns the story into an unrelenting thrill ride. Act Two is now sandwiched between a fateful knock on a door and a fated bullet in the brain.

I like. A lot.

Easy to see why it sold so quickly. Finish the read, contemplate the changes, ponder the chain of events leading to my here, my now. Not sure whether to feel proud or stupid. Anonymity nulls success. Way it is.

Destiny or density? With the one-year anniversary of my reclusive quest looming large, jury might very well be hung.

THROW ME THE WHIP,
THROW YOU THE IDOL

Heading toward the hornet's nest. Driving Share's BMW into Beverly Hills. She's in the passenger seat, dressed to the tens for her birthday. At a stoplight on Little Santa Monica, she adjusts my collar, says, "Thanks for doing this."

"No worries." *No worries? Really?*

At Crustacean, we valet the car, walk to the door.

Share whispers in my ear, "After dinner we'll bolt. Promise. I'll tell him we're meeting my friends, and he'll want no part of that."

Grab the door, open it for Share, spot a sign displayed on the glass: Closed Tonight for a Private Party. Doesn't register. Not until . . .

"Surprise!" the entire restaurant shouts. They're all standing, staring, waiting for us. They begin to sing "Happy Birthday."

Share beams, spots Lackey, and raises her hands in surprise as the crowd hits the song's second line. She leans into me as they sing her name. Ventriloquists from behind her smile, "I don't know any of these people."

That's funny. I know them all.

Patrons usually find Crustacean's Asian décor inviting. Usually.

We navigate the walk-on-water entrance, a winding glass floor featuring an aquarium underneath leading from cocktail lounge to dining room. It's the shark-infested waters on this level that have me fearing for my livelihood. Everyone's suited in Armani and Hugo Boss, dressed in Versace and Gucci, holding martini glasses and champagne flutes.

Share and I plot a course through the crowd. I shake hands with individuals I met during my tenure at Foster's office, yet they act like they're making my acquaintance for the first time. Out of sight, out of mind. A few double-take when their eyes bounce from Share to me. Ultimately they glance back at her, amid smiles and forced laughter, forgetting me.

Might somehow get out of this, anonymity intact. Might.

The procession leads us to Lackey, who's clothed head to toe in Prada.

"Justin. What is all this?"

"Happy birthday, Sis. What we have here is a roomful of Hollywood's elite. If you're really interested in furthering your career, well, this is my present to you. I'll introduce you to everyone here tonight."

"Too much," Share says, unsure what to make of the gift.

"You too, Bateman. If you want," Lackey says with a shit-eating grin. "For old times' sake."

I seethe.

Share grabs my arm as we follow Lackey into the fray. "Drink?"

I nod, certain a fistful of ice, generous pour, and bubbles will not soothe my plight.

For close to an hour, we rub elbows with the upper crust of the industry. Heads of Development at Warner Bros., Sony, Touchstone, FOX, and Paramount shake our hands and toast the night. Producers, show runners, and directors buy us rounds of drinks. Agents, managers, and casting agents hand us their cards, compliment Share, ask what I do for a living.

Tell them, "I'm in advertising." Cling to the lie.

A few reporters ask our names, documenting the evening's festivities.

I am not here. This is not happening.

We finally sit, and Share grabs my hand under the table. "Bateman. I'm sorry. I had no idea."

"I know, but I should have."

Share looks distressed, her brow furrowing.

Afraid she's going to cry. On her birthday. "C'mere."

She does.

"All I care about is being here with you. Happy birthday."

Our kiss is showered in light, captured by a hired photographer.

Lackey approaches, places two boxes in front of Share. "Thank you all for coming tonight," he bellows. "It means a lot to me. My sister is talented, and I want the world to know that. So tomorrow I want you all to e-mail the world."

He gets a laugh from the room.

"I know you're all drunk and looking forward to

soaking up the booze with what Crustacean does best. I recommend the roasted crab, by the way. But before they take our orders, I want to deliver some gifts."

Share smiles. "Thank you. For everything. You really shouldn't have."

Justin leans in to kiss her cheek.

"Open it up." He takes a seat across from us.

The crowd watches as Share rips the wrapping paper, revealing a shirt box, which is odd because it's covered with Louboutin logos and Louboutins are shoes.

Share slowly lifts the lid, revealing a small metallic card amid a bunch of tissue paper. One side of the card is black, the other red. Suspect it's a gift card, God knows for how much. "Justin. Too much."

He grins. "I know how much you love your shoes." Then, "Show the crowd."

She lifts the card. A murmur overcomes the room. Apparently it's not merely a gift card. It's a VIP card for Louboutin's Shoe of the Month Club—twelve pairs of limited edition shoes, one pair waiting for her every month over the next year.

"Justin," Share gushes after she's brought up to speed.

"You deserve finer things in life," he says.

Feel like it's a compliment with a backhand directed at me, but it's nothing compared to what comes next.

"Is this another present?" Share says, holding the card while moving the empty box to the chair to her right.

Lackey smirks, takes a swig of his scotch. "Oh, that. Actually that's not for you. That's for your man. I know he's important to you and you've been together for so long. I figure I've probably missed a birthday of his. That gift is for him."

BOOM!BOOM!BOOM!

Share looks my way, slowly slides the box over.

I clear my throat. "I'll open it later."

"Come on. Where's the fun in that? Everyone," he says with volume, "we all missed Bateman's birthday. Do you all want to see what I got him?"

They cheer. Share pats my back. Think everyone in *Star Wars* said it best when they said, "I have a very bad feeling about this."

I rip the paper to reveal a plain white box. Open it to see about 120 coffee-stained pages bound by two gold brads, cover page inked in Courier 12.

```
         Nobody Moves, Nobody Gets Hurt
                      by
              Brice Allan Kirkpatrick
```

Hands shaking, mouth suddenly dry, heart providing the bass.

Even Share goes, "Oh no."

Lackey raises his glass, takes a swig, and addresses his handpicked audience. "Ladies and gentlemen, few know what I'm about to divulge, but a third script by the elusive Meyer Holden surfaced not too long ago."

Murmurs tidal wave the room.

"Don't get too excited. Meyer Holden's peculiar ways make the script a lame duck. It's not on the table anymore, and unfortunately it's a movie that will never get made. That end result is not my fault, but I can and will admit that I let the opportunity slip through my fingers. And I won't let that happen again." He laments for a moment, then looks to me. "But I digress. My friend and former associate here is quite a fan of Mr. Holden. I do believe he's been on a quest to find The Man for some time, but he won't admit it."

Share squeezes my thigh.

"He's a talented bloke, one I am trying to convince to come work for me. So tonight I throw him the idol, hoping he throws me the whip. I present him with the rarest of the rare, a copy of Holden's third postwar effort."

Oooohs from the crowd.

"Happy birthday, Bateman. Whenever the fuck it was."

Crowd applauds.

Share whispers, "Bateman."

"Not your fault. Doesn't matter anyway. It's over." *I'm done.*

We eat. Couldn't tell you what anything tastes like. Throughout dinner, the upper crust come to shake my hand, this time their attention fixed solely on me. They marvel at the Holden, ask too many questions, poke, prod.

"Mike Lipper with Synergy. Do you have a card?"

"Angie Reynolds, *Variety*. So how long have you been on the hunt?"

"Hey. Brooklyn Marx. Head of Development at New Line. I wanted to see it up close. Didn't think there would ever be another."

Lackey doesn't eat, roves the room, palms his drink, gloats, furthering my stellar opinion of him.

After dinner, Share mingles, thanks most everyone, hugs her brother.

We make our escape as Lackey calls for everyone's

attention, aiming to make yet another announcement. *No, thank you.*

Hit the door just as he begins to sermonize. "Here's the thing about writers. They're a cantankerous lot. I'm not a fan of them, but I am a fan of their end result . . ."

Outside, inhale deep. Fresh warm air helps calm me.

Valet brings around the car.

Toss the gifts into the trunk.

Tip the man holding the car door open, get inside. He shuts it.

"Bateman—"

I cut her off. "Share. I don't want to talk about your brother or Meyer Holden or the industry for the rest of the night. It's your birthday. And I want my girlfriend to have the night she deserves."

She bites that lower lip of hers.

"Now can I show you what I had planned?"

She nods.

At the first light, I type, "Major delay. En route now. There in 20." Send the text and pound the accelerator, speeding us toward Hollywood.

Café des Artistes is a little-known place off Sunset in the shadow of Hollywood High. If you ever take a date there, you're apt to hear her ask, "You're not going to kill me, are you?" as you drive down the dark desolate street or approach the nondescript building. It's not until you walk down a small alley and turn the corner that you reap the rewards. Faces are guaranteed to light up when they catch sight of the French courtyard.

Share's face lights up, all right, but it also has to do with the bulk of her friends there to greet her with, "Surprise!" They also sing, but the song sounds so much more appealing this go-around.

She turns and grabs my shirt, pulls me in for a kiss. "Much better," she whispers.

Agree.

Fish Get Drowned

Share's birthday celebration continues deep into the night. The restaurant keeps the place open late for us, champagne flowing the entire time. After, we head to The Well for a nightcap. Before we call it a night, I drive Share up to the Yamashiro Restaurant off Franklin. It's closed, but that's the point. The place is situated some three hundred feet above the avenues, and the parking lot provides an inspiring view of Tinseltown.

We park, get lost in the sea of lights.

Lights everywhere twinkle, look so inviting, but it's a trick. I know it.

"Thanks," Share whispers, finally breaking the silence. "For tonight."

Look over. Chestnut eyes shimmer. No trick. Sure of it.

Head hits pillows. Share's asleep. Stare at the ceiling for almost an hour, get out of bed at four. Read the script, a masterful heist film. Contemplate its greatness upon finishing.

Doze off on the couch just after six.

Wake three hours later, forgo Runyon, grab the trades, the paper coffee. It's 10:05 when Share calls out from the bedroom, "Who's Stacy Stevens?"

"Writes an entertainment column in the *Los Angeles Times*. Why?"

"Justin sent a text. Said we might want to read her today. Why won't he leave us alone?"

Question goes unanswered as I push the *Hollywood Reporter* out of my way, pull the Calendar section from the *Times*.

The Plot Thickens . . .
by Stacy Stevens, *Los Angeles Times*

For years, I've heard rumblings about treasure seekers here in Hollywood reading countless scripts, hoping to unearth the camouflaged work of Meyer Holden, a screenwriter with a golden pen, author of such gems as *Fielder's Choice* and *The Living End*.

If you don't know, Holden walked away from Hollywood about seven years ago but continues to write scripts under undisclosed pen names, which keeps some people in this town up nights looking for Holden between paper covers.

I'll admit I used to think this clandestine behavior sounded more like a plot in a movie than sensible in reality. However, last night I had the pleasure of meeting two of these treasure seekers, both former protégés of the great Jon Foster.

No, no, no. Not here. Isn't happening.

This reporter looked these swashbucklers in the eye and shook their hands. They made me believe another elusive Holden could indeed be found and that they're precisely the men for the task. Therein lies the conflict and the crisis to make this story so compelling.

I learned both have plans, though radically different ones. While the previous scripts dramatically dubbed Holden Tickets were found by chance, these treasure hunters have designed strategies which, dare I say it, remove luck from the equation.

One of them has devoted close to a year searching by means of resourceful under-the-radar tactics. The other utilizes the system, casting a wide net as far as money allows, employing a legion of readers and rewarding them handsomely.

One man searches for Holden confidentially. The other screams his intent from a mountaintop. I will say both men's bravado is heartfelt. The question is not *if* one of them will find the next Holden Ticket but *when*.

If they were stocks, I'd invest heavily in them. If we were in Vegas, it'd be a matter of betting on either red or black—take your pick. If I were Hollywood, I'd watch out for both of them. They're on the hunt and on the rise.

What are their names? Justin Lackey and Sam Bateman.

I read it half a dozen times.

Share's fallen back asleep.

Must clear my head.

Head to Runyon, reach the peak in a sprint in record time. Pass dozens of unfamiliar faces on the way up. Swear most of them recognize me.

That's him. That's the one. He was there last night. He's one of the two she wrote about.

Have to believe Lackey fucked us both. Thought that last night. Ten times worse this morning thanks to Stacy Stevens. Fucked. Anonymity is the key to Holden's game. Believed that from the get-go, and now my cover has been blown.

Panting, I turn, face the Hollywood sign. It's laughing at me.

Look away, look down, close my eyes. I'm drowning.

Don't want to be here. Gotta get the fuck out of Coldfuckcold. Gotta disappear.

Almost home, I end the call I'm on. "Sounds good. Send me all the info."

Hang up, enter the apartment.

Share's on the couch, Stacy's column on the coffee table, the Holden opened in her lap. She pushes the script away, jumps off the couch to greet me.

I stop her with a palm in the air. Put an index finger to my lips.

She freezes, looks at me like a hot chick looks at the guy dressed like Darth Nihilus at a Star Wars convention.

Walk to the stereo, power on, press play on the iPod, next track to number four. Radiohead's "Weird Fishes" emanates. Turn the dial to eleven, grab Share's hand, lead her to the middle of the room. I move close, put my mouth against her ear, so no one can hear, so no listening devices can pick up what I am about to say.

"Don't want to be here. Need to get out. Want to whisk you away. Somewhere warm. Hawaii." I pull away to see the look on Share's face.

It does not disappoint.

I lean in. "This weekend. Leave Friday morn. Four Seasons. Seven days. Pack your bags." Pull back to see the look again.

Her gaze darts over my face.

Lean back in. "Why are you looking at me like that?"

She shifts her head, puts her mouth to my ear. "Why are you telling me this in the middle of the living room with the music blaring?"

Shift. "Because I saw it in a movie. Thought it looked cool." I feel her laugh. "You thought I was losing it, huh?"

She nods once.

"Hawaii? Whadda you say?"

Nods abound. Shift. "What about . . . ?"

"Told you. It's over."

Fourth Season

Pack.

No scripts.

Rush, rush, rush from taxi to LAX to gate until we're taxiing on the runway to fun.

Worth it. Getting away. Out of Coldfuckcold.

In first class, mimosas already downed, Share's foot snakes up the cuff of my khakis, toes tickling my ankle under the blanket draped across her lap. She knows how much I love this, somehow having sensed it on our first date and never relenting.

"Seven days," she whispers.

"Seven days."

Maui. Wailea. Four Seasons Hotel and Resort. Paradise.

Feels so damn good to get away. By three, we're lounging by the pool, soaking up the day's remaining rays. After a sunset walk on the beach, we get ready for dinner. Enjoy a meal at a place called Joe's.

Day two, lounging by the pool, getting our tan on, enjoying the lavish amenities the resort provides.

"Let's move here," Share says, all sun-drenched and just fine.

"Into the Four Seasons? Done."

Her BlackBerry vibrates on the little table between our lounge chairs. She glances at the screen. "Care if I get this?"

"Not at all."

She gets up, answers it.

Watch her sway away. Close my eyes when she's out of sight, relax in the sunshine, decompress in serenity.

"Mister Bateman?"

I wake from a nap, open one eye to see a concierge hovering over me.

"Sorry if I woke you."

"No worries."

"This arrived for you. Marked urgent."

She hands me a yellow envelope, walks away. My name on it, stamped *urgent*, no address, no postage. Tear the side, pull out a postcard, one of two versions we printed up to advertise *Flowers in the Addict*.

BOOM!BOOM!BOOM!

Flip it, read the print:

> *Second show was the best. If not for the first-act gaffe, opening night would have taken the prize. Third night, everyone seemed to be going through the motions. As you so eloquently put it, way it is. MH*

Read it over and over. Look at the envelope. My name, *urgent*, no address, no postage.

"Excuse me," I call to a passing pool boy. Can you leave a note for my girlfriend, tell her I'll be up in the room?"

"Of course."

Get up, grab my shoes. On my way to the elevator, I spot the concierge. Make a beeline for her desk. "Excuse me."

She looks up, smile already in season. "Yes, Mister Bateman."

"Yeah. This postcard. Where did it come from?"

"It was delivered to the hotel today."

"But how?" I show her the envelope. "No postage. No address."

She looks up at me and squints.

"You can tell me. They are addressed to me. I just want to know how they got here."

"Oh. I see. I just don't want to ruin the surprise."

"Surprise?"

She looks down, thinks, for some reason looks to her right before admitting, "Well, we did get four more cards with instructions to deliver them while you're staying with us."

BOOM!

I smile wide. Shake my head. Think. Laugh. "Smitty. That's great. My buddy Smitty was supposed to be here along with his wife. But they had to cancel. His wife is pregnant, and they need to save money."

"Oh, congratulations to them."

"Yes. It is great news. And this was a pleasant surprise." I hold up the card.

She smiles.

I almost turn to walk away, then, "You know. I can take all the cards now. Save you the trouble of delivering them every day."

She hesitates, contemplates.

I pull out a twenty. Push it across the marble.

She slides open a drawer. "Here you go, Mister Bateman." She hands me one large yellow envelope addressed to the hotel, postage in the upper right corner.

"Thank you . . ." Glance at her name tag. "Thank you, Claire."

"My pleasure."

Walk away clutching the envelope. Head to the elevators. BOOM!BOOM!BOOM!

Up in the room, I spill the contents onto the bed. There's a page of typed instructions for the hotel staff along with four envelopes bearing my name and stamped *urgent* just like the one I was handed by the pool. Paper-clipped to each are small pieces of paper marked Day 2, Day 3, Day 4, Day 5.

I tear open Day 2. *Flowers* postcard, version two. Turn it over:

> *Hope I didn't come across as a cynic. Really enjoyed the play. Damn fine actress you got there. MH*

Day 3. Postcard depicts Dale Wennington, all-star right fielder for the Chicago Cubs from Holden's masterpiece *Fielder's Choice*. Back reads:

> *Did you know they wanted Costner to play Wennington before I threatened to walk with the script? Viggo did well with the role, but I always wondered what Crowe might have brought. No regrets, though. MH*

Day 4. Picture of Warner Bros. studios circa 1935. On the back:

> *Ever wonder what kind of damage old souls like us could have done in the day and age of the studio system? I do, every drink. MH*

Day 5. Card depicts Alan Ladd in the 1953 film *Shane*. *Enough with the postcards. I'm done. It's been fun.*

You're wasting your time if you keep sending. Time
to move on. MH

Standing, staring at the enigma before me, I hear Share
at the door. Before she gets the keycard to work, I collect
the postcards and envelopes, toss the collection into my bag.

She tiptoes into the room, puts a palm in the air, then
an index finger to her lips. She walks to the stereo, powers
on, presses play on the CD player. Luau music emanates.
She turns the dial high as it can go, grabs my hand, leads me
to the middle of the room. She moves close, puts her mouth
against my ear.

"Remember that pilot episode I was cast in a few
months ago? The drama?"

I nod.

"The show got picked up. The network ordered thirteen
episodes. Shooting starts next month."

Shift. "Holy shit. That's the best news. I'm so happy for
you."

Shift. "What's wrong?"

"Nothing. Nothing. Think the breakfast didn't exactly
agree with me but not going to let that spoil this."

Lips to my ear. "It's happening, Bateman. It's really
happening."

We celebrate. I leave thoughts of Holden up in the
room. He can wait. This cannot. On an island in the Pacific 2,482 miles from Hollywood, I drink and dance with
a star of ABC's upcoming drama *Cross Examination*. The
pilot episode shot a few months ago follows Nathan Cross,
played by Billy Bob Thornton, as he assembles a crack
team of investigative lawyers, including Share's character,

Gwendolyn Miller. She's the book smart beauty of the team and a valued asset because she studied medicine prior to jumping over to law.

Script for the pilot read like *House* meets *Law & Order*. I imagine each episode will present a new case, followed by investigation, culminating in cross-examining a key witness—hence the name of the series. That action will, of course, solve each case and tie up the loose ends. All in an hour minus commercial breaks. It's formulaic but sure to be a hit.

Next morning in bed, I enjoy an upside-down view of the abstract painting hanging above our bed for a half hour before Share stirs, wakes, finally says, "Hey."

"Hey."

"Are you as hungry as me?"

"Well, I got some beans I'm dying to spill."

"What?"

"Meyer Holden sent me a postcard yesterday, and when I asked a hotel worker where it came from, she gave me four others that he also sent."

Share sits up. "Shut up. How could you not tell me?"

"How could I? You had big news."

"This is big news."

"But yours was huge."

"That's what she said." Share laughs at her own joke, then outstretches her hands. "Let me see. Let me see."

We order room service and spend the next hour analyzing every card, every word.

"Hmm, he thinks I'm a good actress."

I shoot her a look.

"I mean . . . he came to see the play. That must be freaking you out."

"Understatement."

"Think he might be lying?"

"Not sure what he gains from that. Plus, his assessment of the shows is accurate."

"True. True. You know, this would all seem so random, but the fact they were sent together makes it so calculated."

"What I thought when I got them yesterday."

She reads one over again. "I mean, think about it. He obviously wrote and mailed them all together, but they read like a week of his thoughts."

"Well, he is a damn good writer."

Share hops on my iPhone, wants to see if Crowe was ever considered for *Fielder's Choice*.

I continue to scrutinize the cards.

Few minutes later she says, "Bateman? Who's Sal Burton?"

What the fuck is happening here? "Writer. Friend of Holden's. Why?"

"Someone spotted Holden in LA last week, snapped a picture." She hands me my iPhone.

On the screen is a page from a writers guild blog featuring a blurb about the alleged Holden sighting. Pic was taken inside Father's Office. Caption reads, *Meyer Holden kicking one back with Sal Burton, as if he never abandoned Hollywood.*

The guy Sal is drinking with is indeed Holden. They look deep in conversation. I put my thumb and forefinger on the screen, spread them, enlarge the photo.

"Fucking A," I whisper.

"What? What?"

"Share, you're going to think I am crazy . . ."

"Already do."

"Nice. But I swear, those two are talking about me."

"Bates, I think you're crazy."

"Told you."

Be easy to think I go mental the next five days, get island fever brought on from the need to hightail it back to LA. Could think that, but you'd be wrong. Maybe it's something in the postcards, mainly the way Holden ended the fifth: *Wasting your time if you keep sending.*

Then again, maybe it's actually something on the island—brunette, chestnut eyes, primetime body that's getting more tanned by the day, looking hotter by anyone's standards, led by mine. By day four her skin's darker than the burnt-orange bikini that's become my favorite.

"What are you looking at?"

"Why did you stick with me?"

Share puts her hand to her face to shield the sun from her eyes as she glances at me. "Hmm. Not sure if you recall this, but when we got together again, we ate lunch at that Ammo place . . ."

"Yeah, I remember."

"Well, when we were leaving, I stopped to help out this couple. I could tell you were antsy to get home, get back to your work, and when I was running to catch up with you, I thought you were going to yell at me. Instead, you smiled." Share pauses.

I put my hand near my face to cast a shadow so I can see her.

"Even though I was attracted to you from the moment we met, I honestly wasn't really sure about you, especially given your super-secret everyday activities. When you smiled, I remember thinking, *Maybe, just maybe, he'll surprise me after all.*" She grins. "I saw promise and hoped one day you'd get the balance right."

"And?"

She drops her hand, turns her head back to the sun. "Still got a little catching up to do."

Day six, I stop in the gift shop, purchase a postcard of a Maui sunset. On the back, I print:

> *Know you said to walk away from the postcards*
> *but thought I'd filter this one into the system, see*
> *if maybe you can find it.*
> *Cheers,*
> *Brice Allan Kirkpatrick*

Add a stamp, drop it in the hotel's outgoing mail just before nine.

Seventh day. In love with the island and wishing we didn't have to leave tonight, we vow to return next year. Maybe every year.

"Back to LA."

"Back to LA."

"You ready?"

"Never was ready. Been faking it this whole time."

"Me too."

Approaching LAX, maybe five thousand feet above the sea of lights that is Los Angeles, Share asleep on my arm, a stellar vacation behind us, I realize something. Recently flew past my twelfth month, my fourth season, of this . . .

whatever it is I'm doing. Can't even think of a word for it anymore. Did I used to call it something?

Rest my head near the window, thoughts set adrift, regret scratching at the pit of my stomach. Density.

No regrets.

Ever wonder what kind of damage old souls like us could have done?

Been fun. I'm done. Wasting your time if you keep sending. Move on.

Do believe my second-half complication worked. Got the shark to hunt the hunter. Not patting myself on the back, mind you, especially given the fact I believe he took a long look at me, who I am, what I might have had to offer, and spit me back out.

No regrets. Been Fun. Wasting your time. Move on.

Been a year. Nothing to show. Still bleeding cash. Fuck Coldfuck.

Lights below twinkle, taunt.

"Ladies and gentlemen, United Airlines flight forty-four is now beginning its final descent into Los Angeles . . ."

Now what?

No Contest

Home. Place feels peculiar. Not sure why. Enter the den, survey the stacks. The To-Be-Read pile wanes in comparison to the To-Be-Shred pile, maybe 150 scripts versus 400-plus. Estimate it will take me about three weeks to get through them at my post-Crustacean pace.

Then what?

Contemplate doing some shredding. Dawns on me there's no need to shred anymore. Probably never was. Regardless, cleaning house is not something I aspire to at the moment. Glance at the third pile in the room, the Projects-With-Potential pile.

Atop, *Channel 5uper4ero*. Feeling unmotivated, I reach for it rather than something new. Aim to read a few pages, end up enjoying the entire script. Again. Last page leads to cover page, leads to me picking up the phone. Punch in *67, ten digits, ring, ring.

"Hello."

"Good afternoon. Might I speak to Finn McMillan?"

Silence.

"Ma'am?"

"Yes. This is his wife." Long, uncomfortable pause. "Finn is no longer here."

"I'm sorry?"

"He"—she stammers—"there was an accident."

"Oh." Then, "I'm sorry. I didn't mean to . . ."

"Who's calling?"

"Well, I read your husband's . . . I read the script Finn wrote."

"Ah. I see. You're from that contest?"

"I think so. Which contest are you referring to?"

"I don't recall the name. I sent the copy of the script after seeing the ad."

"The copy? This was the only contest it was entered into?"

"Yes. I really don't know much about things like that. I just wanted someone to finally read Finn's work."

Feel guilty the only contest entered was a trojan horse of mine, but my remorse is overshadowed by a particular word. "Finally? No one's read his stuff before?"

She pauses, whispers, "Finn was a little paranoid."

A paranoid writer. Imagine that. "I see. A lot of writers are, but that's a shame because his work is impressive."

"Well, I'm happy to hear that. I always knew he was talented." She hesitates, seems to want to say something else. "He battled depression for years, until it seems he lost that fight."

Don't know what to say. "Shane Black once said, 'There's a point at which something you're writing becomes more interesting than your own fear, and writing becomes a magic antidepressant.'"

"I don't know who that is."

"He's another writer, like your husband. Another talented writer."

"That's nice of you to say."

"Finn was talented. He is. His script is compelling and entertaining. I've read it five times."

"Really? Did it win the contest?"

Catches me off guard. Don't want to lie to her anymore. Choose my words wisely. "No contest. Once I read Finn's script, I realized his was the best ever sent to me. So, yeah, it wins, hands down."

"Well, that's some good news." Awkward silence. "How much does the winner get again?"

Amazing the context you can pick up in words transmitted via telephone lines.

I tell her what she wants to hear. "Fifteen hundred dollars. My accountant will FedEx the check by tomorrow morning."

"Thank you."

Looking down at the script, I flip through the pages. Brain is working overtime. "Mrs. McMillan, if this is still a good time for you to talk, I'd like to tell you a little bit about me, how it is I have your husband's script, and what we might be able to do with it."

"This is a good time. For me."

An hour later, an amiable click.

I'm still sitting with the phone in my hand thirty minutes after we hang up when I hear Share walk in, back from a run.

"Hey."

"Hey," I whisper, not looking over.

"Bad day?"

"Interesting day."

"Anything I can do to help?"

"No. I need time to think."

No more words. Share knows to leave me be. She showers, changes, leaves.

Twenty minutes later, I press a button on the phone, silence the dial tone by punching in ten familiar digits.

"Foster Films." It's Brett Stussy, old coworker, last-assistant-standing at Foster Films—the new Lackey.

"Stussy. It's Bateman. Listen, know it's going to cost me, but I need a favor."

WRETCHED HIVE

T en days after I speak to Mrs. McMillan, PaperPen-
Inc officially owns *Channel 5uper4ero*. My company
bought the exclusive rights for one dollar, the product of a
candid conversation and a generous agreement drawn up by
lawyers, ensuring that the bulk of all profits generated by
Channel 5uper4ero will go directly to the McMillan family—Cindy McMillan and her three sons, Casey, Peter, and
Finn Jr.

Step one complete.

I take the script to Kinko's, make five copies. One goes
to the Writers Guild of America Registry along with the $20
fee. One is sent to the Library of Congress Copyright Office
in DC along with a $45 check for processing. One goes into
the mail, postmarked to myself along with a copy of the letter
of ownership. Two copies travel with me to Culver City.

Pull onto Washington, park on the street. Walk into
Foster's offices at eleven sharp. Right on time.

Stussy looks up. Nod confirms it's on.

I toss a thick nine-by-twelve envelope in front of him, followed by one of only seven known-to-exist bootleg copies of the film *The Day the Clown Cried*,[31] which he catches in his outstretched hands. As promised, as agreed, he silently watches me pass en route to Jon Foster's wretched hive.

Once I'm inside, Foster looks up. Surprisingly, he remembers my name. "Fucktwat."

I sit.

His eyes dart left, right. "Who the fuck made you? Get out before Pussy out there calls security."

"Five minutes," I say, not asking. Telling.

"Fuckfiveminutes," he spews. "You don't waltz in and fuckfiveminutes me."

"Five. Because, well, you're a dinosaur. What the fuck do you have to lose?"

He stares at me, his hands falling flat onto his desk. "If you have something to pitch, pitch it to Pussy. He'll fill me in and maybe we'll schedule a meeting. On my time."

"You're not listening, old man. Five minutes to decide if I stay the next two and a half hours. Five minutes to decide if you get one more day in the sun or if you cuntfuck it up, like you cuntfucked it up with Meyer Holden."

Foster's face folds in perplexity, then anger. "Look at the gall on you. Cockwipe with a boner thinks he can muscle me. You. Know. Nothing."

"I know *Nobody Moves, Nobody Gets Hurt* would have

31 *The Day the Clown Cried* is the unfinished and unreleased 1972 film directed by and starring Jerry Lewis as a washed-up German circus clown named Helmut Dorque, who entertains children in a concentration camp as they are led to the gas chambers during the Holocaust. Legend has it, the original script was about the redemption of a selfish man, but during production Lewis changed the entire story into a Chaplinesque dark comedy. The end result was such a disaster that Lewis refuses to discuss the project to this day. It was thought Lewis had the only copy of the film locked away in his office. Somehow a few bootleg copies surfaced, and occasionally the film is shown at secret screenings organized by Hollywood insiders.

made one hell of a movie. Shocked as anyone to see Holden write a heist film, but goddamn if I wasn't rooting for the wrong side to win in the end."

Foster's jaw drops. He attempts to hide it by gritting his teeth. His hands try in vain to grab the slick cherry wood. "Five minutes. Let's go, assprick. Let's see what you got up your sleeve."

Stussy shuts the door.

Everything is going according to plan.

Two hours fifteen minutes later, Foster is still sitting at his desk. His palms are getting a workout, been making small circles on the cherry wood for the last few minutes. He has no poker face whatsoever, and this is his tell. When he's excited and needs to think, he polishes tables with his hands. It's always fun to watch, especially today.

He has one hell of a decision to make. On the desk before him is a copy of *Channel 5uper4ero*. He read it behind closed doors, me watching him turn every page. He sat back when he finished, rubbed one of his three chins before he said, "It's a damn good script. Not sure I understand it all, but there's something there."

He eyes me, but I remain emotionless. "Needs some work, but you're probably aware of that. Besides, the author needs to be privy to any negotiation. You know this."

I break my silence. "These are not negotiations. My company, PaperPenInc, bought the rights to the script outright this week. I own it, which means you will not." I slide a letter his way.

He peeks, and it's obvious the big blue notary seal catches his eye.

"Came to you to see if you want to produce, get your name on something big."

He laughs, snarls, "You need me more than I need you."

"Not true. Have a two thirty meeting with New Line. Hence the two and a half hours I allocated to you, of which ten minutes remain."

"New Line. Well, well. Moving up in the world." He grunts. "Think New Line is going to play this ass-suck game of yours?"

"Have a whole other game planned for them. Do you know the head of Development there? Brooklyn Marx?"

He swats the namedropping away with, "Fuck your cumjob." Then, "Why even bring it to me?"

"I have my reasons. And you're desperate."

Foster cleans his teeth with his tongue. "So I get a chance to be a part of this," he says, tapping a fat finger on *5uper4ero*, "if I also agree to purchase this?" Fat finger on his other hand taps a copy of *Flowers in the Addict*.

"Correct."

"How do I know this isn't douchepaper?"

"Because I brought it to you. Don't deal in douchepaper."

Foster makes his lips go, "Ffffpppptttt."

"You can also ask Stussy his opinion. He was reading *Flowers* while you were reading *Superhero*."

Foster leans back, no words as he deliberates for a good five minutes.

I glance at my watch.

"Pussy! Get in here."

Door swings open. Stussy fills the frame.

"Call Brooklyn Marx at New Line. Ask him if he can meet with me at three. Tell him it's important. If he has an appointment, ask him who the fuck is more important than Jon Irvin Foster."

"On it," Stussy says as he swings the door shut.

BOOM!BOOM!BOOM!

Foster stares at me the entire four minutes before the door swings back open.

"Brooklyn no can do," Stussy declares. "Says he has a Paper, Pen, Incorporated rest of the afternoon."

Hear the door shut.

Alarm on my iPhone goes off.

Foster stacks *5uper4ero* on top of *Flowers*, pushes both to the side with a sweep of his arm. "Do you drink scotch?"

ALL'S WELL, ENDS WELLES

"Why take it to Foster, though? Why not that contact at New Line?"

Share and I are celebrating at STK on La Cienega. Told the story beat by beat, and this is her first and only question.

"I have my reasons. I don't know Brooklyn Marx 'cept for a handshake at Crustacean. And there was no way New Line would accept the package, but I knew Foster would bite. Desperation makes for a seller's market. I know he'll produce *Flowers*. Let's just say he's not one to waste any dollar spent. Also, have to admit, it was sweet revenge to sell my father's work to the guy who rejected it."

Share twirls her glass by its stem. "Interesting."

"What?"

"It's kind of scary to see you in action. You could rule this city if you tried."

"Nah." I enjoy a swig of champagne. "King of Coldfuckcold is not a job I want. That's more your brother's goal, not mine."

"Are you ready to order?" the waiter interjects.

"I believe so." I gesture toward Share. "Ladies first."

My phone rings. Seldom does, and the person who keeps *seldom* from being *never* is sitting across from me.

We both look at it.

Caller ID is blocked.

Cue dramatic music.

"I'll come back," the waiter says.

I stop the ringing with, "Hello."

"Sal Burton says you root for the Twins."

BOOM-BOOM!BOOM-BOOM!BOOM-BOOM!

"Sal Burton should stop talking and start writing."

A chuckle. "Truth. So Twins are your team?"

"Truth."

"I root for the Chicago Cubs."

"I know you do."

"Of course you do. I enjoyed the postcards. Poignant stuff."

"Well, I can say yours also had an effect."

He chuckles again. "You know, when they left that scene from *The Living End* on the cutting room floor, that was the first time I realized Hollywood and I were not headed for a happy ending."

"That's a shame. Would love to see it restored sometime."

A light, "Hmph," then, "I picked up the phone for two reasons. One's a question."

Nearly piss my pants when Holden says the word *question*. Trust me, you would too.

"Did you realize how difficult you were making it for me to find out who you were with those postcards? It's not like they have a return address, you know. Was that your idea of payback, or were you testing my resolve?"

"Pot kettle black," I whisper.

Makes him laugh. "Fair enough. I like you, kid, and everyone's a critic, but I don't think you thought your plan through. I would have called to say hello weeks ago had I known who was dropping me those notes. Then I came across that contest. The next Meyer Holden," he whispers, disdain in his voice. "Got me riled, that's for sure, so I hired a PI to poke around and sniff out who was behind it. Then there was the article about you in the *Times*."

Holy shit. Fucking Lackey.

"With that, I had a sneaking suspicion the postcard writer was identified, so I hired another PI to follow you."

"Wow. I suddenly feel stalked."

"Welcome to my world. At times, I need to know who's out there fucking with me. I usually ignore about ninety-eight percent of it, but every now and then I get intrigued. Consider that a compliment."

"I do."

"One morning I wake up to voice mails from both private eyes, both parked outside the same Mail Boxes Etc., both telling me they have their man, caught you red-handed when you went there to retrieve a box of screenplays."

"Unbelievable," I whisper.

Another chuckle. "I was in LA around that time and Sal told me about this kid poking around the Office. He said you seemed like the postcard-writing type."

My turn to laugh.

"Any animosity I had for the guy who created that contest was trumped by the respect I had for the postcard writer. Imagine my surprise when I discovered you were one and the same. That's when I realized you meant business. In part, it's why I decided to pick up the phone. I have to say, well played."

Loss for words. Look up at Share.

Eyes wide, she tilts her head toward me, looking like a safecracker waiting on the click.

"Second reason I called," he declares. "Back to you and the Twins. They're in town next weekend to play the Angels. There will be a pair of tickets waiting for you at will-call for all three games. Really nice seats. Take that pretty girl of yours and enjoy the show."

"Why you doing this?"

"It's my way of saying thanks."

"For?"

"For," he says. "For? For making me think maybe there's some hope out there in Hollywood. Hollywood after the war," he adds in a dramatic voice. He exhales. "Hollywood died on me as soon as I got there. Welles said that, not me. But damn if he didn't nail it, you know?"

"Agree. Love that quote."

"I heard about your script sales. Bully for you."

"You heard about that?"

Chuckle here, chuckle there. "Yeah. I know people. I anticipate seeing what you put up on the big screen."

Life of me, I cannot think of anything to say. Have him on the line, cannot reel him in. *Not here. Isn't happening.* Then, "Will you be joining us? At the game?"

He snickers. "Nothing's ever going to come to you that easy, kid. But, hey, you got the girl." Click.

I drop the phone away from my ear.

"Bateman. You going to tell me that was him?"

I nod.

"Oh my God, you did it."

I shake my head.

"You didn't do it?"

"He said a bunch of stuff but nothing remotely optimistic. It's like he just wanted to chat." Brain's drowning, trying to float on his words. "He knew about the script sales."

"What? How?"

"No fucking clue."

"Think he'll call back?"

"Don't know what to think."

It's the first and last time he will ever *67 me.

Thirteen months, 414 days, 3,022 scripts in, I will pack it in.

Twelve months in, I began realizing I'd attempted the impossible.

One week ago, I started to move on.

In eighteen days, I will stop searching for Meyer Holden.

Time off for Good Behavior

The blurbs debut in *Variety* morning of the first ball game.

Channel 5uper4ero -- Finn McMillan (Foster Films)

The first of two spec ventures for Foster Films, both in partnership with the newly formed development outfit PaperPenInc. Parties involved are keeping logline under wraps. **3/23**

Flowers in the Addict -- Henry Bateman & Sherilyn Lackey (Foster Films)

It's a posthumous first deal for Henry Bateman, whose dark drama caught the eye of producer Jon Foster, and a first deal for cowriter Sherilyn Lackey. It is the second deal to emerge from the development outfit PaperPenInc, both in partnership with Foster Films. **3/23**

Read them several times. Favorite line: *caught the eye of producer Jon Foster.*

By noon, Share and I are seated in section 110, third base line, first row. Nice seats, indeed. Seventy-seven degrees, sunny, my beloved Minnesota Twins playing Share's adopted Angels. Joe Mauer, the Twins' catcher and team MVP, goes four for four with three runs, six RBIs, and a HR. Twins win seven to three. Good day. Good memories.

"Happy?" Share asks after the seventh-inning stretch.

"Content," I say, looking at my girlfriend in her Angels red ball cap, ponytail pulled through the opening in back. Way content. "You know, sometimes you're always right."

"I know." She keeps her eyes on the field, trying in vain to stifle a grin.

That night we attend a party at LACMA, a career retrospective for Clint Eastwood. The producers of *Cross Examination* extended an invitation to Share and a guest. So here we are. My first official LA event since being escorted out of the Hollywood scene, since going legit with Paper-PenInc and all the insanity in between.

I'm at the bar, getting us some drinks. While I wait, I watch Share mingle, all dolled up, from little black dress to brand-new Louboutins. Marvel at the fact it's the same girl who was in a tank top and Angels cap hours before.

"Service blows," guy next to me says.

"What are you going to do?"

"Complain."

I laugh. "Well, I'm the wrong guy to complain to."

The bartender finally looks my way.

"Champagne. Two. And whatever he needs," I say, pointing to the guy.

"Two Red Bull and Kettle Ones."

Bartender turns, gets busy with our drinks.

"What are you in for?" I ask to pass the time.

"I'm a writer."

"Screenplays?"

"Yeah. You?"

"Art critic. What are you working on?"

"Right now? Peddling a script I finished a few months ago. It's a suspense horror flick."

"What's it called?"

"*Big Hand on the Hate.*"

"Ah. I read that. Good idea, great title, but the characters need a lot of work."

Kid's face morphs into a ball of confusion. "What? You read it? Thought you said you were an art critic."

And what you wrote ain't art.

"How did you get a hold of my script?"

Busted. But does it matter anymore? "Don't recall how it fell into my hands. Regardless, the idea is good, but it needs work."

"I worked on it for eight months."

It's quality, dude, not quantity.

Bartender places two flutes in front of me.

"Look, what do I know? But if I were working in development, I'd tell you to spend some time on those characters because right now they are paper-thin stereotypes."

Grab the drinks, turn, walk away, realize you can't teach a dumb dog smart tricks.

In the week that follows, the To-Be-Read pile dwindles, but that's because the pipeline has been shut down.

Pulled all the ads last week. Closed down the websites too. FedExed the fifteen hundred to Cindy McMillan two weeks ago. Also sent checks to three more faux contest winners. Kelly Garcia wins the first annual Vision on Paper Screenplay Contest for her drama *Soon*. Hank Monaghan and Malcolm Aldean win the New Voices in Hollywood Script Competition for their comedy *Punchin' Judy*. Finally, Terry Campbell takes the grand prize in the 12-Point Courier & Don't Forget the Brads Contest for his action script *Means Justify End*.[32]

Decide to wait about a week before Sam Bateman with PaperPenInc will call them, congratulate them on their accomplishments, inquire if they'd be interested in meeting to discuss the potential development of their projects.

Three thousand five scripts read. Thirty-three remaining. Estimate I'll be done sometime on Monday.

I dispose of all the To-Be-Shred. Den is actually starting to look like a den again.

PaperPenInc version 2.0 officially moves in. Decide to call it home until the company has done enough damage to merit some office space. No idea when that will be, but it's good to dream.

I spend a few days building a company website, then place an ad in a few choice spots. It reads: "Upstart development company seeking imaginative, conceit-filled scripts. Period."

---

32 No one comes close to winning the first annual *So You Think You Can Write Like Meyer Holden* contest despite the fact the contest generated the most submissions of any of my faux competitions. Go figure.

How to Reappear Effectively

"Sam Bateman with PaperPenInc calling for Brooklyn Marx."

"Brooklyn is on the phone at the moment. Can I have him return the call?"

"Certainly." Share leans into the speakerphone in the den. Check that. The office.

She provides Brooklyn Marx's assistant with my vital information, repeating my name and company, adding the phone number. After she hangs up, her fingers tap-dance across the keyboard, recording the contact details on the iMac.

She gets up and, as she leaves the room, trips on a fugitive script from the To-Be-Read pile.

"Bates, you need to tend to the clutter in here. That or get me some worker's comp."

"I'm working on it. The clutter I mean." I wave the script I'm reading in the air without taking my eyes off the Courier.

"That was the last one on the list. Twenty-five calls, which will hopefully lead to a busy afternoon for you."

"Much appreciated."

"My pleasure. Now I gotta get ready. My call time is eleven."

Daily, development companies like mine place calls regarding projects they're pitching, whether they're aiming to send out a script or follow up on ones already delivered. Of course, the fat cat executives being phoned are always "on another call" or "in a meeting." That is, unless you're someone of proven importance. And if you are, they're probably expecting your call.

Every morning, assistants across the city are driven mad by this barrage of calls. The juggling act typically lasts from nine to eleven, depending on how fat the cat.

After the barrage, the messages are logged, dissected, researched, and prioritized before being delivered to the executive in a comprehensive list. Valued assistants will often provide personal tidbits along with the what-where-when-why of who called. Information such as names of spouses, significant others, children, pets, things in common, location/date of any social interactions, etc. This crutch helps the too-busy-for-such-details executives appear less socially awkward when conversing. Lackey always did this for Foster and trained us to follow suit. Thought it was a brown-nosing tactic at first but swiftly learned it to be essential in this business of show.

Not bragging, but I don't need these types of cheat sheets. Able to recall facts from conversations I've had much like I can remember details from scripts I've read, regardless whether it was yesterday or last year. Okay, that does sound like bragging. Guess I'm a braggart.

The goal of these calls is to put together the best possible package of cast and crew to a screenplay. These attachments can help secure financing for film or vice versa. If you own a script, as I now do, you begin at the top with the above-the-line talent. It's an everyday chess match of contacting and schmoozing the executives and companies that have previous/healthy relationships with preferred actors, directors, and cinematographers. Basically you're selling them on the project, and once aboard, these executives and the companies they represent will invest in the film and vie for a slice of the pie, the profits upon release. This is why you often see several companies credited with producing a film.

The morning calls are customarily returned after lunch, and you can pretty much tell where you fall in the food chain by when your phone rings. If it doesn't ring by the end of the business day, well then, the writing on the wall says it all—you're pond scum.

"What time is Foster?" Share says from the bedroom.

"Ten."

"Sweets, it's ten."

Glance at my watch. She's right. "Shit. Fuck."

"Preparing for your meeting, I see."

"Baby, will you do that thing? That thing you do?" I say as I enter the office, pick up the phone.

"Bates, I gotta get out of here."

"Do that one thing, and then you can take the rest of the day off. Promise."

I hear clicks across the hardwood. Share enters wearing bra-panties-heels. Talk about *that thing you do*.

"I'm not getting paid enough."

She's getting paid zero-point-zero. "I'll double your salary."

"Ha. Ha," she deadpans as she sits in my lap and dials the phone.

Elvis starts singing as the phone rings. Share wiggles her hips. "Stop," I whisper.

Third ring, I hear Stussy's voice. "Foster's Films."

In an impeccable English accent Share says, "Sam Bateman, PaperPenInc, telephoning for Jon Foster."

"Hold."

Takes less than ten seconds before Foster picks up. "PenisPussyItch. What can I do you for?"

Share's jaw drops in exaggeration as she looks over her shoulder at me. She turns back to the speaker to deliver, "Please hold for Sam Bateman."

"Oh. Sorry, toots. Pardon my French. Thought I was talking with the Buttman."

"No worries. I'll put you in queue for one moment. Cheers," she adds before putting the dinosaur on hold. She sets the receiver on the desk, squirms some more in light of Elvis' standing-room-only performance this morning. She sighs. "Enjoy your call, Buttman. I gotta go."

She doesn't get up. Instead she leans into me. "I absolutely must depart. Fear I'll be tardy," she reiterates.

"Don't be cruel."

She giggles, gets up, escapes my grasp. "Take your call. Give the bastard hell," she says, her bum doing that thing it does as she returns to the bedroom.

I punch a button on the phone. "Foster."

"Well, well, well, Fucktwat. Got yourself a hoity-toity English secretary. Little company of yours must be heading up, up, and away. Don't forget the little people when you're at the podium."

Elvis wilts at the sound of his voice. "Let's get started, Jon. We have much to cover, and I have calls coming in."

"I started two minutes ago, Twatsack. Catch up."

"Any word from Brillstein? Can you call your guy again?"

"I don't want to push so soon. They only got the thing yesterday. Plus I don't even know why we went to them without any secured financing."

"I know, Jon. You made that abundantly clear the other day, and I told you we do this my way. Anyway, I'm working on it."

"Who you talking to?"

"I'll tell you when it's in place."

"Cumjob. Tell me now. I'm a partner in this."

"Yes, you are, Jon, but you know you second-guess every name ever provided to you."

"Err on the side of caution," he protests.

"More like on the side of paranoia. When the financing is in place, I'll provide you with one of those explain-it-all PowerPoint presentations you love so much. One with all the bells and whistles. I promise."

"Mmmm. Mister I-Have-All-the-Answers, how did you get so smart?"

Throw him a bone to shut him up. "I paid attention while doing time at your office."

"Shit-fucking straight, you did. Got that shit-fucking straight."

Another line on the phone rings. Area code 310. Beverly Hills. I glance from the caller ID to the log sheet still up on the computer screen. Scan down, down, down. At the bottom, a match. Brooklyn Marx is calling. It's 10:06, and Brooklyn's returning my call.

"Foster. Got an incoming call I have to take. Want to

hold? Or call you back?"

"Call—"

Tap a button with an index finger, and he's gone. Tap another to connect to line two. "This is Sam Bateman, PaperPenInc."

"Please hold for Brooklyn Marx, Mister Bateman."

"Thank you."

"Good morning, Sam. This is Brooklyn Marx with New Line. My assistant said your office called."

"That is correct. Thank you for returning my call."

"My pleasure. Don't know if you remember, but we met at Crustacean a few weeks back."

"I do. You were eager to get a look at the Holden, we were both drinking gin, and you informed me about the brand Leopold's, which I have yet to try."

"Impressive memory."

"Well, to be honest, I wouldn't have called this morning if we hadn't met and seemed to have similar tastes."

"I can say the same thing. You left quite an impression. You and Stacy Stevens' article."

I cringe at the mention, but I'm also beginning to think my phone calls are being returned by the likes of Brooklyn Marx thanks to Lackey and Stevens. Seems there is no such thing as bad press after all.

"I also saw your company's name on my calendar a few weeks back. But then you cancelled prior to the meeting."

"Apologize about that. Long story."

"Water under the bridge. So what can I do for you, Sam Bateman?"

"I wanted to talk to you about a property I control the rights to, a script I'd like to send over to you today. It's called

Channel Superhero."

"Read it," Brooklyn announces.

"You read it?"

"Two days ago."

"Um, where did you get it? If I might ask."

"Well, shouldn't be telling you this, but after the blurbs in the *Reporter*, I had my assistant calling around town trying to locate a copy of both scripts. Like I said, you impressed me when I met you, so I was eager to see what you had acquired. Plus, I'll admit, that cancelled meeting sort of piqued my curiosity. You sent *Superhero* to Paradigm earlier this week, I suspect to get a star or two attached. Well, a former assistant of mine who works there helped us secure a copy."

"Why not ask me for it?"

"Well, where's the fun in that?"

I laugh.

"I was actually hoping you might contact me sometime soon," he says. "And I always like to be prepared."

"I read that about you."

"Don't believe everything you read."

"So what do you think? Of the script?"

Brooklyn pauses. "Hmm. I love it. The script's stand-alone potential is obvious, but it also has franchise written all over it. I know you know this, but with the extensive action and such a large cast, the choice of director will be paramount."

"Which is why I called."

"I figured. Who did you have in mind?"

I lean back in my chair. Breathe in, take the bull by the horns. "Well, I think Fincher would be perfect but not sure superheroes resonate with him. Nolan might not be keen to take on the genre again, plus he and his brother gravitate toward things they have a hand in writing or rewriting, which is something I am not comfortable with. That leads me to Favreau or the Wachowskis."

"Directors I have worked with in the past."

"This is a true story."

He laughs. "Well, you've validated my hope that you had vision for a property like this one. You named two of three I pegged for it."

"The other?"

"Bigelow."

"Kathryn? *Point Break* Kathryn Bigelow?"

"Yes, but she's about to be known as *Hurt Locker* Kathryn Bigelow. You see it yet?"

"No, not yet."

"Well, check it out. When you do, you'll know why she should be on your list."

"Done."

"Listen, while the script has that traditional male hero, big-name star leading the way, the story—and I'm suspecting the franchise—will fall upon the shoulders of that female lead. The daughter. Think about it. That'll resonate with Bigelow, and she might be perfect if this thing takes off. Plus, between you and me, I get the feeling superheroes are something she'd like to sink her teeth into. Before you try to get her attention, though, I'd recommend having that male lead attached. You'll need the supporting actor who'll play the villain too. Those two names will be critical."

"Completely agree."

Share enters the room. She leans in for a kiss, but I shoo

her away with a wave of my hand. She gets the idea, shoots me a well-excuse-me face. Peck on the cheek, and she's gone.

"Who did you have in mind?" Brooklyn says.

It's all a test. Yes, we're having a dialogue, but he doesn't know me. I'm unproven. I know he'll eventually disclose his thoughts, but first he needs to see if we are on the same page before he'll even think about championing the script and endorsing me along with PaperPenInc.

"Every time I read the thing, I can't help but see Brad Pitt as the Sentry. Maybe Josh Brolin, but I'm certain Pitt would turn the part into something unforgettable. He hasn't done superheroes yet and he could give the aged Sentry such depth. For Omni, I'm torn between Philip Seymour Hoffman and Russell Crowe."

Brooklyn is silent for a moment. "Hoffman. That's brilliant. Thought of Crowe, but I think you're onto something with the Hoff. Smart casting. Any word from Brillstein Entertainment regarding Pitt?"

"They're reading it."

"So why are you calling me today? It's a bit cart-before-the-horse, don't you think?"

"Well, truth told, for a company like mine, it's more chicken-and-the-egg."

"Appreciate the candor. Look, the script is top-notch. It's going to attract A-list talent. But I think you're going to have to be patient. On another note, might I ask how you found it?"

"Well, my off-the-record quote would be, 'It's the first thing I ever read I thought might have been written by The Man.' It wasn't, but nonetheless, I couldn't pass up an opportunity to option it."

"I concur. It does have that Holden feeling."

"Which is why my call isn't premature. Everyone at Brillstein is going to love it. In fact, I'm pretty confident they'll call today to tell me Pitt has already been sent the script and covets the role."

Brooklyn laughs. "I like your confidence, but that's because I happen to agree. Tell you what, if you get that call and if Pitt is on board, I want in. I'll get it in the hands of Favreau, Wachowski squared, and Bigelow. Maybe get some free press if they all fight to helm it. How does that sound?"

"Sounds like a plan."

"To clarify—because if I'm going to get behind this, I need to clarify—you're saying if the cards fall accordingly, you're comfortable granting New Line first rights refusal on financing this thing, details of course to be worked out later, all this contingent upon marrying the project with one of the three directors?"

"That is exactly what I'm saying. And yes, if the cards fall, we'll let the lawyers do their thing."

After a second of silence, "Good-good. Well, I'm glad I picked up the phone this morning."

"I second that emotion."

"One more thing, if you have time."

"I do."

"I have a favor to ask," he says.

"Shoot."

"Like me, I believe you see that lead actress, the daughter, being played by a relative newcomer."

"I do. Believe it's a breakout role. One that could carve a career for someone."

"Well, I might know that someone. Actually my better

half, whom you met, represents a girl you need to consider."

"Cynthia," I say. "Your wife's name is Cynthia, right?"

"That's correct."

"She's with Aspire."

"Correct again. And again, I'm impressed."

"Well, I'm intrigued. What's the girl's name?"

"Last name Cionni. First name Meg. I realize the suggestion might be a bit cart-before-the-egg, but you're going to love her. I envisioned her in the role from page twenty onward. So did the wife. She read the script too and would love to set up a meeting with you and Meg when the time is right."

"Might you have a reel you could send my way?"

"I'll make it happen. E-mail me your address, and they'll courier a package over this afternoon."

"Look forward to it."

"Let's touch base later this week. Unless Paradigm gets back to you, that is. Then call me right away."

"Sounds good."

"We'll talk soon." Brooklyn's gone with a click.

I hang up. Ponder what's transpired. *Here. Happening.*

I smirk, pick up the phone, dial. "Stussy. Bateman. Get Foster on the line."

A few seconds later, "What?"

"Call Brillstein. Poke around with your contacts and see where their heads are. It's not too soon. Trust me."

THE SPACE BETWEEN

Wednesday. Still no word from Paradigm. Trying to be patient. Key word, *trying*.

Haven't heard from Foster since Monday, which is odd because he's been calling on average four times a day. More I think about it, his absence is a good thing. Suffice to say, he can be a pest. In turn, I have not touched base again with Brooklyn. Still hope to give him a call on Friday with good news.

Decide to spend the day away from the office. I need a break. Walk to Barney's Beanery to watch the Twins and clear my head. Despite my intent, throughout the afternoon I find myself jotting down ideas for PaperPenInc on napkins and coasters. I also end up creating a lengthy to-do list.

Great thing about the Beanery is they serve the 5. It's been a while, but I enjoy getting reacquainted. Too much. After my fourth 5, I stop jotting. After six, I'm seeing twin Twins on the TV screen, have to shut one eye to watch Joe Nathan close out the ninth.

Twins win. Twins win.

Head home. Zero-point-zero messages waiting for me when I get there.

Fall into bed before eight. Pass out. Sleep tight.

Share's sleeping next to me when I wake up at four in the morning. Didn't even hear her come home.

Head hurts. Get out of bed, piss, down a bottle of water. Slip back into bed.

"Hey, babe. How was your day?" Share whispers, half asleep.

"It was blah." Lower *b* and *h*, capital *LA*.

Thursday afternoon. Couch. Full immersion.

Seven Years Back, a taut thriller, has me in its grasp. It's a revenge flick that follows Carrie Miller, who is stalked, tormented, and threatened by the recently paroled Rick Holman, a man she sent to prison for raping her seven years prior. Standard revenge flick stuff. However, when the second-half complication takes hold, I suddenly see the conceit. Turns out Carrie fabricated the rape story when, at seventeen, she found herself suddenly pregnant. In one chilling scene, the hero becomes the villain, the villain the hero. Rick Holman hovers over Carrie Miller, wanting the seven years he can never get back. Feel like I'm in a cineplex watching the action on the big screen, packed house, edge of my seat, *kill the bitch*.

"Bateman?"

"Mmmm."

"Got a sec?"

Outcome will have to wait. Close the script, toss it on the coffee table. "What's up?"

"Help me run through these sides?"

"Sure. Audition?"

"No, it's for my acting class."

Girl never stops. Amazes me. She's in production on her TV show, taping every day, yet she's still taking classes and even working on writing an original pilot. *Energizer Bunny, this one.*

Share gives the script pages one last glance, committing the lines to memory before handing them to me. She stands.

I follow suit. "Who am I?"

"Cody."

"And you?"

"Ashley. Only two names on the page, Bateman."

"Okay. Cut me some slack."

We run through the scene.

I stop midway through.

"Your line," Share prompts me.

"Where did you get this?"

"That's not your line."

"Share. Where did you get this?"

"I said—from Howard Fine's class . . ."

Losing patience. "I know you said that. But where is it from? Who is the writer?"

"I don't know. It's something someone is workshopping, I think."

"Can you find out?"

Share squints. "I can ask."

"Ask. Can you get a copy of the whole script?"

"I can try. Bateman. What's up? You're acting like that guy again."

I read the scene over again.

Share interrupts, "Bateman?"

I read.

Share fidgets.

"I need the script," I whisper, not looking up.

"And I said I'll ask for a copy at class."

"When?"

"When I'm at class."

Jaw clenches. "When is class, Share?"

"Saturday." She reaches for the pages. "Can I . . ."

Yanking the pages from her fingers, I say through gritted teeth, "Goddammit. Just. Get. It."

Share's face goes stone.

I exhale, relax my body, and take a step into the space between us. Extend my arms.

She pushes me. Hard.

Reach back and stop my fall with an arm against the couch, but she makes me timber with a few swings, two connecting, chest and chin.

I fall.

She heads for the door.

Moments in every relationship can torpedo the ship. Depends on the collateral damage. Reaction to it. Recovery from it.

Hull's been hit. And bad.

"Fuck you. Honestly. Fuck this." Last thing she says before the slam.

Don't call out. Don't chase after her. Don't do anything but sit there reading the pages over and over.

Fifteen, maybe twenty minutes later, finally snap out of it.

Try calling Share.

She won't pick up.

Head to her place.

Not there.

Back at mine. Nothing to do but wait.

Reread the sides.

Scene is good. Hard to tell what the whole script is like out of context, but there's one word midway through that sticks out, resonates, echoes in my well-read head.

Infectious.

in·fec·tious *adj.* Capable of affecting the attitude and emotions of others: *an infectious laugh*

In the sides Share got from her acting class, it appears as follows:

```
Ashley laughs an infectious laugh.
```

It's so trivial, but I am the spin doctor of Holden's entire oeuvre. Read every work countless times, aimlessly searching for clues. Recall Holden's initial screenplay, *This Time of Night*, the first of two spec scripts he finished prior to writing and selling *Fielder's Choice*. In it, he introduced a character named Sarah French in a way I've never forgotten.

```
SARAH FRENCH, 24, a keeper, laugh so
infectious, it's contagious.
```

Infectious.

It's one word on one page in one script. One word

floating in an endless sea of spec. One word makes me stumble, fall off the wagon.

Losing my mind.

Just then, KNOCK!KNOCK!KNOCK!

McCartney-Watson-Sundance

KNOCK!KNOCK!KNOCK!

My door seldom gets knocked, and the person who keeps *seldom* from being *never* is missing in action. Spot Share's keys in the bowl by the door. She forgot her keys. Cue uplifting music.

Jump off the couch, barrel down the stairs, unlock, swing open the door.

"Expecting someone?" Lackey says.

Heart sinks. Shoulders follow. Should be caught off guard. Certain he envisioned it that way, but I don't care anymore.

Let go of the knob, turn, walk upstairs.

Lackey shuts the door, follows. "So this is where it all happens," he says upon entering the apartment. "This is where you've been hiding for the last year. This is where the search for Meyer Holden goes down."

Mention of Holden makes me realize the screenplay pages are sitting on the coffee table next to a few scripts, which Lackey of course notices.

"Ah, hard at work, I see," he says, reaching for the top script, reading the title page. "*Seven Years Back*. Any good?"

I don't answer.

He flips through it, says, "Might it be a most elusive Holden Ticket?"

Silence on my end.

"Doubt it." He tosses the script on the stack, current of air moving the pages a few inches across the table.

"Heard about Foster. Congrats. Not sure why you'd want to get into bed with that fuck but ballsy move on your part. Real Gordon Gekko–type stuff. Stussy filled me in on most of what went down."

"Good old Stussy. Sure it came at a cost."

"It was worth it." He shifts gears, says, "Did Foster tell you what The Question was?"

His question answers one I have. He definitely isn't here about Share. "Is that what this is about? That's why you're in my home?"

"No, that's actually not why I am here." He turns away from the couch, paces. "Bateman, we've been through a lot together. As much as I hate you, I respect you."

Wish I felt the same about you.

"I know you respect what I do because I'm good at what I do. Maybe the best. But I also realize two minds are great-er than one. Lennon needed McCartney. Holmes needed Watson. Butch Cassidy, the Sundance Kid."

He stops in the middle of the room, spins to look at me.

Before he even says it, I think, *This again?*

"Come work for me."

The tone of Lackey's words there, then, tells me something I did not know a moment ago, makes me smile, makes me happy to say, "You need me more than I need you. Way it is. You're McCartney, Watson, Sundance."

He scoffs. "Not true."

"Then might you answer one question for me?"

Lackey raises an eyebrow.

"Why are you here?"

Lackey bobs his head a bit. "I'm here because now that you have Foster and what he knows in your pocket, combined with my company and its army of readers, we can do this fucking thing. Together."

I laugh at Lackey's dramatics. *Now that I have Foster and what he knows in my pocket?* "Wait," I say, recognizing. "He didn't tell you The Question, did he?"

Lackey stops, looks all caught-you-can't-pretend-you're-not-caught.

"That's why you're here," I add.

He stews. "Look at the big brain on Brad." Claps a few times for added effect. "That's right. When Foster was wearing that glass of scotch, courtesy of me, he didn't really feel the love, didn't feel the need to confide in me at that juncture."

I laugh again. At him, not at what he says.

Lackey looks to the right, studies the wall a moment. He walks around the room, grasping for confidence.

"Let me rephrase my question. I know words are important to you, and I chose them wrong a moment ago. Come work *with* me. Together we can fuck Hollywood into submission."

I scoff. "Interesting choice of words there. But I'm not looking to fuck anyone. So with all due respect, go fuck yourself."

Lackey's salesman face goes awry, then comes the fury.

"You think Holden or one of his fucking scripts will just show up on your doorstep one day? Is that the dream? Is that what you tell Share?"

"Don't go there."

"I won't, because I know she's happy. Wonder how long that will last, though."

"Don't go there. Will not say it again."

Lackey stares. He scans the room. Seen this look before. He's choosing words to follow prudently. "When you went into business with Foster, of course I had to do a little detective work."

He's pacing again, working the room.

"This *Channel Superhero* of yours is an enigma. No one in town knows what it is. No one has ever seen a copy."

Getting bored by this.

"*Flowers in the Addict*, different story. Good old Stussy got me a copy of that one. Compelling tale there. And I'm not talking about the words in the script. I'm talking about the story that comes with the name on the cover page."

Don't. Go. There.

"Henry Bateman. Wow," Lackey says, laughing. "For a guy chasing pseudonyms all day, you think you would have given your dad one before selling his script. And I say that because of the facts attached to his name, the name you chose to type on that cover page, the name you advertised in *Variety*."

"You should stop."

"Oh, no-no-no. The tale is only starting to get compelling. Lovely family you have there, Bateman. Norman Rockwell–type stuff. I talked with your sister the other day—"

Don't let him finish.

Rush him.

Tackle him.

Both of us crashing into lamp and plant and wall. Then floor, with a resounding BOOM!

Lackey struggles but didn't see me coming. Have upper hand and now he feels my upper cut. Shuts his mouth up good. Paint his face a new color with my fist.

"Stop," he cries.

Lackey's tone tells me something. I hold my punch, what would be my third.

"Get the fuck off me." No more fear in his voice.

Fist shakes midair until I start breathing again, relax, lower it.

He pushes me away into the wall.

I lean against it, breathe.

Lackey rubs his jaw, tries to open his mouth wide, cringes from the pain. "Asshole," he says all cotton-mouthed. "I was trying to get a rise out of you. I didn't know you . . ."

"Just . . . let it go."

We sit there for a bit on the floor. I get up first, slowly. Tired. Shuffle to the couch, fall. It catches me.

Lackey gets up. Sits in a chair. Rubs his face. Breaks the silence with, "You ever hit me again, I call the cops. That's fact. Look, I could give a shit about your fucked-up family."

I sit, listen, avoid eye contact.

Lackey leans forward, grabs *Seven Years Back*, pulls his phone from his pocket, hits a few buttons, writes something on the back of the screenplay. "Do what you will with it, but . . ."

He tosses the script onto the table. The sides flutter another few inches.

"Your sister would really like to hear from you." Lackey gets up, turns, walks to the door. "I didn't speak with her long, but it was pretty apparent she'd like to know who you are."

Slam my eyes shut, grimace, quell emotion.

His footsteps stop. "Bateman." He pauses, like his sister does, waits for me to acknowledge.

I exhale, open my eyes, look up.

"When you see Share, don't tell her about me calling your sister. She already thinks I'm an asshole, and even I can admit I shouldn't have crossed that line."

When I see Share.

Lackey lingers in the doorway, contemplating. "You don't really think you can win, do you?"

"No. But I expect you to lose."

Lackey laughs, shakes his head. "You force my hand, Bateman. You actually think I didn't have a Plan B? Come on. You know me. You know what I'm capable of."

I'm done. With this. With him. Everything. "Get out of my house."

He doesn't listen. "I came here to give you an opportunity, but you're so damn stubborn. You'll never learn. You'll always be the loser in this game. Way it is. Oh, and enjoy *Variety* tomorrow morning. Probably see you on my front lawn." He walks out, leaves.

Sit there on the couch for a good hour.

His threat echoes.

The sides mock.

Sister's number beckons.

Share's absence worries.

I lament.

Thoughts set adrift.

I flashback . . .

"So you gonna ask?"

"Ask what?"

"What The Question is."

"The question?"

"Are you the only fucktwat in Hollywood that doesn't know what someone is talking about when they say The Question?"

Good to see nothing has changed even though everything is different.

That day in Foster's office, half hour after Foster poured me that scotch, after he poured himself a second, informing me we had a deal in between, he spelled it out. "Do you want to know what Holden's magic question is? The key to his little fucksuck game?"

"I'll pass."

Foster almost falls out of his chair. "You'll pass?"

"Pass."

"Greatest secret this town has ever fostered, and you'll pass?"

Nice use of the word foster, Foster. "I'll pass."

"Bullfuck. Why?"

I lean back. "Not sure. Doesn't feel right, I guess. Knowing the question and never finding the man would forever haunt me. Other way around, if I ever did find myself face-to-face with him with that knowledge already in my back pocket, I'd feel like I cheated."

Foster looks at me like a father whose son just told him he'd rather try out for the cheerleading squad than the football team. "Son of a bastard."

And we leave it at that.

Flashback over.

Establishing Parting Shot

*E*verything is falling . . .
Everything is falling . . .
Everything is falling apart.

Eight a.m. Still in bed.

Grab phone. Dial Share. Get voice mail. Hang up.

Roll over. Stare at ceiling. Fifteen minutes expire.

Rise. Shower. Dress. Head out. Grab coffee, no words. Pick up the trades, brown bagged. Back home, bowl of cereal, sip of caffeine, ready to face whatever damage Lackey has done.

Headline in *Variety*. Jaw clenches. Gut wrenches.

"Mthr."

ESTABLISHING SHOT ACQUIRES FOSTER FILMS

"Fckr."

This ends. Today.

Century City. West LA. A cluster of high-rises gleaming in the sun.

Park. Make a beeline into the building, fake a call, charge past the front desk into an elevator.

Twentieth floor. Ding!

Receptionist. Words required. I improvise. "Sam Bateman here to see Justin Lackey."

"Ah, Mr. Bateman. They've been waiting on your arrival."

"They? Waiting?"

"It's Conference Room A. Down the hall, to the right. You can't miss it."

Know it well. Same place Lackey met with all the readers.

Walk down the hall, turn the corner. Through the cracked doorway, I see Lackey hanging up the conference room phone, craning his head to see me barreling his way.

Kick open the door. Enter the room ready to battle it out. Surprised to see it full. Entire company must be present.

Room begins to sing, "For he's a jolly good fellow. For he's a jolly good fellow . . ."

Feel like an idiot standing there. Lackey's making a mockery of all of this. Spot Foster sitting at the head of the table like Vader in *Empire*. Stussy's here. Kevin Mills too. There are other suits, some recognizable faces, but names escape. Bulk of the room is filled with pasty-skinned young'ns. Must be the readers. There are at least sixty of them. Sixty times eight scripts a day is over three thousand a week, more than thirteen thousand a month.

That's no moon. It's a space station.

When the room is done serenading me, they applaud. Then Lackey speaks.

"Everyone, this is the man I've been telling you about, Sam Bateman. Sam, this is everybody." Lackey laughs. "We here at Establishing Shot want to welcome you. Let you know we're putting the full-court press on you until you're convinced, until you're ready to join us in our quest for Hollywood greatness. We'll wine and dine you. We have reservations at Chateau Marmont tonight. Table for ten. Bring Share, of course. But first things first. How about we start with a tour of the compound?"

I stare at Lackey.

He laughs nervously. "What do you say, Bateman? Ready to call Establishing Shot your home?"

I turn to walk out, walk away.

Stop.

Turn back to Lackey, smile, address the room. "The other day, when I was speaking with Meyer Holden . . ." I pause, let the words have their effect.

Look on Lackey's face alone is worth the price of admission.

". . . he said something to me, quoted someone. He said, 'Hollywood died on me as soon as I got there.' Love that quote. But for me, it's not true. Hollywood was dead, facedown in the water, long before I ever arrived, thanks in large part to the likes of you. All of you."

Everyone swallows hard.

"Now carry on." I smile, turn, walk away.

Almost to the elevators when I hear the clump of Lackey's shoes. I press the down button. Third elevator over, doors slide open. Enter. Press the button that lights up a capital *L*. Again. Then again.

Doors slide together until Lackey stops them with one arm.

He enters. "Dramatic exit there. Is it true?"

Don't answer. Hands become fists as the doors slide closed. *Everything is falling . . .*

"Doubt it's true. But well played." He pauses. "Told you, you forced my hand."

"Why would you do this?"

"Don't worry. I'll see that *Flowers* gets made. I know how important it is to you. And to Share."

"If you think you're getting your hands on *Superhero* . . ."

"Get over yourself, Bateman. I didn't buy Foster out for your little superhero script. Or *Flowers*. Or his contacts. Open your fucking eyes. I bought the question. The Question."

He grins, cat-ate-canary-like. "I'm stronger than ever, Bateman. I know the answer."

"Don't you mean The Question?"

"Same difference. Now when I find Holden, and I will, I'll be ready. All the more reason you should join me. With our combined strength, we can end the conflict and bring order to Hollywood. The offer is on the table. I'll leave it there. And if you join me, well, we can call *Flowers* a signing bonus."

Clench my fists.

Lackey flinches. "Chill the fuck out, man. This is business."

"Business?"

"Business."

Raise my right fist, relax it, point, jab a finger at Lackey's chest.

"Listen to me. Get this through your thick fucking skull. I. Will. Never. Work. For. Or. With. You." Jab. Jab. Jab. "Ever."

Lackey swats away my hand as the elevator stops. Doors slide open.

I walk out, squint from the sunshine pouring into the glass lobby.

"You cannot hide forever, Bateman."

I stop, turn. "Don't need to hide anymore," I say, smiling. "Remember?"

Lackey's face goes cold. "What you said up there can't be true. No way. No fucking way. No way you can or would keep that secret."

I knee-jerk, speak before thinking. "Oh yeah? Well, you can confirm all reports with Share. Your sister was there."

Lackey blinks twice. More words aimed to punch him in the gut. I grin. He pulls out his phone, hits two buttons, puts the device to his ear. Grin vanishes.

BOOM!BOOM!BOOM! *Mistake.*

"Hey, Share. Got a sec? Have a question, and I'd appreciate your honesty." There's a pause. "Can you confirm Bateman talked with Meyer Holden this week? . . . What? . . . Yeah, I'm here with him right now." Another pause. "Share." Lackey squints. "Wait. What did you say? . . . What? Hello? Hello?"

Everything is falling . . .

Lackey pulls the phone from his ear. Looks at me.

"She said for me to tell you, 'Good to know where your priorities lie.' What the hell is going on between you two? What happened?"

"None of your business."

"Whatever. She confirmed nothing. And if there was something to confirm, if something did go down last week, why no blurb? Huh, Bateman? Why no blurb?"

I say nothing. Stare at him, until the confidence drains from his ugly mug. Works every time.

"This isn't over."

"Yes. It is. For me, it was over weeks ago, a Hollywood lifetime ago."

I turn, walk away. Again.

His parting shot: "I know Foster didn't tell you The Question. Nice bluff yesterday. I'll give you that. But you're walking around blind without a cane, pal. So whatever you think you have up your sleeve, Bateman, you better hurry. You better play your cards before I'm dealt the winning hand."

I walk away—from him, his voice, this place.

Pull out my phone. Dial Share. Goes directly to voice mail.

"Fuck."

Everything is falling apart.

MIND THE GAP

Sunday night. Been four days. Still no sign of Share.
Do the math. Been to her apartment four times. No sign of her whatsoever.

Been to Maggie's. She assures me she has no idea where Share is.

Cindy and Lisa, two other friends, have not seen her.

Been everywhere.

So I thought.

Around eight, my phone vibrates from a text. I snatch it off the table and see, "If I tell you where Share is, will you reconsider my offer?"

Lackey. *Dolt. You just told me where she is.*

BAM!BAM!BAM!

Lackey answers the door, snarls a hello.

"Where is she?"

"Who?"

I stare at him.

"She doesn't want to see you."

"I know. Coming in anyway."

"Wow. I didn't see that one coming."

"Where is she?"

He breaks eye contact with me, glances up the stairs, involuntarily answering my question. He flinches as I pass.

Barrel upstairs. "Share?" Start opening doors, peering in bedrooms. "Share?" Third door's a charm. "Share."

She's sitting, reading, doesn't look up, doesn't acknowledge me.

"Share."

Nothing.

She puts down her book, gets up, attempts to move past me.

I grab her.

She squirms away.

Grab her again, bring her close.

She resists, never looks up, stomps on my foot with the heel of her boot.

Ow.

She stomps on my other foot.

"Ow!"

She almost squirms away. I corral her back in. Hold on until I feel her push become a pull, until the her and me divided by Coldfuckcold is us again.

"Bateman."

"Yeah?"

"Let go of me."

I oblige.

She moves away from me, past me, composes herself. At the door, she grabs the knob, shuts the door, faces me, and whispers, "Took you longer than I thought."

Not sure what she wants me to say. Shake off that notion, say what I'm feeling. "Got here as soon as I figured out where you were."

She nods. She looks pissed, distant—rightfully so on both counts.

"That phone call on Friday." She closes her eyes for a moment, rubs her brow, as if she's trying to erase the memory.

"There were mitigating circumstances."

She laughs. "Mitigating circumstances. Lovely."

"I'm sorry."

She purses her lips, walks to a desk, bends to reach in her bag on the floor. She flings a white mass my way.

It flutters for a sec, pages making that noise they do when flying across a room.

I catch the script, glance at the cover page.

God Moving Over the Face of the Waters
by
Whitney M. Ellsbury

"Let me know when you're done."

"Where are you going?"

"Downstairs."

"Share. When are we going to finish talking about this?"

"That depends. How long does it take you to read one hundred twenty pages?"

"Talk to me."

"Read," she says before she exits. "Then we'll talk." She shuts the door.

Do what I've done for the last thirteen-plus months, albeit in a couldn't-have-predicted-it-if-you-tried locale. I read. One hundred twenty white pages colorfully painted with black ink, like all the rest, but like none before.

It's a drama, a compelling romance involving generation gap–leaping lovers, unfolding amid brilliant nonlinear storytelling that pulls you in with every turn of the page, every action and reaction of the characters, every line of dialogue uttered.

Action speeds from the Couriered pages. Not of the car-chasing, guns-blazing variety, but action set in motion by advanced characters acting and reacting at the precipice of conflict, providing edge-of-your-seat entertainment.

Infectious.

It's unlike anything Holden ever penned, yet it's as Holden as a Holden could get.

Turn the final page, come up for air, reenter reality. Shut my eyes.

Script in my hands, feel like I'm clinging to Queequeg's coffin.

How apropos.

Exit the room, walk downstairs, see Lackey talking on the phone, Share sitting in a chair, staring through a living room window. She snaps out of it as I reach the bottom step, sits up, looks my way.

"Hey."

"Hey. Put that down over there," she says, referring to the Holden in my hands, motioning with her head toward the coffee table. "Sit down on the couch."

I follow the orders, place, sit.

Share gets up, walks toward me. She takes a seat on the edge of the coffee table, right beside the script, right in front of me.

Glance up at Lackey, who's hanging up the phone, suddenly interested in the events transpiring.

Look to Share, who's not making eye contact.

"Share," I implore.

She looks at me. "Choose."

"What?" I whisper.

"Choose."

"Share."

Lackey moves in closer.

"Choose."

On the table before me is my choice. I get it but still I ask, "What are you talking about?"

"Choose," she repeats for the final time.

Every father's son recalls pivotal moments that define the man he grows to be.

When I was a teen struggling with the bully that life had seemingly become overnight, I came home to find my dad unwinding from his day, easy chair and glass of spirits together as one. Imagine he was probably dealing with his own grown-up bully, but no matter, he took the time to listen when I spoke. I vocalized my frustration over some daily event teenagers find crucial at that juncture in life, something so trivial by today's standards. "Just once I wish I was given the chance to succeed."

My dad studied my face for a moment, then smiled and responded in his even-keeled voice, a voice I miss so much. He delivered wise words, familiar words, a mantra I used to think was inspired by the loss of the family he once held dear. Now, however, I ponder whether ill tidings from Hollywood might have prompted it.

"Sammy, it's choice, not chance, that determines your destiny."

I admit those words did not resonate there, then.

Never really resonated until here, until now.

Choose.

Share sits before me, waiting, eyes closed, the Holden on the table beside her.

I rise, grab the script, feel the weight of the words in my hands. I toss it to Lackey, who catches it, gawks at the bundle, the cover page before him.

"Let's go," I say to Share, hand outstretched. "No choice. Choose you."

Share looks up, maybe a bit surprised.

Lackey chimes in, "Have you lost your fucking mind?"

Share shoots him a look.

"Sorry, Sis, but if this is what I think it is, you got yourself a lunatic there."

She looks to me, takes my hand.

Touch of her skin confirms what I already know. *Destiny.* "Let's go home."

Together, we exit Lackey's place, me limping a bit.

"Think you broke my toe," I say.

"You deserved it," Share whispers.

We walk to my car.

She breaks away before we reach it, saying, "Give me a second. I need to talk to Justin."

She scampers back to the doorway, where he's framed. They talk.

I get in the car.

Lackey's demeanor changes. Looks like he was punched in the gut.

She kisses him on the cheek before turning and heading my way.

Lackey sits on his front porch just as Share reaches the car and gets in.

"Let's go home," I reiterate.

"Bateman. Sorry for the drama. I just had to know."

I shake my head. "Sorry I even put you through this. I really am."

The pause between us feels like it unites us.

"I read it," Share whispers.

"You did?"

"Yeah. Good stuff. Amazing stuff. Why do you think it was called *God Moving Over the Face of the Waters*?"

"No idea." I start the car. "Actually didn't get that when I read it, but what are you going to do?"

"Funny thing about scripts." She pauses in that way she often does.

Turn my head.

Eyes meet.

"Funny thing is, if you take away the cover page, no one would ever know what a script is called or who wrote it." With that, she pulls a folded piece of paper from her pocket, hands it to me. "Sorry for the drama. But I had to know."

I look up.

Lackey's still sitting on his stoop. He shakes his head, raises his arm, extends a finger to me.

I look away, to Share, then back down to the paper. Try to make sense of it all, what it is I'm holding, what it all means. Think I know what's in my hands, but if it is what I think it is . . . "So inside . . . if I chose the script . . . ?"

"You would have lost us both."

I unfold the page, until the 8½ x 11 with three holes punched on its left side is revealed.

MIND THE GAP
by
Sarah French

Boom.

WHAT MAKES SAMMY READ?

I enter the Will & Ariel Durant Branch Library, a stone's throw from Sunset and La Brea, at exactly nine thirty in the morning. The bums I pass—one camped out in the building's shade, another passed out in the corner of the doorway, and the third one with the Van Winkle beard reading *Time* magazine on a bench—have me worried. *Maybe they're onto me, sent these deep-cover guys to observe. Place is probably already bugged.*

I'm kidding.

Have the conference room reserved until close. Plant myself inside, sit, wait for my meet and greet with Sarah French. Talked briefly with her last night, set up this meeting. She played the part of the writer of *Mind the Gap* to a T, even had an infectious laugh.

Nice touch, Holden.

I'm wondering where he gets these people to play his pseudonyms—*does he cast them, are they people he knows, past associates maybe?*—when The Man, The Myth, The Legend walks through the door.

Pretty certain my heart stops.

He looks like he does in all the photos I've seen amid my research—not a day older than when he left Hollywood, seemingly more relaxed. Hair's longer, skin a bit more tanned, but his trademark five o'clock shadow, blazer, and black T-shirt have not changed.

He speaks to a librarian who is doing a balancing act with a stack of books. The employee juts his chin in my direction.

Holden turns, spots me, approaches, stride after stride. Face-to-face.

Hand outstretched. "Mr. Holden . . ."

"Meyer."

"Meyer. I'm Sam Bateman."

He laughs. "Nervous, kid?"

"Actually not nervous at all."

"Well, I know who you are. Congrats on that. But don't make me regret anything, okay?"

I nod. *Why am I nodding?*

Meyer sits, surveys the scene, scrutinizes me. "Sal said you looked like a good kid. Grounded. Not some Hollywood phony."

Makes me smile. "Sal said that?"

"He also said you were a prick who called him a has-been to his face. So don't get cocky, kid."

I nod once.

"I'm curious. Did I make it too easy for you?"

"You didn't exactly hand it to me."

"Yes, but I put it where pretty much only you could find it. When I found out your girl takes acting classes with Fine, the path became apparent. Howard is an old friend. So I called in a favor."

"Still had to know what to look for."

"Truth. But still." He thinks for a moment, then, "I guess I wanted to see if you were paying attention, and you were indeed." Meyer turns his head, looks out the window. "To be honest, I was kind of rooting for you to find it. Better you than the Justin Lackeys of this world."

Mere mention of the name makes me knee-jerk. "You know Lackey?"

"I know of him." He's still staring at the world outside. "He is one grandiose motherfucker."

Wow. Everybody knows his name.

"The Lackeys of this world are the reason I went AWOL." Something makes him chuckle, and he shakes his head. "Of course I know Lackey and his . . . how did Stacy Stevens put it? His legion of readers hunting for me day and night. Guys like him think they're sharks in some strobe-lit ocean. They never realize we're all just specks in a lonely sea and opportunity is merely what you make of it."

He turns his head, looks at me.

"My knowledge of him goes back to his days with Jon Foster, even before he or whoever it was found *Nobody Moves, Nobody Gets Hurt*. Sure, Foster was the one who blew it, but I'm betting all I've got in the bank that even if Lackey were in that room, he wouldn't have had the answer.

Answer. To the question. *The Question.*

"For the record, kid, it wasn't that you sent a string of postcards. Anyone could have done that. It's what you said in them that intrigued me and helped you get a seat at this table. You made me reassess my own work. You made me laugh. And as I said before, you instilled a little hope in a place I thought was dead to me. All that in a postcard. Now, that's some effective writing." He pauses, grins, shakes his head. "That last postcard you sent, though—the one you signed Kirkpatrick. That one told me you were persistent. In a good way. Might I ask how you got hold of *Nobody Moves*? Did Foster give you a copy?"

I deadpan, "Not sure I'm willing to divulge that information at this juncture."

Meyer smiles, squints. "You have any questions for me?"

Every time he says the word *question*, my stomach turns.

"Yeah, I do have one."

"Shoot."

"How did you know about Hawaii, where I was staying?" Then I add, "How did you get my phone number? How did you know about the sales so quickly? And how in the hell did I not see you at the play?"

Meyer laughs. "Well, that's four questions, kid, but they're all the same." He shrugs. "You'd be surprised what money can buy. And at the play, you were preoccupied. Distractions tend to do that. I even walked right by you one of the nights, shook your girl's hand another." He looks away, looks to the door, into the library. "If you're done, I have a question for you."

Remember when I said I wasn't nervous? Me neither. "Shoot."

He leans back. "I'm going to ask it once. Once." He raises an index finger, like an exclamation point on a threat.

I nod.

"So tell me, Sammy. What have you read lately?"

Honestly taken aback by The Question. There, then, a stone's throw from Sunset and La Brea, 13 months, 414 days, 3,022 scripts in, I get it. Greatest fuck-you a writer ever pulled was a strategy aimed to turn the system upside down.

Fifteen years ago Meyer Holden won the lottery. Now he's turned that lottery onto the machine once in control. His needle-in-a-haystack game got a notoriously lazy town to read everything in hopes of striking gold. Problem is, once a Holden was discovered, the wrong people got in the room, the ones paying the readers to do the reading, the ones allergic to putting in the time.

Can't help but smile. Can't help but laugh.

Meyer's fixated on me, clearly trying to make sense of my reaction.

Don't know quite where to begin. Nonetheless, I tell The Man what he's been waiting to hear.

Like to say *Mind the Gap* sold for a record amount. Like to say DreamWorks produced a critical hit starring Robert Downey Jr. and Emma Stone, one that cleaned up at the box office, winning one of the three Oscars for which it was nominated. Like to say Share had a supporting role, knocked it out of the park, furthering her blossoming career. Like to say PaperPenInc has done some damage to an industry that never saw the likes of me coming. Like to say Meyer came out of hiding, worked under the umbrella of hope my company provided. Like to say the partnership flourishes to this day. Like to say all this, except it's one o'clock and we're still in the library conference room. I'm still talking. Meyer's listening, chuckling, shaking his head, drawn in by the story I'm telling. Been answering his question for three hours. He listens for two more.

Meeting ends with a rock solid handshake deal. *Mind*

the Gap belongs to me. *Nobody Moves, Nobody Gets Hurt* as well. Will be the cover story in all the trades, all the papers tomorrow morning.

I'm here. It's happening.

In the parking lot, I shake hands with Meyer again.

We part.

Get into my car, tempted to call Share, can't wait to tell her. Can't wait.

Start the car, want to do it in person, need to see her face, her reaction.

I pull out of the lot, approach Sunset, merge without apprehension.

The Man Holden Found

Esteemed writer joins forces with PaperPenInc
By Lena DeFlores

RELATED ARTICLES:

Got Holden? wild postings milk city's attention

Hollywood ending escapes Holden once again

Living End nets Holden a blockbuster last laugh

Holden reappears with *The Living End*

Hollywood celebrates the *Mourning*

Holden surprises Hollywood with pseudonym

Holden severs ties with Hollywood

Lo and behold, there's a surprise ending to the saga of Meyer Holden. It suddenly seems the greatest trick a writer ever pulled was making the world believe he did not want to be found. While Hollywood was busy searching for Holden, it appears it was Holden who was diligently hunting for a trustworthy counterpart. At least that's the popular water-cooler theory in light of today's dramatic announcement that two new Meyer Holden screenplays have been uncovered and optioned.

This helps explain the seven-year game of mysterious pseudonyms and grave questions Holden played with the Industry. That game, of course, delivered us *The Rising Sons of Mourning Park* and *The Living End* along with the not-so-successful Holdenless sequels to *The Living End*.

Now we can add two more scripts to the list along with the name of the man Meyer Holden was apparently seeking all these years. Sam Bateman, founder and CEO of PaperPenInc, has reportedly obtained the rights to Holden's two newest screenplays, *Mind the Gap* and *Nobody Moves, Nobody Gets Hurt.*

"I met the kid (Bateman) today and we talked for several hours," Holden stated in a brief press release. "I had a few questions for him, he answered them, and long story short, I came away impressed. Sam Bateman now owns my two most recent screenplays, and I look forward to collaborating with him. End of story."

Rumors regarding the existence of *Nobody Moves, Nobody Gets Hurt*, a 99-page heist script, have run rampant throughout Hollywood for months. *Mind the Gap*, a 120-page drama, was reportedly discovered by Bateman earlier this week, which led to the face-to-face meeting with Meyer Holden.

When reached for comment, Sam Bateman's assistant, who would not divulge her name, stated, "PaperPenInc confirms a meeting with Meyer Holden took place, during which an agreement was reached concerning the screenplays titled *Mind the Gap* and *Nobody Moves, Nobody Gets Hurt.* PaperPenInc has secured exclusive rights to both properties. Details forthcoming."

Pressed for further comment regarding what some are calling a Hollywood coup d'état, the PaperPenInc rep cryptically responded, "Don't ask us about our business," before hanging up amid apparent laughter.

Acknowledgments

I want to thank Jennifer Zalokar, who helped me edit/polish a raw manuscript prior to sending it to anyone, back in the days when it was called *Ass Eyes in a Sea of Spec*. I'm certain you would not be holding this book in your hands today if not for her efforts and enthusiasm. Thank you for everything, Monster. Thanks to all who read the work in progress and provided feedback—Brian, Ben, Paul, Rich, Meg, Mark, Karen, Logan, Deb, Dan, David, Stan, Joe, Pat— you all give good notes. Thanks to Scott Allen Perry for championing the book and helping me get the manuscript into the hands of everyone at Medallion. Thanks to Medallion Press for reading, enjoying, and acquiring the manuscript—I'm so happy to be part of this family. Thanks to Emily Steele, my editor at Medallion, for every single note and correction and improvement. Thanks to Michelle Tomallo for leading me to my lawyer, Peter Smith. Thanks to Peter Smith for every minute of your time. Thanks to Writers Boot Camp, of which I am an alumnus. As a result of my studies there, I was able to craft the character of Sam Bateman, screenwriting savant. Specifically, I'd like to thank two dynamic characters—Michael Lippman and Jeff Gordon. Special thanks to my family for all their support and encouragement throughout the years. I love you, and I love you for that. Thanks to all my friends, too—you are family to me. And thanks to my oldest friend, who years ago sat me down on the first bench in Runyon Canyon and told me if I wanted to pursue writing like I talked about in the past, I should move to LA. At the time, I was a tourist vacationing in the sunny/75 for a few days, and I remember thinking, *There's no way I could ever see myself living here—ever.* A year later, I found myself driving across the country, heading in the left direction because I finally realized it was the right direction. Thanks for the push, Rich. Finally, LA—I still hate you, but I do love you.

Author's Note

This book is not about me, nor you. While I do reside in LA and while much of the mood and many of the details of this story were garnered from my time here, this story is a product of my imagination.

However, as mentioned within the legal at the top of the book, all the screenplay/movie concepts (the good and the bad), titles, characters, pages, and summaries contained within this novel are original ideas of mine and have been copyrighted and registered with the Writer's Guild of America, West. This includes: *Fielder's Choice, Channel 5uper4ero, The Living End, The Rising Sons of Mourning Park, You & What Army, Sheer Evidence, A Blue Christmas, methODone/Flowers in the Addict, Punchin' Judy, Mind the Gap*. A few exceptions: *SOD* and *Under the Cottonwood Tree* are titles of scripts written by good friends, Paul Meyer/Rich Varga and Paul Meyer/Carlos Meyer. *tv babies* and *Triple Ex-Girlfriend* are in collaboration with Rich Varga. *déjà vu déjà vu* is in collaboration with Kip Watson.

The idea for *After Birth* is merely a joke, although it'd probably turn a nice profit.

A handful of screenplay/movie titles are references to songs/albums, an intentional gesture on my part to evoke certain moods in the reader.

Elements within chapter 12, "Father's Office," specifically Sal Burton's body of work, are an homage to a favorite band of mine, The Blue Nile. The review from *Queue Magazine* that appears in the book is a modified version of Johnny Black's review of *Hats* from *Q Magazine* (1989) and is used with permission from *Q Magazine*/Paul Rees.

MEDALLION
P R E S S

Be in the know on the latest Medallion Press news by
becoming a Medallion Press Insider!

<u>As an Insider you'll receive:</u>
· Our FREE expanded monthly newsletter, giving you more insight into
Medallion Press
· Advanced press releases and breaking news
· Greater access to all your favorite Medallion authors

Joining is easy. Just visit our website at
<u>www.medallionmediagroup.com</u> and click on
Super Cool E-blast next to the social media buttons.

_____

medallionmediagroup.com

MEDALLION
P R E S S

Want to know what's going on with your favorite author or
what new releases are coming from Medallion Press?

Now you can receive breaking news, updates, and more from
Medallion Press straight to your cell phone, e-mail, instant
messenger, or Facebook!

For more information
about other great titles from
Medallion Press, visit
